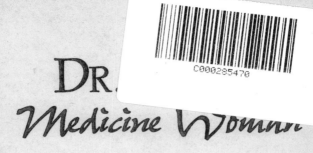

DR. Quinn
Medicine Woman

The phenomenally successful *Dr. Quinn, Medicine Woman* series has quickly become a part of the lives of millions of television viewers. Its sensitive portrayal of a young woman who sets out for untamed Colorado Springs to pursue her dreams of becoming a doctor underscores the important role women played in the development of a burgeoning nation.

Now, for the first time in print, comes an exciting, all-new story based on this hit television show.

THE BOUNTY

Don't miss the other book in this series!

Dr. Quinn, Medicine Woman—
the untold story of how Michaela Quinn became one
of the nation's first woman doctors.

DR. QUINN
Medicine Woman
THE BOUNTY

Teresa Warfield

B⬡XTREE

First published 1997 by Boulevard Books,
The Berkley Publishing Group,
200 Madison Avenue, New York, New York 10016, USA

This edition published 1998 by Boxtree
a division of Macmillan Publishers Ltd
25 Eccleston Place, London SW1W 9NF
and Basingstoke

Associated companies throughout the world

Published by arrangement with CBS Enterprises,
A Division of CBS Inc.

ISBN 0 7522 1166 8

9 8 7 6 5 4 3 2 1

A CIP catalogue record for this book is available from
the British Library.

Printed by Mackays of Chatham PLC, Chatham, Kent

For Michael, Amy, Brittinie, and Jennifer—
the new members of my immediate family

DR. QUINN
Medicine Woman
THE BOUNTY

1

"Reckon that's a good thing for a baby to play with?" Brian asked as he and Mr. Bray watched Katie's eager fingers grasp at the pretty music box that rested on the counter. Mr. Bray grinned and chuckled, seemingly unworried that Katie might break the box. But Brian worried. "I don't think she oughtta play with that."

He didn't mean to be disrespectful. It's just that the box had one of those fancy tops, a "chromolitho" something-or-other, according to Mr. Bray. He'd explained it to Brian as colored stones or plates being laid out in a pattern.

Mr. Bray had a lot of them—the music boxes with the chromolitho tops—at least five or six. They looked breakable, and that didn't sit right with Brian. He had just enough money saved to buy himself a Daisy printing press. Nothing that would give Miss Dorothy's *Gazette* any competition. The Daisy printing press was just a toy, after all, a neat-looking contraption he'd spotted in one of Mr. Bray's catalogs. Still, it *looked* like a real press, one Brian could tinker with. That music box looked like it might cost a lot of money, at least as much as Brian had saved to order the press. And if Katie broke the box, he'd feel like he had to pay for it—which meant he couldn't even think about ordering the press.

Brian had entered the mercantile with Katie propped on his right hip, and she'd cried every time he'd tried to wander away from the glass-covered case that held the boxes. Mr. Bray had shaken his head, grumbling about crying babies. Frustrated and wanting to look at a few things, Brian had started to take Katie out to Ma and Pa, who stood just outside the door, talking to Matthew and Emma.

"Oh, c'mon back here," Mr. Bray had grumbled over Katie's squalls, and so Brian had returned to the counter.

Mr. Bray had reached down, taken one of the music boxes out of the case, and set it on the countertop. And *then* he'd said it was all right for Katie to touch and play with the box.

The chromolitho on the box Katie fingered formed a picture of a girl, her hair in braids, sitting on a swing. Brian had seen Katie break things before, and he *knew* the box was too pretty for her to be grasping at. Her tears and squalls had melted Mr. Bray, however—they melted a lot of people. But when Brian thought of how responsible he'd feel if Katie broke the box, responsible enough to give Mr. Bray every cent he'd saved for the press, his stomach turned and quivered. He didn't care how much Katie cried and squalled—if he were Mr. Bray, he wouldn't let her touch that box.

Brian watched her fingers, knowing he must look pretty nervous.

"Oh, let 'er play with it," Mr. Bray said, his face crinkling at Brian. "She ain't hurtin' nothin'."

Katie managed to get her fingers under the lid, and she looked up at Mr. Bray as she squealed and bounced on Brian's hip. She'd be banging the music box on the glass in a minute! That was a terrible thought. Big tears still dripped from the corners of her eyes, although she was as happy as could be now that she had hold of the box.

2

"Where's yer tobbacer?" a stranger asked Mr. Bray, pressing up to the counter.

A quick glance at the stranger revealed that he was scraggly and dirty, but other than that, Brian paid him no mind. His eyes were focused on the tiny fingers that had hold of that pretty, *expensive* music box.

"On that shelf over there," Mr. Bray responded, distracted. He was too caught up in watching Katie to worry over a man wanting tobacco. He was grinning and chuckling at her delight.

Someone slammed something down on the counter, making Brian, Katie, and Mr. Bray jump.

A pistol, Brian saw, and he jumped a little more, especially when he glanced at the owner of the hand that rested on the weapon's handle. The hand belonged to a different man than the one who'd spoken; it belonged to a big man with mean blue eyes and thick brows. Another man stood behind that one, wearing all black clothes and a beard so thick, it looked like birds could nest in it.

"We ain't used to waitin'," the man with the pistol growled. The muscles around his left eye twitched.

Katie had sucked in a big breath when the pistol slammed down. About thirty seconds passed before she decided to cry again, this time because she was scared. Brian sympathized—he was a little scared himself right now. It wasn't every day that strangers wandered into Bray's Mercantile and got mean. And Brian could see by the way Mr. Bray was eyeing that pistol that he was nervous, too.

"I was gettin' to it," Mr. Bray said.

The big man jerked a quick nod. "That's good. Tobacco—and bullets. .45s."

Mr. Bray's face suddenly had more lines. "Well, you'll have to turn your guns in to the sheriff. People ain't supposed to carry guns in town."

"Is that so?" the man asked, his eyes narrowing slightly.

Brian felt the urge to turn and run. But he didn't want to leave Mr. Bray alone with the mean men. The big man's

3

pistol had cracked the counter glass. Only a little, but enough to be noticeable. The man oughtta have to pay for a new glass top.

Brian bit back that remark. No telling what the man might do if he said something like that and made him angry. The men were already angry over Mr. Bray's not paying them much attention at first.

"That's the law," Mr. Bray said, and then he turned away to collect a box of bullets from the shelf behind him.

The slamming of the pistol on the counter had made Katie lose interest in the music box. She grabbed hold of Brian's ear, twisted around in his arms, and tried to bury her face in the side of his. She was really scared.

Brian wrapped his arms around Katie and rubbed her back. He told her everything was all right, and he stepped away from the counter. He'd have a look later or tomorrow at the things he was interested in. Until the mean men left the mercantile, he wouldn't come back. Especially not with Katie.

"That thing there hushed her," the big man told Brian, jabbing a finger at the music box. "G'on—let her have another look at it."

Brian forced a shrug, trying not to seem frightened. "Maybe tomorrow."

"I *said* g'on and let her have another look at it."

Brian didn't like the man's low, fierce tone of voice or the way he reached for the box and pulled it to the edge of the counter. He tried to turn Katie around anyway, because the box *might* calm her down and make her stop crying. He had a feeling that if she didn't stop crying, the man was going to get really mean.

Katie twisted back toward Brian's face, arching her back and refusing to cooperate.

"Take Katie to the clinic," Mr. Bray advised Brian, turning back toward the counter. He had a box of bullets in his hand now, and a look of warning in his eyes. Like maybe he was thinking Brian ought to take Katie and *run* to the clinic. But Ma and Sully were just outside.

Brian turned and spotted Sully standing in the doorway, watching the happenings in the mercantile. He knew Pa was about to get involved, because Sully had a familiar, serious look on his face.

The mean man stepped in front of Brian. He still had his back to the door—and to Sully.

"You ain't thinkin' of cuttin' out after I told you to do somethin', are you?" the man asked Brian in the same threatening tone he'd used before, this time like he didn't believe what he was seeing—that Brian would disobey him.

"Our ma . . . she's expectin' us at the clinic," Brian stammered. "Truth is, we shoulda been there already."

A few seconds passed.

The man's face broke into a grin. He laughed. "Well, then, I reckon you'd better git."

The man's two friends laughed, too.

Brian made a dash for the door with the squalling Katie in his arms just as the mean man said something to Mr. Bray about putting items on his account.

Brian reached Sully at the doorway just as Mr. Bray growled that he didn't open accounts for strangers. Dr. Mike had moved up behind Sully, an alarmed look on her face. Sully stepped aside so she could take Katie from Brian to comfort and quiet her.

"My name's Hagan," the big man told Mr. Bray. "Now we're not strangers." The mercantile went quiet suddenly, like the big man expected Mr. Bray to accept that revealing his name meant that he and Mr. Bray weren't strangers anymore, and therefore Mr. Bray would open an account for him.

"You're still a stranger," Mr. Bray said. "I've had people leave town still owin'. I can't do it. You pay, or you leave empty-handed, simple as that."

Pa wore moccasins today, and Mr. Hagan never heard him approach from behind. The two other men saw Sully

5

and tried to warn Mr. Hagan. But it was too late. Sully knocked the box out of Mr. Hagan's left hand and the pistol from beneath his right hand—all before the mean man could twist his head completely around to have a look at what his friends were trying to warn him about.

The pistol went flying off the counter, and Brian ran and grabbed it without thinking, without even considering the danger he might be putting himself in.

"Michaela, Brian—go," Pa ordered, not taking his eyes off Mr. Hagan. The man looked real angry. He hunched and squared off like he was ready to fight Sully. His two friends had backed up, like maybe they were a little scared now.

Brian didn't want to go. He wanted to defend Sully, and he wanted to defend Mr. Bray and the mercantile. He didn't want to see everything smashed up in here, the glass case broken and all those pretty chromolitho music boxes scattered in pieces everywhere. He reckoned Mr. Bray had spent a lot of money for those boxes and that he needed to sell them to get his money back and to maybe even make a little.

But Brian had never disobeyed Sully, and as much as he wanted to stay and help Mr. Bray and Sully, he wouldn't disobey Sully right now.

Brian hurried toward the doorway, where Dr. Mike grabbed him by the shoulder and pretty much pulled him outside with her and Katie.

It hadn't taken Sully long to figure out what was going on inside the mercantile. Loren was being bullied—and so was Brian as he held Katie and tried to quiet her.

Loren being bullied was enough to anger Sully. To hear his children be bullied was more than he could tolerate, or that he'd stand for. Anger had bubbled like sour bile in his stomach. If not for thinking about the condition of Loren's store afterward, he'd have already put the man who called himself Hagan through one of the front windows.

As Hagan had argued with Loren about the charge account, Sully had had the quick thought that he'd heard the man's voice before. He knew the name, that was for sure; it

6

was a name he'd once wished he'd never hear again. And now, as he stared at Hagan, he realized he knew the face, too.

George Hagan . . . Pike's Peak. . . .

"What are you doin' here?" Sully demanded under his breath.

Hagan stared at him, confused, for a few seconds. It didn't take him long to realize whom he was looking at.

"Byron Sully. . . ." Hagan's face wrinkled. "Lookin' like a damn Injun! Didn't get around to turnin' in those nuggets, did you? You should've—"

Sully crouched and tackled Hagan around the waist so fast, the breath shot out of him. He plowed the man toward the door while, behind them, Loren and Hagan's low-down friends shouted. Loren worried about the things in his store. Hagan's friends whooped it up, enjoying the fight.

Loren didn't have too much to worry about. Sully drove Hagan clear out to the walkway, then shoved him onto the street.

Hagan slid a good two feet through the dirt, stirring up more dust than a team of horses.

Sully didn't give the man time to regroup. He was on him within seconds, jerking him up and hitting him hard in the gut. Hagan grunted and fell backward. He swung his fists and tried to roll out from under Sully.

Aware of Michaela shouting at him—"Stop, Sully. Stop it!"—Sully backed off, crouching low and watching Hagan carefully. But he backed off only to let him get to his feet. This fight had been a long time in coming, and Sully wouldn't let it go anymore than he knew Hagan would.

Hagan came at him, and Sully was ready.

As fists flew and arms and legs tangled, a crowd gathered in front of Loren's store, Jake's barbershop, and across the street in front of Michaela's clinic. George threw Sully off, then came up with a knife, a nine-inch blade that glinted in the afternoon sunlight.

"Throw it down!" Matthew said, breaking through the crowd to Sully's left.

Sully didn't dare take his eyes off of Hagan's knife. If he did, Hagan would have him slit throat to groin in no time. But Hagan made the mistake of looking away—at Matthew.

Someone grabbed Hagan around the waist from behind; Sully had no sense of who did it. Right then, he went for the hand that held the knife, grabbing Hagan's forearm before he could slice the air with the blade.

People in the crowd gasped and shouted. Sully freed the knife, and whoever had attacked Hagan drove him to the ground.

Just as Sully realized that the attacker was Hank, Matthew was on Hagan, too.

In a short time, Hank had Hagan lying flat on the ground on his belly. His right knee held Hagan in place while he pulled Hagan's arms around to his lower back. Matthew handcuffed Hagan while Hank and Sully—and practically the entire town—watched.

This wasn't how Sully wanted this battle to turn out. "Let him go," he said.

Matthew peered at him like he'd gone crazy. "He had a knife!"

"And he had a gun in town," Loren said.

"'Let 'im go?' What're you talkin' about?" Hank demanded as he pushed hair away from his face.

"That's the craziest thing I've ever heard," Loren grumbled. "He oughtta be thrown in jail!"

"Let him go," Sully repeated as he stared at Hagan. He couldn't believe George Hagan had shown up. He'd lost track of him—and that had been just fine with him. But now, here the man was, stirring up dust and trouble in Colorado Springs. It was time to deal with him. He'd vowed that if he ever ran across Hagan again, he'd deal with him.

Michaela stepped forward with Katie in her arms. "Sully—"

8

"I can't just let him go," Matthew told Sully. He jerked his head toward Loren's store. "What happened in there?"

"I'll tell you what happened in there," Hagan said, licking at a small cut near the corner of his bottom lip. "Me 'n' Sully here . . . we know each other from the minin' camps."

Sully's fists itched again.

"You mean you haven't told no one how you almost got yourself hung for stealin' a man's gold?"

Sully plowed into Hagan again. He had no sense of rational thought, that he might take Matthew down, too. He'd not stolen a thing from anyone in his life, and he wouldn't let George Hagan tell these people—his family and friends—that he had.

He took Hagan to the ground again.

At least he had time to do that much before Hank grabbed him and struggled to pull him off. Jake helped, saying, "You'll get yourself in trouble, Sully. Let it go." It wasn't so much of a shock anymore to hear concern from Jake. He'd become friendlier in recent years, at least accepting.

Jake and Hank together finally managed to pull Sully away from Hagan. Sully struggled against the two men while Matthew pulled Hagan to his feet.

"Don't, Sully! *No!*" Michaela cried, placing her hand on his forearm.

He glanced at her sweet face and saw the concern and fright in her expression. And there was Katie, with big tears in the corners of her eyes.

Not wanting to frighten Katie and Michaela, Sully stopped struggling against Hank and Jake.

Matthew now had Hagan on his feet and was telling him to move, that they were going to the jail and that he'd spend at least one night there.

"Get out of here, Hagan," Sully said below the rumble of the townspeople's conversations, below whispers and shouts, some for them to stop fighting, and some for Sully to beat the man. "Get out of Colorado Springs."

9

"I'm an American," Hagan spat at him. "I've got a right to be here."

"Get out."

"What if I don't?"

Sully stared at the man for a few seconds. Hagan wouldn't leave, not even after Matthew released him. Especially now that he'd encountered Sully. Hagan was a troublemaker. He enjoyed the conflicts he stirred up. That hadn't changed. "I reckon I'll make sure you do," Sully promised.

George spat laughter. "Dead or alive, huh?"

Sully fell silent.

Michaela pressed on his arm. "Brian wants a slice of Grace's apple pie."

He'd never let anything threaten her or Katie—or Brian, or anyone he loved. And as long as Hagan roamed the streets of Colorado Springs, he was a threat to Sully's family and friends.

"That your woman?" Hagan asked, looking Michaela over, up and down. "Well, now, that's a fine lookin' filly."

Sully went over the edge, from managing to calm himself a little to seething again. "Dead or alive," he confirmed under his breath.

A lot of people couldn't hear him. But Matthew did, and so did Hank and Jake. Hagan had a good idea of what Sully had said—he grinned and turned like he wasn't scared, and like he planned to go along with Matthew without a struggle.

Jake and Hank both glanced at Sully, looking bewildered, almost shocked. He'd threatened George Hagan—they'd never heard him threaten anyone.

Michaela shot Sully a troubled look. "I think Grace has that pie waiting," she said. She tugged on the inside of his elbow, trying to get him away from the explosive situation so she could cool him off.

Brian handed Matthew the revolver he'd grabbed in

Loren's mercantile. Sully again looked down at Katie, who held her arms out like she wanted him to take her.

He melted. Certain things, and people, could make him consider walking away from a bad situation. Katie was at the top of the list.

Sully brushed the dust off of his buckskins, then took Katie from Michaela.

As he pressed the baby's head to his shoulder, he caught sight of Matthew shaking his head at him, silently wondering what this business with George Hagan was all about. Then Matthew walked off, giving Hagan several shoves to keep him going.

2

Michaela placed the sleeping Katie in her cradle and spread several knitted coverlets over her. She withdrew slightly from the cradle, and began buttoning her night shift. Katie stirred, shifting her legs and turning her head to the other side, and Michaela paused, wondering if she would need to rock the baby more. Tonight Katie hadn't slipped into as sound a sleep right away as she usually did. She had fussed off and on since the trouble in the mercantile that afternoon, and Michaela had to wonder if the baby would rest well tonight.

A few moments slipped by, and Katie settled into a comfortable position. She stopped turning her head, and her breathing deepened. She looked content, like a tiny pink angel. And was she growing! An inch and several pounds a day of late, it seemed. She ate certain table foods—plenty of them—but she still nursed, too, more than ever.

"She's growing more hair," Sully said. He'd stolen up behind Michaela, being as quiet as ever with his steps.

Michaela laughed softly. "Yes, she is, finally." Katie's hair had a red tint to it, especially in the sunlight.

"It'll be long an' pretty, like her ma's," Sully said, lifting Michaela's hair.

She turned a smile on him.

He rubbed her hair against his face, closing his eyes and inhaling its scent.

Michaela felt a flicker of excitement.

He wore only his nightshirt, and she wasn't quite as tired today as she had been for the last several days. He smelled delicious—like the hickory fire over which he'd roasted venison for their supper. He drew closer, wrapping his arms around her, and she felt the warmth of his breath and the softness of his lips as he kissed her temple.

"I love you," he whispered.

That was her complete undoing. Her hand strayed from the buttons. She turned, and her arms encircled his neck and shoulders.

Their kisses were soft and gentle, then urgent. She had been so tired, and then he had been gone—off hunting with Brian for several days. Sully awakened her easily. After only a few kisses, she felt breathless and aroused.

As they kissed and his hands strayed, she realized that he was the same Sully she knew so well: the strong yet gentle man. His touches and caresses were still tender and sweet. And yet, this afternoon she had seen a side of her husband, an aggressive side, that she'd previously seen only in the Indian villages when he tried to negotiate with soldiers.

Sully had been distant since this afternoon, quiet and faraway in his thoughts. Michaela felt a need to be close to him physically and emotionally. This afternoon he'd pulled away, falling into silence, a brooding, distant man. In the hours since, she had given him space and time. Now she wanted him back. Her heartbeat and breath quickened, reminding her of the physical hunger for Sully she had experienced on their wedding night.

He wasted no time in picking her up, cradling her against him, and carrying her to their bed.

There, he laid her down in his gentle way. He smoothed

14

the hair back from her face, and he kissed her again, sweetly and tenderly, while his hands caressed her, and she fell into the sensual pace of his lovemaking.

Afterward, they lay in the flickering lamplight, her head on his shoulder. She placed her flattened hand upon his chest and watched it slowly rise and fall with his breathing. This was the closeness she loved more than any other with him. She cherished lying with him like this in the quiet of the night, feeling the warmth of his skin and, if she pressed her head to his chest, the strength of his heartbeat.

He was almost asleep; his breathing changed, became deeper and slower. But she didn't want him to fall asleep just yet. She needed answers to a few questions.

She didn't understand certain things about the events that had happened this afternoon inside and outside of Bray's Mercantile. She had asked Brian several questions, and he'd told her what he knew, what he had witnessed and been a part of: George Hagan and those two other men trying to badger Loren into letting them purchase items on credit. And then there was Mr. Hagan's bullying of Brian, which doubtless had been what made Sully so angry.

"Sully, who is George Hagan?" Michaela asked. Her voice was naturally soft; the hour was late, and Brian and Katie were sleeping.

He missed a breath; tensed, too. Whether he was aware of his reaction, she couldn't know.

She felt him withdrawing emotionally again, closing up inside, becoming distant and strange, and she raised up on her elbow and looked down at him. "Don't," she whispered. "Sully, I love you. Something is wrong. Don't close the door on me. Let me help you." Before this afternoon, it had been a long time since he had withdrawn from her emotionally, falling into such brooding silence. Even supper had been eaten with a heavy hush hanging over them.

"He's someone I don't want around my family an' friends," Sully said finally, fierceness edging his voice.

15

He meant George Hagan. "Why?" Michaela couldn't help but ask.

She waited. He didn't answer.

"Sully—"

"I know him from the camps, Michaela," he said impatiently. "Men like Hagan made the camps rough places. They were rough anyway, an' justice was fast. A group of citizens got together, a few questions were asked, an' a hangin' took place if that group wasn't satisfied. If a man came up missin' his gold, whoever he accused usually was hanged. I caught George Hagan stealin' gold three times. The first time, I didn't say anything—I didn't want a hangin' on my conscience. The second time I made him give the gold back. I caught him again, an' by then he was scared I'd tell somebody. He made it look like I was guilty. I escaped a hangin' by runnin'."

None of what he had said was pleasant. It all made George Hagan sound like a horrible person. But Michaela believed in forgiveness and time's ability to change or mellow a person. Her mother's attitude about her becoming a medical doctor had certainly improved with time. Elizabeth Quinn had mellowed, and if she could, anyone could.

Sully felt vengeful, and that was understandable. But things, life, had changed for him since his days in the gold camps. "That was a long time ago, wasn't it, Sully?" Michaela asked softly.

He inhaled deeply, as if expecting, and dreading, her unspoken words about forgiving and forgetting. "Yep. I thought I'd forgotten his face."

"He could have changed since then."

Sully grunted. "That's why he was tryin' to bully Loren into lettin' him get things on credit. That's why he wore a gun into town. That's why he used it to try an' get what he wanted."

His jaw was set. His eyes were cool. His mind was fixed where George Hagan was concerned, and that frightened Michaela. She would get nowhere trying to convince him that Mr. Hagan could have changed between their days at the mining camps and now.

She and Sully had come a long way in overcoming their individual stubbornness. But Michaela knew her husband well enough to know that despite hours of talking to him, she would not sway his opinion of George Hagan.

"I don't want him around my family an' friends," he said again.

"He won't be here for long, surely. Many people do nothing more than pass through Colorado Springs, Sully. They don't always stay. Perhaps they come through to settle in other places, or simply because they're traveling. Mr. Hagan surely doesn't mean to stay."

"How do you know?"

She shook her head. "I don't."

"Exactly. The minute you think you know what he's thinkin', he does something different. I saw him shoot men for lookin' at him wrong, Michaela. I ain't got reason to think he's changed. First time I've seen the man in years an'. he's bullyin' people, an old man an' a boy. He ain't stayin' around here. I'll make sure of that."

She had seen Sully bite his tongue where soldiers at the Indian settlement were concerned. She'd seen him frustrated and angry and in a near panic when the rations promised by the federal government were delayed, or when the rations never arrived as promised, and still he'd tried to deal diplomatically with government officials. She'd seen him handle patiently, in a dignified and civil manner, many problems that came his way, yet she knew how stubborn he could be, because she'd seen that, too, on a number of occasions. She saw his stubborn side again now, only she had a feeling, a heavy one, that this time he would react more stubbornly than she'd ever seen him react. This was the first time she'd heard him talk about running someone out of Colorado Springs.

"Please wait and see what his plans are," she said. As stubborn as he was being about George Hagan, she didn't want to tell him what she was really thinking—that the man had a right to settle anywhere he wanted to settle.

"His 'plans' usually mean trouble."

"Perhaps he has no plans for Colorado Springs, Sully. Perhaps he'll simply move on in a day or two."

He glanced at her, looking skeptical. Seconds later, he rose and blew out the lamp on the table near the bed.

The subject was closed to discussion.

Once back in bed, Sully gathered her close again and pulled the coverlet up over them. *I love you,* his actions said. *George Hagan is my business,* his silence said.

Michaela snuggled against him. Wind rattled the windowpanes and whistled beneath the eaves. Coyotes yapped in the distance, and Michaela imagined Wolf's ears perked at the noises.

After a time, when she thought Sully had gone off to sleep, she began to drift off herself.

"I hope you're right, Michaela," he mumbled.

That kept her awake for a while longer. She worried and fretted, knowing how strongly he felt about not letting George Hagan stay in Colorado Springs for any length of time; his stubborn silence and refusal to be swayed revealed that.

She kept seeing Mr. Hagan, his evil grin as Matthew urged him toward the jail. He had enjoyed taunting Sully by raking her with his lecherous gaze, knowing she was Sully's wife and that looking at her in such a way would anger Sully. He had *enjoyed* angering Sully. He had *enjoyed* the trouble he'd caused—and instinct told her, as much as she would like to believe differently, that Mr. Hagan indeed planned to stay in town and cause further trouble.

Sully had told Hagan that he would leave Colorado Springs dead or alive. He hadn't really meant that, had he?

The question chilled Michaela, almost as if the wind stretched its cold fingers inside the house and touched her.

Since he had been fired as an Indian agent, Sully was no

18

longer allowed on "federal lands." Since Cloud Dancing was not allowed to leave the Indian lands, the two men, "friends for many moons," as Cloud Dancing often said, were forced to meet secretly. They usually met at night, when Cloud Dancing could sneak past a guard who had nodded off or who simply did not have "night eyes."

Michaela worried about Sully and Cloud Dancing during the secret meetings, knowing, from past experiences, that most of the soldiers looked for excuses to harass the Indians. The meetings usually took place close to the homestead or at the homestead, which meant that Cloud Dancing indeed left the federal lands. He could be shot on sight by a soldier, and Sully could be arrested for aiding Cloud Dancing in defying government authority. But nothing, no threat or fear, kept the two men from meeting.

Michaela sometimes sat on the porch in the darkness, a shawl or cloak warming her shoulders, and listened to the sounds of owls and distant coyotes as she waited for her husband to return. She always sent food with Sully for Cloud Dancing—cinnamon muffins or a dish of stew. More recently she had sent slices of roasted turkey and potatoes coated with butter and sprinkled with basil and salt and pepper. Thanks to Colleen and Grace, she had learned to cook well. The Cheyenne did not add much flavoring to their food, and Cloud Dancing liked the taste of the herbs and spices she added to her preparations.

Sully had been forbidden to visit the Arapaho and Cheyenne, and a few scattered Pawnee on the federal lands. But Michaela visited the Indian village every few weeks, if not once a week. She tended the ill or, more commonly of late, the broken down and dispirited. She detested killing in any form. If Chivington and Custer, and other U.S. officials and soldiers, had wanted to break the once nomadic Cheyenne and Arapaho people, there had been no need for the slaughter at Sand Creek and later at the Washita River. Forcing the Indians from their ancestral lands and limiting their hunting and their religion would have been enough.

Michaela had seen more Indians die from broken hearts than from disease, wounds, or complications of wounds.

Michaela usually took Katie with her to the Indian encampment. She was sometimes gone for the entire day, and she didn't like to be separated from Katie for so long. While she helped Cloud Dancing tend those Indian people in need of medical attention, she usually left Katie in the care of several Cheyenne women, who treated the baby as if she were one of their own. Many times Michaela had returned to find Katie laughing or playing contentedly with Indian children and toys—banging wooden spoons on overturned bowls or making noise with the turtle shell rattles the women made for their children. Nearby the women might be stitching or scraping hides, or cooking.

Many of the soldiers expressed disbelief and disgust that Michaela placed Katie in the care of the Indian women. But Michaela usually put down their objections with a few calmly spoken words—"She's my child, and they love her and care well for her"—or, occasionally, a defiant look whenever a soldier, or soldiers, spoke about her actions in a hostile manner.

That didn't happen as much anymore. Of course, occasionally new soldiers arrived and Michaela was forced to defend her actions, as well as the Cheyenne women who cared for Katie, all over again.

This week's visit was no different. Michaela handed Katie off to the Cheyenne women, then she went to Cloud Dancing's lodge, where he sat cross-legged and ready, expecting her.

She and Cloud Dancing purified themselves with the minty smoke of burning pine needles and sweet grass. Opposite the blackened area where the pine needles and sweet grass burned were heaped the "gifts" recently presented to Cloud Dancing—requests from people that he tend their sick or ailing relatives. Cloud Dancing held the pipe he had been given by a father on his daughter's behalf. He drew briefly from the pipe, then handed it to Michaela,

20

so that she might do the same. She had learned, shortly after her arrival in Colorado Territory, to be completely respectful of the Indians' religious and healing beliefs. That respect came not from a desire to humor the Indians but from her witnessing firsthand the healing abilities of many herbal powders, dried preparations, and mixtures. She always took part in this now familiar ceremony with the utmost respect— and with the belief that it would indeed cleanse and purify her.

She laid the pipe across her thighs as Cloud Dancing began to chant. He leaned forward slightly, letting the smoke from the pine needles and sweet grass cover his face. Michaela closed her eyes and listened to his melodic chanting, the sometimes harsh, throaty syllables with which Cloud Dancing began each healing ceremony.

Presently, Cloud Dancing sprinkled ground juniper, dried and pulverized mushrooms, and powdered bitterroot over the smoking leaves and grass, producing a thicker, more earthy scented smoke. He urged Michaela to go first, and she drew the smoke her way with a wave of her hand toward her forehead. She kept waving, lowering her hand as she went, inhaling, surrounding and engulfing herself in the purifying smoke. When she finished, Cloud Dancing did the same, waving the smoke his way. Then the medicine man and the medicine woman went off to tend those in need.

Cloud Dancing shook his "medicine," a rattle, over the rash on one man's leg. With the smoke of slow-burning sage filling the tipi, he prayed in his native tongue that the bad spirit would be driven from the man's lodge. From a pouch at his side he produced buffalo hair, stones, and several lizards. He placed them on the rash while he prayed again. Then he removed the objects, which signified that he was removing the cause of the rash. He chanted again, and then he moved aside to allow Michaela to apply the healing balm she had produced from her black leather "medicine pouch."

In this way, the healers worked together, as they always did, moving from tipi to tipi, somberly and steadily. The

21

soldiers usually left them alone; in fact, for quite a length of time, there had been no trouble from the soldiers during a healing ceremony, and Michaela was grateful. Cloud Dancing considered trouble from them "bad medicine," and anytime there was trouble, they began again, going back to his lodge, where he burned more pine needles and sweet grass and chanted, asking for purification.

"She cut off her finger while butchering a bull," he told Michaela about a woman who came to see him. She was Arapaho, and normally she would seek out an Arapaho medicine man. But the Arapaho had been separated, displaced, and scattered like the Cheyenne, and they had no medicine man here. Many Southern Arapaho and Cheyenne were now on reservation lands southeast of here. They had been relocated in the Indian Territory, where Custer had slaughtered so many Cheyenne in Black Kettle's camp along the Washita River. The militant Dog Soldiers had tried to come to the rescue, but they had been too late.

Immediately after severing her finger, the Arapaho woman had applied hot ashes to the stump, effectively cauterizing the wound, which, Michaela noted, was healing nicely.

After leaving the Arapaho woman, they encountered a Pawnee man with a severe limp. Concerned, Michaela watched the man, but Cloud Dancing gave him only a brief glance. Moments later, Cloud Dancing told Michaela that since coming to the Federal lands for food, the man had been unable to put aside his bitterness against the Cheyenne— the Pawnees' ancestral enemies. The man would rather die than accept Cheyenne medicine.

Another woman had been vomiting most of the morning, and after examining her and deciding her condition was not serious—no intestinal obstructions or other conditions— Michaela boiled wild mint leaves and offered the woman a soothing tea. A hour or so later, the woman felt much better, and she gratefully offered Michaela a small deerskin bag decorated with quills and beadwork.

The Indians had so little, and Michaela hated to accept the

gift, or payment. On the other hand, she would deal the woman a great insult if she refused the gift. So she accepted the bag, smiling and thanking her in the Cheyenne language.

Michaela and Cloud Dancing were standing outside the woman's lodge, and Michaela had just slipped the drawstring over her wrist, when she heard the thunder of horses' hooves. Many of the Indian people heard them, too; women and children scattered. Some older men slipped off quietly to their lodges. Others remained in place, refusing, like the younger men, to run and hide.

Cloud Dancing waited, tilting his head back, a familiar defiance sparking in his eyes. *What now?* his look said, and Michaela wondered that herself. The Indians here lived quietly. There was rarely trouble—only an occasional drunken Cheyenne or Arapaho. Who rode toward the encampment at such a pace? And for what reason? A number of soldiers had emerged from tents and had paused to raise their rifles and stare toward the sound of the approaching hoofbeats.

Breaking up grass and stirring dust, George Hagan and the two men who had accompanied him in Colorado Springs two days ago, when he had disturbed Loren and Brian and Katie in the mercantile, rode into the Indian camp. They dodged tipis and the soldiers' tents. Hagan spotted Michaela, made eye contact with her, and slowed his horse. Seconds later he reined the animal in front of her.

Michaela and Cloud Dancing were forced to breathe the gritty dirt the riders unleashed into the air. Hagan didn't bother to dismount; perhaps he felt like a bigger man, staring down at her and Cloud Dancing from atop his horse. His friends reined in beside him, and they didn't bother to dismount either.

"I'm trackin' a man," George Hagan grated. "Levi Willard. Wanted for murder. He stopped in on some settlers outside of Colorado Springs this morning. From there, the trail leads here, to this Injun camp. Imagine that."

Michaela glanced at Cloud Dancing, whose gaze was

locked on George Hagan. He knew the man meant to cause trouble.

"We do not harbor criminals," Cloud Dancing responded in a low voice. George Hagan's insinuation that the Indians harbored the outlaw angered him, Michaela could tell. She knew Cloud Dancing well, and his succinct way of speaking and the way he stood, with his legs slightly parted and his arms tense and straight alongside his body, gave him away.

Cloud Dancing, like many of the Indians, was allowed to carry a knife, a rifle and other firearms, and necessities for hunting. Although he carried no rifle at the moment, he did carry a knife, and Michaela wondered if he itched to unsheath it. He felt threatened by the way George Hagan had ridden up and by the man's accusation, so she couldn't imagine that he had no thoughts of using the knife.

Cloud Dancing could not afford to be embroiled in trouble, especially not with a white man. He'd be sent away again. He knew that, and he exercised a great deal of self-discipline now, standing still and silent before George Hagan and his men.

"Well," Mr. Hagan drawled. "You claim you're not hidin' him, so you won't mind if we look around."

"He told you Mr. Willard isn't here," Michaela said. "I know Cloud Dancing to be a man of his word."

"He's a Injun," one of George Hagan's friends remarked. Mr. Hagan grumbled an agreement.

Captain Fuhrmann, Sergeant O'Conner's replacement, and a group of soldiers appeared between two tipis, hurrying toward Michaela, Cloud Dancing, and the men on horseback. Worry knitted the captain's thick brows. He walked with determination and purpose, obviously sensing trouble, his saber swaying with his steps.

"Someone tell me what's happening here," he ordered when he had almost reached the gathering.

Michaela opened her mouth, intending to tell him that Mr. Hagan and his friends felt they had tracked a wanted man to the Indian camp and that they were bent on searching the lodges. But George Hagan said, "Injuns are hidin' an outlaw," before Michaela had a chance to utter one word.

"We do not harbor criminals," Cloud Dancing repeated, his gaze still fixed on Mr. Hagan.

"Who are you?" the captain demanded of George. "A federal official?"

Mr. Hagan met the captain's scrutiny. He worked his jaw back and forth, and shifted the reins he held from one hand to the other. "Name's Hagan," he said finally. "I'm lookin' for a man by the name of Willard. He's robbed and murdered. There's a price on his head."

The captain's eyes squinted a little more. One side of his mouth twitched. "I see. . . . And you're after that price."

George placed his hands on the saddle horn and shifted his position. He laughed under his breath. "Well, now, I'm lookin' to see that justice is done. Not that that money wouldn't be a nice thing to have. I reckon it would be. Even split three ways, it'd set us up pretty nice. Wouldn't it, boys?" he asked, glancing around at his men.

Captain Fuhrmann nodded slowly. He was no friend of the Indians—Michaela knew that. He was a soldier, and he'd been sent under presidential order to restrain the Cheyenne and Arapaho people and confine them to this piece of land. She had heard that he dealt harshly with troublemakers, and that he kept an especially close eye on Cloud Dancing, who was regarded as something of a troublemaker by the soldiers.

"You're on federal property, Mr. Hagan," the captain said. "As far as I can tell, you're not a federal marshal. If the Indians here are hiding an outlaw, I'll find him and have him delivered to the marshal in Denver. Then I'll deal with the Indians responsible for hiding the man. Right now, I'm ordering you off federal land."

George Hagan's eyes narrowed. He worked his jaw back and forth again, then rubbed it, as if he'd been hit. His men, cowards really—Michaela had seen the way they had disappeared when he and Sully fought in front of the

25

mercantile—glanced worriedly between Mr. Hagan and the captain.

"I mean to collect that bounty, Captain," George said, his voice deeper and lower now. He eyed the soldiers behind Captain Fuhrmann, who held rifles they would undoubtedly discharge if the captain ordered them to.

"That's fine, Mr. Hagan, just as long as you don't ride onto federal land and try to collect it."

"Are you gonna order a search, Captain? Or are you just gonna stand there?"

"Turn those horses around and get out of here," the captain commanded, and this time the soldiers' rifles came up, aimed at George Hagan and his friends.

Cloud Dancing pulled Michaela back, trying to remove her from the direct line of danger in case any firing began.

But Mr. Hagan was smarter than he acted. He had no wish to be wounded or to die, it seemed. Especially not when he hoped to collect what must be a rather large reward for that outlaw. He jerked his horse's reins to the right, prompting the animal to whip around. Without another word to the captain or to Cloud Dancing, he sped off, his men following.

The captain gave another order, and the soldiers dispersed. With a slightly suspicious look at Cloud Dancing, the captain warned, "I'd better not learn that that outlaw is being hidden here."

He knew Cloud Dancing was a leader, that the people looked to him for strength and guidance. If the outlaw was hidden in the encampment, or anywhere close by, he assumed that Cloud Dancing knew about it. He would punish Cloud Dancing *because* he was a leader and because his spirit was strong, making him an example. Breaking the Indians was important to the army.

Cloud Dancing did not respond. The captain went off without another word, marching back toward his tent.

"Thank you for coming today," Cloud Dancing said to Michaela. He always thanked her, but there was no need.

She came because she wanted to come, because she was needed here.

"Cloud Dancing . . . you don't suppose that man is here anywhere, do you?" She couldn't stop the question; she was afraid for him and for the Indian people. It seemed she was forever afraid for them. She didn't know what would become of them—if it would be anything good. She sometimes wondered, as she knew Sully also did, if they eventually would be wiped out, annihilated. The thought caused physical pain to grip her chest. She helped them with her medicine for now. But could she help them overall, in the end?

"I have no reason to believe that he is here," Cloud Dancing responded. But he wondered now. She could tell. His eyes had slanted more than normal, and they had a worried look to them. His jaw was tense.

Nodding, she squeezed his hand. "I'll return next week," she said, and then went off to gather Katie from the Cheyenne women.

3

That evening, at home, Michaela didn't say a word to Sully about what had happened at the Indian encampment. It was selfish of her, she knew. She feared that he would want to get involved, and she didn't want him involved. The captain regarded him as a troublemaker, and would not hesitate to arrest Sully.

George Hagan was a sensitive subject where Sully was concerned, one Michaela didn't think she and Sully could discuss amiably. Sully had wondered why Mr. Hagan was in Colorado Springs, and after this afternoon's events at the Indian village, Michaela knew. If that outlaw was hiding somewhere around the Indian encampment, surely he wouldn't stay there for long—at least Michaela hoped not—not with Mr. Hagan and his men tracking him. Sully wouldn't see things that way, however. He was convinced, for whatever reason, that George Hagan was here to stay and that he would have to drive him away.

Over supper, Brian was full of excitement over having ordered a Daisy printing press from Mr. Bray. "It might take a while to get here," he said, "bein' shipped from Chicago

29

an' all. In the catalog, it looks just like a real printing press, only it's smaller."

"You still gonna work for Dorothy or are you gonna start your own paper?" Sully asked.

Brian paled at the question. "I wouldn't take over printin' my own paper. That might hurt Dorothy's feelin's."

Sully shrugged. "Everyone has to get used to the idea of competition."

"I just want a press of my very own, that's all."

"Just to investigate?" Michaela queried.

Brian nodded eagerly. Katie was seated next to him in the high chair Sully had built for her. She squashed a carrot, then clapped her hands together, squeezing the orange pulp between her fingers. She squealed with delight, then held her hands out to Michaela as if to say, "See, Mommy?" She was so proud of her mess, Michaela couldn't help but smile.

Brian groaned and clapped his hand to his forehead. "Katie, you need a bath," he said.

Michaela and Sully both laughed and agreed.

"She probably did it just so she can take a bath," Sully remarked.

"You're right, I'm sure," Michaela said.

"I'm sorry 'bout havin' her in the middle of all that trouble yesterday, Ma," Brian said.

He meant in Bray's Mercantile, and Michaela didn't want to talk about that trouble. Talking about it would lead to talking about George Hagan. Then Sully might learn she was hiding something. He knew her well enough to tell when she was nervous.

"There's no need to apologize, Brian—it wasn't your fault," she said. "There's no need to bring it up again."

Michaela had finished her meal. She rose and took her plate to the basin that sat on top of the cabinet where they washed dishes. There she set the plate down and returned to the table with a damp cloth in hand, prepared to wash Katie's face and hands.

Katie never enjoyed having her face and hands washed.

She wriggled and squirmed and sometimes cried. She would rather have a bath, and if she were older and capable of doing more than babbling in baby language, she might have told her mother that.

"Oh, no," Brian said when he saw Michaela coming with the cloth. "She ain't gonna like this. She never does."

Sully sat back in his chair and grinned, as if preparing to watch the show.

It was a battle, washing Katie's face and hands, just as Michaela had known it would be. Katie twisted and spat. Her face reddened, and she let out a squall that could have deafened someone at the top of Pike's Peak.

When Michaela had finished washing Katie, she picked her up and pressed Katie's head to her breast, trying to assure her that she wasn't being mean, that she still loved her.

When Katie kept crying, Michaela took her to the rocking chair, where she sat and rocked her. Katie rooted around, wanting to nurse, but Michaela knew that at this hour the baby might fall asleep. She still had dried carrot in her hair. They'd have to put off the nursing and sleeping until after she had a bath.

Michaela held Katie against her, stroking the baby's arms and face, and finally Katie began to quiet. Michaela brushed away the baby's tears as familiar feelings of happiness and delight surged through her. She always felt a swell of emotion whenever she looked at Katie. The baby had altered her life, and certainly the lives of her family members, but everyone had adjusted gladly. Things had been chaotic for a while—the feedings, Michaela trying to take on her full patient load again when Katie was only weeks old—but everyone, including Katie, had settled down somewhat. Of course, with a baby around, there was little routine anymore. Still, she, Sully, and Brian had adjusted even to that, dealing calmly with situations as they arose.

"I'll heat water," Sully volunteered.

"You haven't finished eating yet," Michaela objected. But she knew he'd go after the water anyway.

He shrugged, pushing back in his chair and heading for the front door. He meant to dip water from the well, then bring it inside and pour it into the big kettle that sat on the stove.

"I'll get towels and a dry blanket," Brian offered, and he rose, too.

Michaela smiled, silently thanking him. Throughout the months of adjustment, he and Sully had been wonderful. How many times since Katie's arrival had she had to say to Brian "later, please," whenever he asked for something, or for a little private time with her? How many times had she put off Sully's advances or had their private time together interrupted by Katie? And yet he rarely complained.

"I don't know why you ever worried that you might not make a good mother," Sully said from the front door. "You're the best one I've ever seen."

Michaela's lips parted in astonishment. What a truly sweet thing to say. But Sully wasn't just being sweet. He usually meant exactly what he said. She prized the openness that had begun between them during their courtship. Which was why his withdrawing from her on the day of his confrontation with George Hagan had upset her so much. He had been withholding information about something that troubled him deeply, and that in turn had troubled her.

She felt a twinge of guilt.

Wasn't that exactly what she was doing? Withholding information about Mr. Hagan's visit to the Cheyenne and Arapaho encampment? She didn't want to tell Sully about the visit and about what had transpired because she didn't want him to go in search of George Hagan and make sure the man left the Colorado Springs area.

That was exactly what Sully would do if he knew. The other day Mr. Hagan had posed a threat to Mr. Bray, Brian, Katie, and then to Michaela herself. Today he had posed a threat to Cloud Dancing and the Cheyenne and Arapaho people, and Michaela knew how Sully felt about anything that threatened the Indians, particularly Cloud Dancing. Since being fired as the Indian agent, he had exercised a great deal of restraint in staying away from the Indian encampment.

So while she might feel guilty about not sharing today's events with Sully, her actions were prompted by concern for his safety. If the captain and his soldiers hadn't stood in George Hagan's way, he might have killed a few Indians in order to search the lodges. If he felt that Sully stood between him and that bounty money by trying to force him to leave the area, he might think nothing of killing Sully. Actually, after the events that had taken place in Loren's store and outside the mercantile, George Hagan might *enjoy* the opportunity to kill Sully.

She *was* withholding information. But she was doing it with Sully's safety in mind—and she meant to give a performance worthy of much praise.

Her performance didn't last long. The following morning, Sully burst into the clinic. After shutting the door, he fixed a hard stare on Michaela, and she knew her secret was out. How, she couldn't be certain, but it *had* been discovered. She stood at the examination table, folding the sheets and bandages she paid one of Hank's girls to launder. She had frozen when Sully first entered the clinic. Now she resumed folding, but at a slower pace, waiting for the explosion she knew would not be long in coming.

"Why didn't you tell me George Hagan was at the village yesterday?" Sully demanded.

A lot of good she had done by keeping the information from him. He was angry, as she had known he would be if he learned that Mr. Hagan had visited the reservation while she had been there, that he had been aggressive and hostile—and that she had not said a word of what had happened. That she had, in fact, spent a quiet, normal evening with her family.

"He didn't stay long," she said, attempting nonchalance, "and there was no trouble."

"There was no trouble." He threw his hands up. "Only because the captain saw fit to make him leave. *That* happened only because Hagan intruded on government land."

"Well, at least the captain did make him leave."

"There *was* trouble, Michaela. You're not tellin' everything."

He looked wounded, and she couldn't stand that.

She turned away, stopped folding.

"Michaela."

She put down the half-folded sheet and went to him, taking his hands in hers. Suddenly she was afraid again.

"Listen to me, Sully. Please listen to me. After the confrontation between you and Mr. Hagan in front of Loren's store, I didn't think it was a good idea to tell you about his visit to the village. How—how did you find out he was there?"

"Cloud Dancing. He came this mornin' after you left with Brian an' Katie."

"This morning?" That immediately concerned her, because Cloud Dancing rarely left the village before dark. "Why?"

"To ask for my help. That outlaw . . . Willard. Hagan was right. He's hidin' out on federal land. Captain Fuhrmann didn't find him when he searched 'cause he doesn't know the land like Cloud Dancing an' the other Indians do. Some Pawnee are hidin' him. Cloud Dancing found out Willard paid the Pawnee in food an' money to hide him after he realized Hagan was on his tail. Food an' money . . . that's like gold to the Indians right now."

Michaela inhaled and released a deep breath. "If Captain Fuhrmann finds out the Indians are hiding a wanted murderer, the army will have yet another excuse to kill them."

"Right. You should've told me Hagan was out there, Michaela," Sully scolded, gently squeezing her shoulder.

She shook her head. "I knew there would be trouble. I

34

couldn't risk it. What do you plan to do?" He planned to do something, of that she was certain. Sully couldn't stand by while the Cheyenne were in danger.

He didn't hesitate: "Go find that man an' turn him in to Matthew."

She knew it. . . . She had known he would go after the outlaw if he knew the man was hiding on Indian land, endangering every Indian in the village. But she had been through enough situations with Sully involving the Indians to know that her insisting that he not go would do no good. He was going, and if he was killed by soldiers while he was hunting the outlaw, in his mind he would die an honorable death. Honor was the one thing no one could ever take away from Sully.

"Don't go alone," she whispered. "Take Matthew and some of the other men."

"Onto federal land? An' have Captain Fuhrmann wonder why a group that looks like a posse's out there? I can't do that. The captain would guess the reason. Then the Cheyenne and Arapaho would be in trouble right alongside the Pawnee. Anymore the government an' the army don't care what tribe an Indian's from. He's just an Indian. One's killed as easy as the next."

"You're going *now?*"

He nodded. Then he embraced her. "Don't worry about me. Cloud Dancing's goin', too. He'll make the soldiers think he's gone huntin'. After we find Willard, I'll bring him in. Then it'll be over."

Michaela kissed him. "Be careful, Sully. Please be careful."

He smiled and caressed her face. "I will."

When he turned to go, she said a silent prayer for him, that God would watch over him and bring him safely back to her. He smiled at her over his shoulder, then he closed the door behind him.

• • •

Over in the sheriff's office, Gwennie Hall, a local girl Grace had recently hired, had just brought Matthew dinner. He'd been about to ride out to the Tennessey ranch and check on things there; the Tennesseys had had several head of cattle stolen a few days ago. He hated the thought of rustlers in the area. Then again, he hated the thought of someone going hungry. No matter how hungry they were, he'd still have to find and arrest the rustlers. Stealing was stealing, and he took his responsibilities as sheriff seriously.

"Smells good," Matthew said, taking the basket of food from Gwen and setting it on his desk. He'd become interested in Gwennie a few months ago, shortly after Emma had left town to join up with that actress who had passed through. He'd kissed Gwen one day last week after they'd taken their boots off and dipped their feet in the creek. He hadn't tried to kiss her again since then. It wasn't that he didn't want to. He just didn't want to scare her off.

"It tastes pretty good, too," she said, blushing a little. "I know—I always sample while I'm cooking."

Grinning, he reached for her. Her dark curly hair was tied back with a ribbon. She wore a baby blue dress trimmed with white lace, and she looked as fresh and perky as a lone wildflower in the summertime. She definitely stood out among other women he knew. "I wasn't talking about the food. I was talking about you. *You* smell good."

Her blush deepened. "Matthew," she chided.

"Well." She *did* smell good, like a whole meadow of wildflowers.

She slithered out of his reach and lifted the lid on the basket. "Let's see, I brought roast and potatoes and carrots. Oh, and spice cake."

He laughed in surprise. "Whoa! What's the occasion?"

She turned around, leaning back slightly against his desk. Tilting her head, she smiled in her shy, engaging way. She never smiled at anyone else like that. He loved that smile, but it also frustrated him. Why smile at him like that when she was uncomfortable with him getting too close to her?

"You," she said. "You're the occasion. I know you've been keeping a night watch out there at the Tennessey place, and riding out there several times a day, too. You couldn't be getting decent sleep or food. I haven't seen you at Grace's for dinner since this all started. So . . . I thought I'd bring dinner to you."

"Grace won't get mad at you, will she? She doesn't need you at the café right now?"

"She also knows you haven't been eating properly."

"All right. Well, let's eat," he said, satisfied that she wouldn't get in trouble. "The food smells good."

She turned to lift dishes from the basket, and he moved to help her.

The office door rattled open. When Matthew turned to see who had opened it, in stepped Sully. He didn't often visit the sheriff's office, so Matthew had to wonder why he was here.

"Hope I'm not interruptin' anything," Sully said.

Gwennie's face fell. "We were about to—"

"No, no," Matthew told Sully. The sight of Sully in his office was such a rare occurrence, he wanted to make sure nothing was wrong. Sully looked all right. He hadn't hurried in, and he didn't look like he was in a panic. All the same, what was he doing here? "Something wrong?"

Sully shook his head. "Just wonderin' if you have a poster on a Levi Willard."

Matthew raised his brows. Now why would Sully be asking a question like that? Why would he be interested in such a person? Unless maybe he'd seen the man or knew where to find him?

"Matter of fact, I do," Matthew said. "Came last week from Denver. I try to memorize the faces when the posters come in. Or the facts if the posters don't have sketches."

"Can I see it?"

Matthew nodded slowly. "Sure." He rounded his desk, heading for the wall on the other side. It was littered with wanted posters and notes to himself about things he didn't

37

want to forget. "Not thinkin' Willard's around here some-where, are you?"

He reached for the poster, and when Sully didn't answer him, he turned around, wondering if Sully *was* thinking Willard was around here somewhere.

"He might be," Sully said under his breath as he took the poster.

"Food's getting cold," Gwen remarked.

Matthew shot her a brief glance. She was right, but if Willard was hiding out somewhere near Colorado Springs, that was what he had to concern himself with right now. Just a few months ago, Willard had shot and killed two men in Silver City, Idaho, and then a saloon girl only last month in Boulder. It wasn't like he'd killed somewhere years ago and was a reformed murderer. He was an active murderer.

Sully studied the sketch of Willard. Like maybe he was memorizing the features. Or like maybe he was thinking he'd seen the man?

"Recognize him from somewhere, Sully?" Matthew asked.

Sully shook his head.

"Why the interest in Willard?"

"Just curious."

Now that was a made-up explanation, one Matthew didn't believe for a second. Sully never just walked into his office suddenly feeling curious about an outlaw.

"If you think he might be around here somewhere, I oughtta be told," Matthew remarked.

"There's a rumor he might be on federal land," Sully said, glancing up quickly.

That took Matthew a few seconds to digest. Federal land. . . . "On Indian land?"

Sully nodded.

"You plannin' on goin' out there?"

Another nod.

Matthew shook his head. Everyone knew Sully wasn't allowed in the Indian village anymore. Federal officials could arrest him if he crossed onto Indian land. Matthew

38

couldn't hunt Willard down out there either; only federal marshals could hunt criminals on Indian lands. "I wouldn't do—"

"Hagan's bounty huntin'."

That made Matthew tilt his head back. There was a five hundred dollar reward out on Willard, so George Hagan's pursuing that bounty made sense. Hagan struck him as an opportunist. The man had tried to get him to play poker while Matthew had him locked in a cell. Matthew had released him the next morning, along with a warning about discharging firearms in town—and also about causing trouble with any of the citizens. That meant with Loren and Sully, and Hagan knew it. He'd grumbled something and walked off toward Hank's saloon, where his two buddies, Curly Bodine and Kenny Standly, had apparently spent the better part of the night in the company of Hank's girls.

"He told me he'd leave town soon, Sully."

"Well, he ain't gone yet. He was out at the encampment yesterday, tryin' to stir up trouble."

"You can't go out to the Indian village," Matthew reminded Sully, putting two and two together. Sully was memorizing Willard's feature because he meant to ride out to the Indian land and hunt the man himself. "General Wooden ordered you to stay away. You'll get arrested if you go out there."

"Somebody's got to go out there," Sully said stubbornly.

"I'll go myself an' talk to Captain Fuhrmann about searchin' the village."

"He already searched. If Willard's hidin' out on Indian land, he's got Indians helpin' him an' Captain Fuhrmann won't find him. Besides, you don't have jurisdiction. I won't be seen or heard unless I find Willard. When I find him, I'll bring him to you."

Matthew didn't like the idea of Sully hunting Willard alone. But *he'd* be met by Captain Fuhrmann if he rode out there, and the captain wouldn't be any nicer to him than he would be to Sully. Captain Fuhrmann liked his command,

and he'd think Matthew was overstepping his boundaries— which would be exactly what he'd be doing.

"Did you read what it says there about Willard?" Matthew asked Sully. He knew Sully's stubbornness, so he was probably talking to deaf ears where this subject was concerned.

"Yep."

"In the last month, I've gotten a dozen wires from the U.S. marshal, all tellin' me how dangerous Willard is. Now you're tellin' me he might be hidin' out near here an' that you're goin' off to hunt him alone."

"Make sure your ma doesn't see that," Sully said, tossing the poster on Matthew's desk. "Or any wires that come in."

Matthew took a deep breath. "Sully, you oughtta at least take some more men with you."

Sully turned away and headed for the door. "I don't want a crowd," he mumbled.

Matthew knew there was no swaying Sully. He raked his hand through his hair. He'd lose another night's sleep tonight, this time over worrying about Sully.

He already was worried. When Willard got it in his mind to kill someone, he didn't balk. Back a wanted man into a corner, which was what Sully was about to try and do with Willard, and he could be twice as dangerous.

But in a way, Matthew saw the logic in Sully wanting to go find the outlaw alone. A group of men—a posse— would attract attention. Sully hunted by being as quiet as the Cheyenne, by stalking, then taking his prey by surprise. If he caught Willard, he'd do it a lot faster and quieter his way than if he took a posse with him.

Matthew didn't try to change Sully's mind anymore. He let Sully go, even knowing he'd sit up worrying tonight.

As soon as Sully shut the door, Gwennie put her hand on Matthew's forearm. "I can't believe he's going alone."

"That's Sully," Matthew remarked. "He's goin', an' chances are he'll come back with Willard. I don't like him goin' alone, but that doesn't much matter when Sully has his mind set."

He snatched the poster off the desk and stuffed it in a drawer. Then he collected the numerous wires about Willard from the wall behind his desk. "I agree with him about these. Dr. Mike ain't gonna see them."

He stuffed the wires in the drawer, too, then he turned back to Gwennie. "Now, pretty lady, let's see what's in that basket. I'm hungry."

Gwen broke into a smile. She turned her attention back to the basket and its contents, and Matthew made up his mind to enjoy himself while they shared the meal she'd brought.

4

"**I** ordered a press," Brian blurted out to Dorothy that afternoon while watching her print copies of the *Gazette*. Something was wrong with her. Every time she had to readjust anything on the press, a lever or a knob, her face turned red and she wrinkled it all up. Several times Brian heard her gasp and watched her drop her hands into her lap. He'd asked her if something was wrong, and she'd told him no. But something was—he could tell. She just didn't want to talk about it.

He'd written a story for this issue about several new families who had come to town and settled: Mr. Freund had come to open a tobacco and cigar store, and Mr. Hayes was an apothecary, newly arrived in Colorado Springs and meaning to open a drugstore. That might give Ma some more competition, Brian had thought when he'd heard about Mr. Hayes.

But then, every growing town had competing businesses. That's pretty much what Sully had said about his press, and it was what Mr. Bray had said when Brian asked him about ordering the press—and he told Mr. Bray he didn't mean to

43

give Dorothy any competition. He'd paid for the press up front, too, feeling real proud that he'd saved so much money. He didn't want Mr. Bray to wonder if he'd have the money when the press came in from Chicago.

"You what?" Dorothy asked. At first Brian thought she was asking him to repeat himself because she hadn't heard him right and couldn't believe he'd done such a thing. Then he realized she wanted him to repeat what he'd said because she hadn't been able to understand him over the noise of her press. "Oh, drat," she said, as if she'd messed up something.

She hadn't said *drat* because of anything that happened with the press or because she'd made a mistake or anything. She'd said *drat* because the puppy she'd agreed to take in for one of Hank's girls kept biting at her skirt. Some man had given the puppy to Sadie Jean, and Hank hadn't wanted the puppy at the saloon. He'd talked about taking it out back and "getting rid of it." That had horrified Dorothy, so she'd grabbed the puppy out front of the saloon when Hank booted it out one day. Right then and there she'd announced that she'd take care of it. But every day since then, whenever Brian came into the *Gazette* office, he'd found Dorothy and the puppy not getting along too well.

"Won't let me get any sleep," Dorothy complained, "an' now he's chewin' on my dress." She booted at him. "Shoosh! Go chew on those pork bones I gave you, an' leave me be so I can print my paper!"

"I ordered a press," Brian repeated, not knowing if she'd hear him this time either. Her attention was on the fluffy brown puppy, who had a good grip on the edge of her skirt. Dorothy tugged on the skirt, trying to make the puppy let go. But the more she tugged, the more the puppy tugged, backing up and growling like a fierce animal.

"You let go, now! Don't know why Sadie calls you Mouse," Dorothy grumbled. "You might be little, an' you might look like one, but there's nothin' mousy about you. She might've warned me. Let—go—of—my—dress!" she ordered, and

44

finally she yanked it free—minus the piece Mouse had in his mouth.

Miss Dorothy was real short-tempered this afternoon. She was usually calm and easy to get along with, but Brian had a feeling no one should cross her today.

Mouse shook his head and sneezed suddenly while Dorothy stood looking down at her skirt, her mouth hanging open in shock. "Why . . . ! I oughtta give you back to Hank. You know what he'd do with you, don't you?"

"You wouldn't really do that, would you, Miss Dorothy?" Brian blurted out. Seeing how furious she was all of a sudden, he wondered if she might. Today, at least, she might.

He got down from the stool he'd been sitting on for a good twenty minutes, reached down, and scooped up Mouse.

The piece of Dorothy's skirt fell out of Mouse's mouth, and she gasped as it tumbled to the floor. She looked down at it in horror. "One of my favorite dresses! Emma made it for me when she was here. He's ruined it!"

"You wouldn't really give him back to Hank, would you, Miss Dorothy?" Brian asked again, stroking Mouse's back.

"Tell me why I shouldn't consider it," she snapped.

"'Cause Hank doesn't want him around. He'd kill him for sure!"

"Well, I'm gettin' to the point that I don't want him around neither. Last night he yapped all night. Look at me—I've got a dozen more wrinkles t'day, an' now I've got a ruined dress."

"You can't give him back to Hank, Miss Dorothy," Brian said seriously. "You just can't give him back to Hank! Please don't do that. He'll settle down, I bet. He's just a puppy, an' puppies chew on everything. An' they get lonely 'cause they're tryin' to get used to being away from their mas. I know what that's like, tryin' to get used to being away from your ma. You *do* feel like cryin' all night."

Dorothy's mouth fell open again, then shut. Her expression and her eyes softened. She wasn't so mad anymore. He'd said something that made a lot of sense to her, he could tell. He'd made her see the world from Mouse's point of view. To him it seemed like he and Mouse had something in common, something that melted Dorothy's angry heart.

"All right, then," Miss Dorothy said, wiping her hands on a towel, real carefully, like maybe her hands hurt or something. "I won't give him back to Hank. But he's gotta let me get some sleep. *An'* he's gotta let me print my paper." She gasped, looking at her press. "My paper!"

The newsprint was all jammed up in the rollers. From the look of things, it had gone in crooked. Miss Dorothy fussed over it now, pulling out the paper and mumbling and grumbling.

"Can I help?" Brian asked.

"I don't need no help," Dorothy snapped.

Brian jerked. He wasn't used to Miss Dorothy being short with him.

"I'm sorry," she said, plopping down on the stool next to the press. She forced a smile. "I'm havin' a hard time t'day. I don't mean to snarl at you. Guess I need to be left alone."

Brian nodded, understanding. He had times like that— when he just wanted to be by himself 'cause something was bothering him and he needed to sort out his thoughts.

"C'mon Mouse," he said to the puppy. "We'll go out an' play so Miss Dorothy can finish printin' the *Gazette.* You can't bother her while she's doin' that." He turned away, thinking he'd take Mouse right outside and run around with him. Maybe then Mouse wouldn't have so much energy.

When Brian reached the door, he glanced back at Dorothy. She was reaching her ink-stained hands toward the press, and now she had tears in her eyes. What was wrong with her? Her fingers were all curled, and he heard her gasp when they touched the jammed paper. Something was for sure wrong with her hands. He realized that she was having trouble uncurling her fingers.

46

At this rate, she'd never get the *Gazette* printed, at least not as many copies as she usually printed.

He thought about offering to help again, then he thought better of it. Seemed the only way to help her was to go tell Ma that something was wrong with Miss Dorothy's hands, that they were hurting her for some reason.

Brian nuzzled Mouse against his face. Once outside, he put the puppy down and raced off toward the clinic. And just as he thought would happen, Mouse ran after him.

Ma wasn't in the clinic. She'd left a note on the door that she'd had to ride out and check on a few patients at their homes. He'd see her later this evening, for sure. But Miss Dorothy was having trouble *now,* and she needed to print more copies of her *Gazette now.*

Brian plopped down on the clinic's front steps, and Mouse plopped down beside him. They'd wait right here for Dr. Mike. That way, they'd be sure to catch her as soon as she got back.

A few hours after he returned from checking on things at the Tennessey ranch, Matthew wasn't really looking for George Hagan. Truth was, he wasn't looking for anything or anyone. But when he started past the doors of Hank's saloon and saw George Hagan inside with one of Hank's girls on his lap and a spread of cards in his hands, Matthew pushed the doors open and walked into the saloon.

"Hey, Matthew," Hank said, greeting him from behind the mahogany bar, half-grinning as Matthew neared the stools. "Come for a drink, Sheriff Cooper?"

Hank knew him better than that, knew he rarely drank. Hagan glanced up from his cards, obviously taking in the sight of the sheriff walking into the saloon. Hagan dipped his head in acknowledgment to Matthew, and Matthew returned the silent greeting. He almost couldn't believe Hagan hadn't made more trouble around town; he'd thought sure he would. Matthew eased onto one of the stools and asked Hank for water.

A minute later, Matthew took the glass Hank pushed his way and swigged a healthy drink of water. He was thirstier than he'd thought.

"Hagan caused any trouble?" Matthew asked Hank as he set the glass down on the bar.

Hank laughed under his breath. He talked low, too, drawling in his usual way: "You know I'da thrown him out if he had."

Matthew nodded. Yeah, he knew that. He just hadn't given the matter much thought before he'd walked in here and approached Hank and the bar.

Matthew didn't always trust Hank—except in matters that straddled the law or that were out-and-out on the wrong side of the law. Most times if he needed to know something about a shady character, Hank was the man to ask. Today, he made up his mind pretty quick to talk to Hank, knowing what he knew about Hank's nature and a few of his less desirable traits.

"Where do you suppose his buddies are?" Matthew asked.

"Curly an' Kenny?" Hank shook his head. "Don't know. Ain't my business."

Nothing was ever Hank's business unless he made it his business.

"Word is, he's bounty huntin'," Matthew told Hank nice and slow, so he was sure Hank heard him well. He lowered his voice another notch, too, when he disclosed the information. Doing that implied that he wanted the information kept under their hats. "Had any strangers stop in lately that I maybe missed seein' when they rode into town?"

"You mean b'sides Hagan an' his boys?"

Matthew nodded.

Hank wiped the bar with a towel. "Nope. Who's he huntin'?"

"Levi Willard."

That raised Hank's eyebrows. *Good.* He broke into

another grin. "Why do it if you ain't goin' for the big money?"

"It ain't such big money when it's split three ways. An' it's dirty money, if you ask me. Bounty hunters are no better than outlaws."

Hank leaned slightly over the bar. "Neither are most sheriffs an' marshals."

That remark made Matthew study his glass. Hank was right, and that was shameful. Most sheriffs and marshals were involved in plenty of shady and illegal activities. The difference was, they found ways around the law so they didn't end up on the wrong side of the cell. Matthew imagined Hank had been involved in his own share of shady activities. But in Colorado Springs, at least, Hank mostly stayed on the clean side of things and kept to his saloon business.

Hank had commenced to rub his jaw. "So . . . if Hagan's huntin' Willard an' Hagan's here. . . ."

"Stands to reason Willard's somewhere near here," Matthew finished for him.

"Hagan don't look too concerned about it," Hank remarked, glancing at the bounty hunter again. Hank's left eye was a little more slitted than the right, and Matthew knew that meant thoughts were turning in Hank's head. *Another good card.*

"He's bidin' his time. He got put down yesterday."

Hank's interested gaze turned back to Matthew. "Yeah? By who?"

"Captain Fuhrmann."

"Out at the Indian village?"

"Right. Seems Hagan went lookin' for Willard out there, claimin' the Indians are hidin' him."

Hank's left eye narrowed a little more. "What're you thinkin'?"

"That they wouldn't dare. They've seen too many of their people slaughtered in the last few years to risk hidin' an outlaw."

49

Hank considered that. "Makes sense," he said finally. "But if that's right, why's Hagan sittin' in here, drinkin' an' womanizin', when he could be out trackin'?"

"That's a good question. Give me more water, would you?"

"Sure," Hank said. He grabbed the glass and turned away. He poured water into the glass from a pitcher, then plopped the glass down in front of Matthew.

"One thing's for sure," Matthew said. "Willard's not anywhere near the village. Captain Fuhrmann searched an' didn't find him. Found some tracks leadin' off of federal land, but his business is the Indians, so he won't bother with the matter anymore." No matter that Matthew hadn't talked to Captain Fuhrmann. For his purposes, he wanted Hank to believe he had. And that Willard was gone from the area.

Hank flipped his long hair back from his face and shoulders. "What about your business? Don't you want that bounty money? If Willard was there an' there's tracks leadin' away, why aren't you on him?"

"My job is to safeguard the citizens of Colorado Springs, not to chase outlaws across the territory. If he rides into town, I'll arrest him. But if he's halfway across the territory . . . I'm not goin' after him. I wouldn't collect the bounty anyway. It's blood money."

"I would," Hank said without hesitation.

Matthew knew that Hank would collect the money if given the opportunity. That was what he was counting on. Although Hank mostly stayed on the right side of the law, Matthew knew he had a greedy side to him.

"Well, you'll let me know if any strangers come in?" Matthew asked.

"You bet." Hank wiped the counter again, then walked off to serve Henry Hughes, a local rancher who'd just taken a seat at the end of the bar.

Matthew rose and tipped his hat to Henry in greeting. Henry responded in kind, then Matthew walked out of the saloon.

Once outside, he went on walking, as he almost always did this time of the evening, watching for signs of potential trouble, feeling confident that George Hagan and his boys would leave Colorado Springs soon. He'd told a few lies, and surely Charlotte Cooper was turning in her grave right now. But he'd told the lies with the best intentions.

He might not want George Hagan gone from this town as much as Sully did, but he wanted him gone all the same.

5

Dorothy had been in pain for some time and just had not told anyone. Her finger joints swelled almost every day now, and they'd woken her up this morning, all swollen and red and painful again.

She'd thought the pain might get better as the day wore on. It usually did. But today, as the hours passed, the swelling and redness worsened, and the slightest movement of her fingers caused her to wince. If she moved her fingers very much, such as when she laced her corset and buttoned her dress, she fought to keep from crying out. She hadn't been able to get warm today either, and that was bothersome.

She didn't want to think something was seriously wrong with her. She especially didn't want to think something might be seriously wrong with her *hands*. Getting the paper out depended on her being able to use her hands. And even without having to do the paper, she needed the use of her hands for regular daily activities.

She put off going to see Michaela for as long as possible. Finally, by late afternoon, when she couldn't even turn the cranks on the press without nearly crying and when she couldn't straighten her fingers and pull out the paper that had jammed in the press rollers, she gave it up and walked to the clinic. Brian was outside playing with Mouse—he'd been a godsend where that puppy was concerned. The problem with her hands was making it hard enough to get the paper out this week. Add to that the care of an annoying puppy, even as cute as he was, and she wouldn't have made much progress without Brian.

When he saw her, he smiled, looking cautious, and she felt bad all over again for the way she'd snapped at him. He'd done nothing wrong, had just tried to talk to her and watch her print, the way he always did. She sat beside him on the steps for a minute or two, and she apologized again.

"That's all right, Miss Dorothy," he said. "Do you need to see Ma?"

She nodded. She reckoned she'd have to. Something sure was wrong with her hands and fingers, and it was so bad now that she couldn't even print the paper.

"She's inside with Mr. Tennessey. But I bet she'll be done with him real soon." Brian petted Mouse on the head. "I told her you might be comin' to see her."

Dorothy raised her brows. "Did you?"

He nodded, looking guarded again.

She smiled. "Thank you."

"You an' Ma, you're friends, an' I figured you might need to talk to her."

"Lord knows I need a friend right now. But I need a doctor, too, an' your ma's both."

About that time, the clinic door opened and there stood Michaela with Mr. Tennessey. He handed her a few coins and she thanked him, then he walked off, greeting Dorothy with a tip of his hat.

"Do you need to see me?" Michaela asked Dorothy. She glanced quickly at Dorothy's hands, not letting her gaze linger there too long. She glanced at Brian, too, then shifted her gaze back to Dorothy. All that shifting around of

Michaela's eyes—especially the knowing look she exchanged with Brian—told Dorothy that Brian had told Michaela something was wrong with "Miss Dorothy."

"I reckon I do," Dorothy said, sighing.

She followed Michaela into the clinic. As Michaela shut the door, Dorothy went over to the examination table. There, she turned around as Michaela approached. Dorothy held out her hands.

"My fingers . . . they're all bent an' swollen an' red. Painful, too. I can't do a thing—almost couldn't button up my own dress this mornin'. Imagine that! I thought they might be sore 'cause I put out more papers than ever last week. You know, what with people comin' to Colorado Springs for Preston's resort an' all. But that was last week, an' they're worse than ever this week! I can't seem to get warm, either."

"How long have your hands been troubling you?"

"A month or more, give or take a few weeks," Dorothy said sheepishly.

"Dorothy!" Michaela scolded.

"I know, I know. I shoulda come to you sooner. I get so caught up in writin' an' gettin' the paper out on time. . . . If I concentrated on every little ache an' pain, why, given my age, that's all I'd ever think of!"

"You're not old—and this is not a small ache or pain." Michaela gently turned Dorothy's right hand over.

Dorothy grimaced. The pain seemed to be coming from *inside* her hands and fingers. That was strange. "Well, what is it then? Whatever it is, surely a little medicine'll take care of it."

Michaela shook her head. "Perhaps." She glanced at Dorothy, concern drawing her brows together. "Perhaps not."

Dorothy held her breath. "What d'you mean? What is it, Michaela?"

"Rheumatism."

Dorothy's jaw dropped. *"Rheumatism?"*

Michaela nodded grimly. "An acute inflammation of rheumatoid arthritis, actually. Painful, swollen joints, fever. . . ."

Dorothy shook her head. "No! Michaela, I can't have rheumatism or arthritis or nothin' like that! I have a paper to put out an' —"

"Dorothy, I doubt you'll get a paper out this week. I can give you sodium salicylate and recommend steam baths, but—"

Dorothy withdrew. "No paper? Why, Michaela, what are you sayin'?" She *had* to put the paper out. She just *had* to! "The town depends on me to write an' print that paper. It's got to go out. I've got to get it printed an' it's got to go out!"

She and Michaela studied each other for several long moments. Michaela's expression said there was no way Dorothy would get the paper out this week because the condition of her hands wouldn't allow her to, and Dorothy was in a panic inside because the townspeople depended on her for the news she delivered to them in the *Gazette*. Since starting the paper she'd never missed printing an issue, not even when she'd had to fight with her first press, that old cantankerous thing that had always given her a battle.

Rheumatoid arthritis? Why, that was almost worse than when Michaela had told her she needed to perform a mastectomy on her because she suspected a breast cancer. Losing her breast had been something to get used to, that was for sure. Losing the use of her hands . . . why, that was a thought she could not tolerate.

"This doesn't mean the end of the paper forever, Dorothy," Michaela said softly. "Perhaps only this one issue. If you take the medicine I give you and take steam baths at least once a day, there's no reason why this shouldn't clear up. I do worry about long-term illness, since you say you've had these symptoms for weeks now and that they were suddenly worse this morning. The sudden worsening and the chills indicate an acute condition. But the ongoing pain and swelling . . . they're something else. Perhaps a chronic condition."

Dorothy swallowed. "Somethin' . . . long-term."

Michaela nodded.

"I can't work my press, much less carry buckets of water in for a steam bath," Dorothy grumbled, glancing down at her hands. Pitiful things. She hated the sight of them right now. They were betraying her when she needed them most. "Oh, Michaela, what am I gonna do about the *Gazette?*"

"The writing is all done? You just need to print it?"

"Yes. I was tryin' to print it. I printed some copies yesterday. Not nearly enough, though, an' not nearly the number I'da printed if my hands hadn't been botherin' me. Today I've only printed a few copies."

"Perhaps you could hire someone to work the press for you until you're better."

She balked at that. "I don't know, Michaela . . . I'm a little protective of my press. I'm the only one who knows how to operate it—"

"Only because you haven't shown anyone else how to operate it. You never needed to. Now you do."

"I never thought this would happen," Dorothy said, shaking her head. "I never *ever* thought this would happen. I finally get goin' with somethin' I'm real proud of, an' I end up with somethin' like this. Arthritis doesn't just go away, does it, Michaela?"

"No."

"Well, I've had to make the best of other situations. I reckon I'll make the best of this one, too." But Dorothy didn't feel nearly as optimistic as she sounded—and she didn't even sound *that* optimistic.

Michaela gave her a powder to mix with boiling water to make a tea, and she advised her to take daily steam baths. Dorothy didn't know where she'd find time to do that, what with having to teach someone else to work her press and all. She didn't even know *whom* she'd teach to work her press. She didn't know whom she trusted that much. Michaela, maybe, but Michaela was far too busy with her family and

57

professional obligations to learn to work the press so that Colorado Springs would have a newspaper this week.

Katie had been sleeping, but she woke and began fussing as Michaela was wrapping the powder for Dorothy. Michaela picked up Katie, rubbing and patting her back, and walked with Dorothy to the front door.

Outside, the reverend was hurrying toward the clinic from the opposite side of the street, dodging wagons and horses, a distressed look on his face. Robert E. followed him, and neither man looked happy.

"What d'ya suppose's wrong with them?" Dorothy asked Michaela.

Michaela shook her head. "I don't know."

"Well, it seems we're about to find out."

"They're comin' real fast," Brian remarked, still sitting on the step.

The reverend looked most distressed, and he was the first to speak once he and Robert E. neared the clinic. "Dr. Quinn? Dr. Quinn, we need to talk to you! We need to gather the citizens and go to Jake and—and figure out a solution to this."

"We don't want no bounty hunter hangin' out 'round here," Robert E. said. "We've got a clean town, an' that's the way we aim for it ta stay."

"*Bounty* hunter?" Dorothy and Brian blurted out at the same time.

"Where?" Dorothy demanded to know.

She looked at Michaela, wondering at her reaction. Michaela knew something about this, Dorothy could tell. She didn't look surprised or shocked. A little unsettled, maybe, that Reverend Johnson and Robert E. were pouncing on her this way, as if expecting her to do something about this bounty hunter person they claimed was in town. But then, people usually looked to Michaela for guidance because she was a leading citizen of Colorado Springs.

"All right, Michaela, what do you know about this?" Dorothy couldn't help but ask. If the reverend and Robert E.

were right, if there was a bounty hunter somewhere in town, that was newsworthy information and she needed to gather the facts, beginning with *who*.

Michaela glanced around uncomfortably at Robert E., at the reverend as he stepped onto the porch, at Dorothy, at the porch planks, then back at Dorothy. Michaela definitely knew something, and Dorothy meant to get the information out of her.

"I . . . ," Michaela began.

"A bounty hunter helps catch outlaws, doesn't he, Ma?" Brian asked.

"Tell," Dorothy demanded of Michaela. "There *is* a bounty hunter here, ain't there?"

"Yes, Brian. Where did you hear such a thing?" Michaela asked the reverend and Robert E.

"It's goin' 'round town," Robert E. said. "Man started talkin' yonder at *that* saloon. Word traveled from there."

"What man?" Dorothy demanded, pressing forward. Her hands smarted, and she winced. Shoo on them. This was important enough that she'd ignore them for now.

"Don' know his name," Robert E. answered.

"Some man who was playin' cards with that old miner friend of Sully's," the reverend put in.

Michaela corrected him. "He's not Sully's friend. How did you find out they worked the mines together?"

Reverend Johnson withdrew a little. "All right then . . . workmate . . . fellow miner. . . . It doesn't matter how I found out, Dr. Mike. That's not the issue. The issue is bounty hunting. Hunting and killing or imprisoning men for money is—"

"No better than hanging them."

Michaela's words made the reverend withdraw even more. Brian went back to petting Mouse, obviously uncomfortable that Michaela seemed so irritated all of a sudden.

Robert E. took Reverend Johnson's place, coming up onto the porch. "We gonna let that man stay here? We've got

59

a peaceful community. We don't need a bounty hunter bringin' trouble here."

"He didn't bring it, Robert E.," Michaela said. "He simply followed it. Or so he thinks."

That intrigued Dorothy. "Followed it? You mean he's tailin' an outlaw an' he's tailed him here? That's what you're meanin', ain't it, Michaela? That he tailed an outlaw to Colorado Springs!"

Katie began crying again. The noise and confusion frightened the baby, Dorothy was certain. But the journalist in her felt relentless, and so she shot questions at Michaela around Katie's cries: "How did you find out about the bounty hunter? What's his name? Who's he tailin'? Sully worked the mines with him?"

"What are we going to do about this?" Reverend Johnson demanded.

"We've got to gather citizens, at least council members, an' go see Jake," Robert E. said. "We've gotta have a meetin' 'bout this. This ain't gonna sit well with people."

"Who're his friends?" Dorothy pressed. She didn't have her tablet with her. Oh, drat! She couldn't write down Michaela's responses anyway—her hands weren't working right.

"Stop it!" Michaela ordered, taking several steps back toward the clinic door. "You're all frightening Katie."

They quieted—Dorothy, Robert E., the reverend. They glanced at each other, and Dorothy was certain the guilty looks on Reverend Johnson's and Robert E.'s faces reflected the one on her own.

"You can't write a story right now anyway, Dorothy," Michaela said. "Stop attacking me with questions."

The words stung Dorothy. Why Michaela would bring up such a sensitive subject in front of other people, she couldn't imagine. Ordinarily she'd never betray a confidence.

"I'm sorry," Michaela said, glancing away again, then back to Dorothy. "I'm frightened myself right now, and I can't talk about it."

Dorothy wanted to ask why she couldn't talk about what was frightening her—the thought of a bounty hunter in Colorado Springs?—but she figured she'd asked Michaela enough questions for one day.

"Have we posted signs anywhere on the roads leading into town that say who can enter and who cannot?" Michaela demanded of Reverend Johnson and Robert E.

"Of course not!" Reverend Johnson snapped.

"Then I don't see the point in holding a town meeting. The man has stopped here briefly. He'll move on soon. For us to dictate who can or cannot enter Colorado Springs would be extreme, wouldn't it? If not unconstitutional. Neither should we run anyone out of town because of who or what they are," Michaela said. "You surprise me, Reverend. So do you, Robert E."

With that, and after shooting both men a harsh look, Michaela turned and entered her clinic, closing the door behind her.

A few moments of uncomfortable silence passed between Dorothy, Reverend Johnson, and Robert E.

"She's right," Dorothy said, suddenly feeling small and humble. "We're judgin' an' we shouldn't be."

"But the thought of it, Dorothy . . . ," the reverend said.

"The thought is disturbin', I agree. But it ain't for us to decide, or to gossip about, or maybe not even to write about. It's news, but she's right—I can't . . . well, I'm havin' a little trouble workin' my press an' I can't write up anythin' right now anyway."

"Why can't you write anything?" Robert E. asked.

Dorothy's chin shot up. "I'm havin' a little medical problem," she said. Then she descended the steps and walked off, hoping to preserve some of her dignity. She'd gotten caught up in Robert E.'s and the reverend's excitement, and she'd forgotten that before she wrote anything else, she had to figure out who was going to help her print this week's issue of the *Gazette*. If she missed a week, she might as well give it up, she'd feel like such a failure.

61

Back at the clinic, Reverend Johnson told Brian, "You've got to talk to your ma. She's got to talk to Jake about this. We need to hold a meeting."

Brian stood and scooped up Mouse. "I don't mean to be disrespectful, Reverend, but I don't think Ma wants to talk to anyone about that bounty hunter."

Reverend Johnson took in a deep breath, then pushed it out. Brian saw a clear path, and he hurried off, just like Miss Dorothy had, only in the opposite direction. He'd go see what Mr. Bray was doing and if he had any good candy today. Suddenly the coins in Brian's pocket needed to be put to good use, and he couldn't think of a better time than right now.

By evening, Sully and Cloud Dancing had closed in on the area where Cloud Dancing suspected the Pawnees were hiding Levi Willard. They'd traveled through numerous ravines and passed by caves and shallow canyons, stopping only to eat the bread and dried venison they'd tucked in their haversacks. They dipped and drank water from cold mountain streams; Wolf lapped up water, then rolled around in the grass, which had turned green only in recent weeks. Occasionally they caught a drift of chilled air, reminding them that winter had not been so long ago, and that the higher into the mountains they went, the colder the air would become.

They'd talked softly about Katie, how big she was growing, and then they'd talked about Michaela, how she still felt tense at times trying to manage a baby and a home and practice medicine, too.

"You are happier than ever with your family and home," Cloud Dancing remarked. Then Sully changed the subject back to Willard.

Whenever the subject of home and family arose between them, Sully never missed the sadness that crept into Cloud Dancing's eyes. Cloud Dancing missed his wife and son. And, Sully knew, his friend missed much more than that. He missed the old Cheyenne ways, the freedom of roaming the land, of going wherever he wanted to go . . . of following the buffalo.

From a low branch Cloud Dancing lifted a piece of brown material so small that the normal eye wouldn't have caught it. He silently showed it to Sully, who nodded, acknowledging the evidence.

They walked on, stepping carefully through the undergrowth and around trees and branches. Sully smelled smoke, but he saw none rising above the trees. Still, he knew there was a fire somewhere close.

A gathering of low-lying hills sat directly ahead of them. A man could hide easily among the boulders and rocky crevices, even beneath the numerous ledges. The normal person—including soldiers who didn't know the land—couldn't find someone who chose to hide here. But Sully and Cloud Dancing could.

It didn't take them much longer to find Levi Willard.

He had made camp in a small open area that was shielded by rocky rises on three sides. Sully started around the open side and happened to glance down at Wolf, who had gone rigid and still. Sully glanced at Cloud Dancing, who'd done the same, and then he heard whistling behind the rocky rises and he knew they'd found the outlaw.

He crouched low, making his way to the far rise. Cloud Dancing followed, their moccasins brushing softly, almost silently, on the rocks and grass. Sully began climbing the rise, grabbing rocks and planting his feet carefully. He couldn't risk a stone slipping, hitting against other stones as it tumbled down the rise; that would alert Willard to the fact that someone was close by.

Sully couldn't believe Willard hadn't escaped down to Indian Territory, a popular place for outlaws to hide out. But maybe he'd known that Hagan was hot on his tail and that sitting tight might buy him some time where Hagan was concerned.

Embers still glowed in a blackened area in the center of

the clearing where a fire obviously had burned full force not too long ago. Sully couldn't believe Willard had risked a campfire—the smoke always rose and carried. With that fire, he'd risked giving away his location.

The outlaw looked grubby and dirty as he sat on a log, chewing on a piece of freshly roasted meat. His clothes were caked with a good month's worth of dirt and dust. A tin cup sat on the ground beside his right boot.

A rifle was propped against a stone ledge opposite Willard, and Sully figured a distance of maybe five feet separated the outlaw from his weapon. Paraphernalia littered the ground to the left of the rifle—a few books, a box of cartridges, several bundles of money, a brown blanket, loose strips of buckskin, a Colt revolver with a fine ivory handle.

Willard didn't wear a belt with holsters—Sully looked—which made him a little less dangerous. Still, Sully didn't intend to give him any time to react.

He dropped down on the outlaw, knowing he'd have a struggle. Any man in his right mind who'd killed as many people as Willard had, knew that if he got caught, he'd hang. Of course, men like Willard who went around killing weren't exactly in their right minds.

Sully grabbed the outlaw around the neck and yanked him to the ground. The roasted meat went flying.

Willard grunted and struggled, and he and Sully wrestled and rolled across the dying campfire. Willard held him down on the hot embers for a minute, and Sully smelled singeing hair and grunted with pain as the embers burned through his buckskin shirt and roasted the skin on his lower back.

Willard was strong. But Sully finally got his knees up and his feet on the man's chest, and he gave Willard a shove that sent him sprawling against one of the rises. Willard's head whipped back and hit hard against the stones.

Sully rolled off the embers, thinking the blow to the head might knock the outlaw out. But Willard bounced off the rise and came at him just as Sully rolled to his feet, crouching, trying to ignore the painful burn on his back. He watched Willard carefully to try and guess his next move.

Willard jerked a small pistol from a holster inside his boot and fired it before Sully had time to react.

The bullet embedded itself in Sully's left upper arm, hitting him with enough force to jerk him around slightly. He hadn't thought the outlaw had a weapon on him. He should have known better.

Cloud Dancing dropped down between Sully and the outlaw and knocked the pistol out of Willard's hand. Then Cloud Dancing was on him, dragging the outlaw to the ground.

Sully didn't like guns and he rarely handled them, but this was an unusual situation—if he didn't get Willard off Indian land, the entire village of Arapaho and Cheyenne would suffer, not just the few Pawnee who had given the outlaw a hiding place in exchange for money and food.

That thought made Sully grab the pistol and aim it at Willard's head.

The move forced the outlaw to stop struggling.

Keeping the pistol aimed at Willard, who watched him through narrowed eyes, Sully grabbed the strips of buckskin. He handed them to Cloud Dancing, and Cloud Dancing pulled Willard's arms behind his back and tied them together at the wrists. Then Cloud Dancing moved away from the outlaw.

"Get up," Sully told Willard. "On your feet."

Willard managed to roll over and sit up. "Might as well kill me an' get it done," he rasped in a breathless voice. He scooted back against the rocks and used them to push to a standing position. "Don't let Hagan get ahold o' me. He'll cut me up an' deliver the pieces to the marshal. He did that with somebody else. Marshal didn't care none. He paid Hagan the bounty money an' Hagan went off."

The man looked scared suddenly, real scared. Sully

shouldn't feel pity for a man who'd killed so many people. But he did.

"Hagan ain't gonna touch you," Sully promised Willard. "I'm takin' you to the sheriff in Colorado Springs. He'll make sure Hagan doesn't touch you either."

"There ain't no way," the outlaw said. "With Hagan after my head, I'll be dead 'fore we ever get to jail." He spat blood on the ground.

Not if Sully could help it. He figured he'd see George coming—and that he'd have enough time to get Willard out of the way and to Matthew.

6

The hour was late, and Sully still had not returned home. Michaela had sat up reading, waiting for him, finally becoming engrossed in the latest issue of the *American Medical Journal*. It wasn't an easy publication to obtain on the Colorado frontier. A year or so ago, Rebecca had begun sending it from Boston, and Michaela was most grateful.

The wind rattled a nearby windowpane. The pane had worked loose, and not much wind was needed to rattle it. The sound seemed much louder than Michaela knew it was, probably because the rest of the house was so quiet at this time of night. Katie wasn't gurgling, laughing, or crying, and Brian wasn't talking, either entertaining Katie or conversing with Michaela.

Michaela heard a coyote howl somewhere in the distance. But she never considered the coyote's howl a *howl* really. That's what everyone called the noise the animal made. Michaela thought the noise was more of a high-pitched squeal.

She pulled her shawl more snugly around her shoulders.

67

Sully might at least have left Wolf. Certainly she could take care of herself—she had long ago learned to shoot a rifle and revolver. Still, Wolf's presence would make her feel safer.

The horses whinnied out in the barn, loud enough that Michaela heard them inside the house. The coyote's noise made the horses nervous, as always. But the animal sounded like it was quite a distance away, so Michaela didn't worry about it attacking the horses. Besides, they were safely tucked away in their stalls, and the barn was closed up tight.

She tried to read more, this time an article about the benefits of purging. She read a sentence, then reread it. Then read the sentence again.

Surely the article made sense, because the *Journal* was a highly respected medical publication. Normally it might make perfect sense. But tonight, nothing could be learned from the sentence Michaela kept rereading. Probably not even from the entire article.

The house was too quiet; she missed Sully, and worried about him and Cloud Dancing. Had they been caught? If not, had they found the outlaw? And if they had, when did they plan to bring him to town? Soon, surely. Were they spending the night under the stars somewhere? She hoped Sully had taken an extra blanket with him. In June the air always warmed in some low-lying Colorado areas, but the ground was still cold. If they were in the mountains, even the air would be cold.

Distracted from reading, Michaela rose, picked up a lantern, and headed for the front door. Just before opening it, she reached for the rifle that hung above it. She took the weapon down and made sure it was loaded. It was.

Outside, pitch blackness surrounded the house, except for the area immediately around the lantern. Michaela sat on the porch steps, listening to the coyote, now joined by others, and the horses.

She always missed Sully terribly when he went hunting and trapping, or when he simply had to be away for a few days—like when he and Cloud Dancing had been involved in that train wreck. Home was not the same without Sully, without him to snuggle up to beneath their coverlet, without him to bury his face in her hair after the lamps were extinguished.

And yet, Michaela was strong enough to know she would survive if something happened to Sully. Her father's death had shown her that she could survive just about any tragedy.

How quickly she had learned, after her initial journey out here from Boston, that only those with stamina and determination and persistence could survive on this frontier. She *had* survived—and now lived comfortably. The rich forests that surrounded this homestead were vastly different from Boston's wide streets and manicured walkways and commons. Here one had to watch out for wild animals rather than "coasters" and mischievous boys like Jimmie Becker. Yet this was a world she had grown to love.

That thought of Jimmie Becker made Michaela smile. What a long time since she'd thought of that childhood friend! Jimmie Becker . . . the terror of Beacon Hill, the dreamer, the adventurer. While she and David Lewis had gone about their childhood activities in a relatively sensible and calm manner—although her mother would doubtless argue that point—Jimmie had been reckless. Eventually his wild nature had led him to enlist in the Union Army. He'd been killed in battle, as many Boston boys had been, and reconciling herself to the fact that she would never see Jimmie again had been hard for Michaela.

Jimmie . . . he had once told her that girls didn't attend medical school, and he'd once implied that even if a medical school admitted her, she didn't have enough basic learning to make it successfully through college. She'd proven him wrong, however, just as she'd proven many people wrong. The fact that she'd been born female had never kept her from accomplishing anything she wanted to accomplish.

If Jimmie could see me now, Michaela thought, smiling to herself in the light of the lantern. He had felt, as many people did, that all properly bred and raised Boston girls eventually settled and did nothing more than raise children and run a household. She was a girl; therefore she ought to be a delicate creature—or so Jimmie had thought.

She shook her head. *If only he could see me now . . . witness the life I've made for myself in the wilds of Colorado Territory.* She made do without water piped in and without gas lighting. She had no maids or servants, and she had a house she loved but that many Bostonians would find horrid. Also a husband she loved but that many Bostonians would find horrid.

Indeed, as her mother had told her many times and as she knew very well herself, she'd never done anything in a conventional fashion. But she didn't necessarily buck convention to defy anyone, as she often had as a girl. She bucked it now to make herself happy, and to follow what was in her heart.

In the end, her inner strength was good for other people, too. They knew they could rely on her to help calmly in times of crisis—which was exactly the reason why Robert E. and Reverend Johnson had come to her this afternoon with their concerns about a bounty hunter roaming Colorado Springs.

A sobering thought.

She didn't like George Hagan's occupation anymore than did Robert E., Reverend Johnson, and Dorothy. In fact, she had strong feelings against one person hunting and capturing or killing another person for money. But to run Mr. Hagan out of town because of his occupation? No one had the right to do that, any more than they had the right to run Hank's girls out of town because of *their* occupation.

The best solution would be for George Hagan to slip away quietly, on his own.

In truth, because of Sully's hard feelings against the man, Michaela didn't want George Hagan to stay in Colorado Springs. That thought created twinges of guilt in her because Mr. Hagan did have as much right to visit or settle in Colorado Springs as anyone else.

On the other hand, Michaela loved the quiet, moral community in which she had become so involved, and she didn't want to see it changed by the lawless ways that gripped so many other Western communities.

She was finally sleepy. She leaned over and propped her head against the porch railing. She listened again to the coyotes. Moments later, she took up her lantern, rose, and went back inside the house.

The bed didn't feel the same without Sully lying next to her. But she was tired enough that she drifted off to sleep in just a few minutes.

Her last thought was of Sully—a mumbled prayer that wherever he was, he was safe and warm.

"Miss Dorothy waited a long time to tell you about her hands hurtin'," Brian said to Michaela as they rode into town the next morning.

The wagon rattled and creaked as Katie sat on Brian's lap, clapping her hands and squealing with delight every now and then. What, exactly, she squealed about Michaela didn't know. Katie simply did that occasionally—almost as a form of self-entertainment. Perhaps she just wanted to hear her voice.

The baby played with her fingers, entwining them, then disengaging them and fitting them together another way. Katie's cheeks were rosy this morning, and a lock of fine auburn hair peeked out on her forehead from beneath the yellow bonnet Michaela had tied on her a short time ago.

As Michaela continued to drive the horses, Brian spoke more about Dorothy: "Now that I think about it, I started noticin' about a week ago that she was havin' trouble workin' the press. Ma, why d'you suppose she didn't go to you then?"

"No one wants to believe anything might be physically wrong with them, Brian. For some people, realizing that something *is* wrong is for them to accept. Some people actually feel betrayed by their bodies. And other people don't want to be slowed down. Perhaps Dorothy thought she could ignore the pain in her hands and carry on as if nothing were wrong."

"Will her hands get better soon, Ma? Will she be able to print her paper? You should've seen her—she couldn't work her press. Every time she tried, her face turned red an' she pulled her hands back."

"I think she'll need someone to help her for a while."

"I could help her," Brian volunteered sweetly.

Michaela smiled. He had such a huge heart, always wanting to help people. "That's wonderful—as long as helping Dorothy print the paper doesn't interfere with school. You've had several free days because Miss Teresa has been gone and the reverend . . . well, I don't quite know what to make of Reverend Johnson lately." He usually taught the children whenever Miss Teresa was absent. But his mind had been on other things of late—namely, the fact that a bounty hunter had taken up temporary residence in Colorado Springs. "Now it's time to concentrate on school again."

"I know," Brian said, sounding a little disheartened. Seconds later he brightened. "I could help Miss Dorothy this evenin', couldn't I, Ma?"

She considered that. "I could bring your supper into town—or send you to Grace's for supper."

"That is, if Dorothy wants to work this evenin'. She usually works on the paper durin' the day."

"Yes, but if she has a helper, especially such an eager one, she might shift her hours. I can't imagine that she wouldn't, the *Gazette* is so important to her."

"She doesn't much like anyone meddlin' with her press," Brian said, looking rather worried; a possible glitch in his plan had just occurred to him.

"Well, she'll be right there. Surely if she's right there, she won't mind. She doesn't have much of a choice right now,

Brian," Michaela said. "Do you remember when I went back to the clinic after Katie was born and I tried to manage just as many patients as I had before she was born?"

Brian nodded.

"My pride and my feeling that I could manage everything—the house, a family, a new baby, and the clinic—interfered with my good judgment. I don't like to feel limited by anything or anyone. Dorothy's the same way. For years, she *was* limited. That paper is her pride and joy. It's something she created by herself, something that makes her more happy and proud than she could ever express. It's almost like . . . well, it's almost like her child. Dorothy might have as much trouble asking someone to help her print the paper as I had in realizing that I couldn't manage all that I was trying to manage."

The road wound around, and Colorado Springs came into sight. The wagon wheels stirred up dust, creating clouds behind them. On either side of the passage, foliage grew in abundance. In the distance, the sight of the snow-peaked, purplish-blue mountains took Michaela's breath away, as always, they were so beautiful. Almost every evening, if there was a clear sky, they were tinted pink, purple, and a deep, beautiful gray.

"She won't have to ask," Brian remarked. "I'll ask *her* if I can help her print the paper."

Again, Michaela smiled at him. Katie gurgled at her, blowing a big bubble. Michaela and Brian laughed at the baby, and Katie laughed, too, clapping her hands together again.

Sully should have known better than to take Willard down the middle of Main Street. He should have brought him into town the back way, to the back of Matthew's office, then around to the front of the building. That way, he could have had Willard in the sheriff's office before Hagan could spot him or have time to do anything.

Cloud Dancing had loaned Sully several horses, and

73

Willard rode one, while Sully rode on another, behind the outlaw, a woolen blanket draped over his shoulders.

The sight of Sully leading into town a man whose hands were tied behind his back was unusual. As they rode past Grace's café, people stopped eating to look at them. Grace stopped stirring food in a big iron kettle and stared as she wiped her hands on her apron. Children glanced up from the schoolhouse steps. Sully spotted Brian among the children and wondered what Michaela had told Brian to explain his absence these past few days. Of course, Brian might think he'd been off hunting or trapping again. He *had* been hunting, actually.

Robert E. stopped shoeing a horse to stare. Numerous men and a few of Hank's girls emerged from the saloon, while Jake and several old-timers rose from their chairs in front of the barbershop.

The clinic door opened, and out stepped Michaela with Katie in her arms. Michaela had that worried look in her eyes—but she was relieved to see him, Sully could tell. He'd be glad when he delivered Willard to Matthew. Then he could kiss his wife and hold his baby daughter. He could have Michaela tend his arm, too. The bullet needed to come out. He couldn't move his arm without breaking out in a sweat because of the grinding pain.

A crowd began gathering behind Sully and Willard, curiously following along. Matthew's office came into sight; Sully was glad, because he was getting nervous. He and Willard were attracting too much attention.

In front of the sheriff's office, Sully was just swinging his leg over the saddle to dismount when a rifle shot cracked the air. People screamed and shouted and ran.

Sully slid the rest of the way off his horse, ducking instinctively. He heard a thud as something, or someone, hit the ground. The horses whinnied and skittered, and then Sully spotted Levi Willard lying still on the ground.

At first he thought Willard had intentionally taken a spill. Then he saw blood on the dirt and a hole in Willard's left temple. Willard was blinking real fast and fighting for breath. His face had gone white, and the right side of it was almost buried in the dirt. He didn't move his head because he couldn't, Sully realized.

Levi Willard was as close to death as a man could be and still be alive. The really bad thing was, Willard knew it—he was still conscious. He sputtered, trying to say something. But all that came out of his mouth was blood and saliva.

Sully cursed under his breath, something he didn't usually do. A lot of protection he'd given Willard! And after he'd promised the man he wouldn't let Hagan get him.

"It came from the saloon," Robert E. shouted as he ran up to Sully.

"Get Michaela," Sully told Robert E. But Michaela surely had seen what just happened and was probably already on the way, her bag in hand.

Sully wasted no time. He shook the blanket from his shoulders and ran toward the saloon.

"Is George Hagan in there?" he shot at Hank as he neared the saloon steps. Hank stood to one side with a crowd of people.

"He was. Upstairs with one of the girls. What're you—?"

Sully bulleted up the steps and shoved open the swinging doors.

Inside the saloon only one man remained—and he wasn't George Hagan. He was seated at a far corner table, and he looked engrossed in the ledger that sat open beneath his forearms. An open bottle of whiskey and a glass were to his left. The man glanced up at Sully, then went back to his ledger and his whiskey, unbothered by the commotion outside or by Sully's sudden entrance.

Sully raced up the staircase, his injured arm throbbing and screaming at him. Once upstairs, he threw open doors, beginning with the first one he reached.

In the first two rooms the beds were nice and neat, and the rooms were unoccupied. In the third, Sully found Hagan lounging back against a headboard, puffing on a cigar. And Hagan didn't look surprised to see him.

Sully was halfway to the bed when someone grabbed him from behind and slammed him against the nearest wall.

"You can't be comin' in here disturbin' my customers," Hank said, holding Sully tight.

Sully fought a grimace of pain. Cloud Dancing had applied a balm to the burn on his back and the gunshot wound in his arm. He'd then wrapped the wounds, stopping the bleeding. But Sully would bet the bleeding had started again. "That shot came from your saloon," he told Hank. "Hagan did it. He killed Levi Willard."

"There's other people up here, in other rooms," Hank said. "You can't say for sure he did the shootin'."

"Search this room. You'll find a gun."

"What do you mean, I killed Willard?" Hagan demanded from the bed. He lowered his cigar, looking startled and alarmed.

Hank kept hold of Sully's shirt while he glanced over his shoulder at Hagan. "Willard's dyin' in the street. Sully here came ridin' in with him an' someone shot him. Sully seems to think the shot came from my saloon. Did it, Mr. Hagan?"

"It did," Sully said. Sure enough, he was bleeding again. He felt wetness on the bandage and on his shirtsleeve.

Hank either felt it, too, or saw the blood. "You're hurt," he said. Sully nodded.

"You got Willard?" Hagan asked Sully, looking real surprised. He ignored Hank's question. He was doing a fine job of acting. He knew Sully had gotten Willard—he'd just taken a good shot at the man. A deadly shot.

Hagan started up off of the bed, reaching for his pants—they were tossed across the foot of the tick—and Sully jerked against Hank's hold. He'd never wanted to get his hands on anyone as badly as he wanted to get his hands on George Hagan right now. He'd promised Willard a safe trip to the sheriff's office, and he'd bet anything the man was dead by now. If Willard wasn't dead, he was close to it, and there was no saving him. Not even Michaela could work that kind of miracle, and Sully had seen her heal many a person he hadn't thought would live.

"You know I did," Sully told Hagan.

Hank brought his face up close to Sully's. "You just hold still now, 'fore you start gushin' an' I have to carry you to Michaela. You ain't doin' yourself no good."

"I ain't interested in doin' myself any good," Sully shot at him.

"You're not thinkin' right, then."

Hagan pulled his pants on.

"Search this room," Sully told Hank again. "Search it an' you'll find the gun he used to kill Willard."

"Well, if Willard's dead, someone did my work for me." Hagan said as he buttoned his pants. "Imagine that. While I'm in here enjoyin' myself."

Sully nearly came unglued again. "You ain't collectin' that bounty, Hagan."

Hagan turned around and fixed a cold look on Sully. "I aim to claim that body—and that bounty. Doesn't look like you're in any condition to challenge me on that."

"By all rights, that bounty belongs to Sully," Hank said, again glancing at Hagan.

Sully didn't want the bounty—blood money. But he meant to see that Hagan didn't collect it. Willard had been wanted dead or alive because he'd done some pretty bad things. But the fact was, he'd been unarmed and defenseless when Hagan shot him down, and Sully wouldn't let Hagan collect the bounty.

Hagan grabbed his shirt and slipped it on. Then he started for the door.

Hank reached out with lightning speed, grabbed Hagan, and shoved him backward. Hagan slammed against the foot of the bed.

"It's a done deal," Hank growled at the bounty hunter. "Sully gets any money that comes from gettin' Willard. You ain't gettin' no money anyway without a body. Might as well give it up, Hagan. Ain't no way you're gettin' Willard's body out of this town. We bury folks that die here. I know the sheriff well enough to know he'll wire the marshal in Denver an' let 'im know Sully brought Willard in."

Hagan tried staring Hank down. When that didn't work, he said, "You're hurtin' your business."

Hank grinned, and his expression was half daring, half devil-may-care. "Temporarily. There's more out there."

Hank tried turning Sully toward the door. Sully resisted, still wanting to turn the room upside down.

Hank tightened his hold and shook his head. "Willard's dead," he said under his breath. "You ain't gonna change that by findin' a gun in here. Even if you do, no one's gonna care too much that Hagan shot Levi Willard. The man killed a few people in his time, remember? He was wanted, an' he was wanted dead or alive. If you don't want Hagan to collect on that bounty, you've gotta get down there 'fore he does, an' claim that body. Then we've gotta get you to Michaela."

Hank had never tried to talk sense into Sully. Usually it was the other way around. Sully stared at him, knowing he was right. From the corner of his eye, he caught a glimpse of Hagan favoring his right arm. It must have hit the footboard pretty hard. If he had a gun up here, he sure wasn't going after it to try and make sure they let him have Willard's body.

Hank was right—there was no saving Willard by trying to prove that Hagan had shot him. Who would care, anyway? The people of Colorado Springs, maybe, because people weren't normally gunned down on the streets here. But after that—who? The circuit judge, after hearing whom Hagan had killed? Not a chance.

Murder was murder in Sully's eyes. But the fact was, Willard had had a Wanted Dead or Alive poster out on him, and beyond the citizens of this town, nobody would care that he'd been killed by Hagan. They'd be relieved that he was dead.

Sully had said he'd make sure Hagan didn't collect on that bounty. He meant that, even if he had to go down and claim that body and bounty himself. He'd brought Willard in, after all, and after making Willard the promise that he wouldn't let Hagan get him, Willard was dead, shot down by George Hagan. Hagan might have killed Willard, but he wasn't going to collect that bounty.

"Let's go," Sully told Hank.

That made Hank grin. "That's better," he said, and they walked out of the room.

Sully didn't especially like the thought of George Hagan coming up behind them. But as they neared the staircase, he saw that a crowd of people—men and Hank's girls—had gathered downstairs, and he felt confident that Hagan wouldn't try anything with so many witnesses. Hagan was underhanded; he didn't do things out in the open, where he was sure to be caught.

Downstairs Sully and Hank cut through the crowd and made their way outside. Questions rose—*Did ya find who did it? Hell, it don't matter anyhow—that's Levi Willard, ain't it? Ain't there a bounty for him?*

Sully ignored the questions and walked down the steps in front of the saloon. He and Hank again cut between people, approaching the sheriff's office. Sully spotted Michaela bending over Willard, her stethoscope dangling from her neck, her fingertips searching for a pulse a few inches below Willard's jaw. She stood as Sully and Hank drew within a few yards. "He's dead," she announced, and Sully nodded.

"Anybody know where Matthew is?" Robert E. asked. "He ain't 'round nowhere."

"Maybe out at the Tennessey place," Loren volunteered. "They've been havin' trouble with rustlers out that way."

"I'll take Willard's body into the sheriff's office until Matthew gets back," Hank said. "Sully needs attention, Dr. Mike."

Michaela's worried gaze swept over Sully, finally landing on his injured arm. The bandage was a bloody mess. So was his shirtsleeve. He felt dizzy, although he sure wouldn't tell anyone that.

"What happened?" she asked, hurrying toward him.

Sully held up his hand and shook his head to stop her. He wouldn't have her fussing over him out here, practically in the middle of Main Street. "Don't let Hagan get him, Hank," he said, looking Hank straight in the eye. "He ain't gettin' that bounty."

Hank grinned. He liked standoffs and trouble. Sully reckoned Hank got bored pretty often in this quiet, upstanding community. He needed something more like Dodge City, and sometimes Sully was surprised Hank hadn't ended up there, or in Wichita, or in a dozen other wild places.

"You got my word," Hank said. Then he walked around Sully and stood just above Willard's head.

He bent down, looped his hands under Willard's arms, and dragged him off. As he started up the steps with him, Robert E. appeared, lifting Willard's body by the boots and helping Hank get him up the steps and into the sheriff's office. Where Hank meant to put Willard once he got him inside, Sully didn't know. He didn't have time to worry over that, because Michaela took him by the arm and began urging him toward the clinic.

Hagan was waiting at the front door, leaning leisurely against the frame, picking dirt out from under his fingernails.

"Excuse us," Michaela said, and Sully knew what her clipped tone meant: Hagan had a second or two to move, or she'd tell him exactly what she thought of him.

"Reckon you know this means me or you," Hagan said in a low voice. He spoke to Sully, looking directly at him.

"Threatening my husband, Mr. Hagan?" Michaela demanded, her feathers ruffled.

"Just tellin' him how it is. That bounty's mine. I ain't gonna let him stand in the way of me collectin' it. I hear he's friendly with the Injuns . . . that Cheyenne medicine man."

"Get out of the way, Hagan," Sully warned.

Hagan looked up. "I want that body, an' I want it before nightfall."

"You ain't gettin' it."

"Then you just might have more bodies to deal with. A few dead Injuns. . . ." Hagan shrugged. "Nobody'll care."

That snapped what little patience Sully had managed to muster. He broke free of Michaela's hold on his arm and moved with lightning speed, before Michaela had time to react and before Hagan had time to anticipate his move. Sully grabbed Hagan by the shirtfront and slung him off the porch. Hagan went rolling in the dusty street.

"For all your threats, you keep gettin' beat lately," Sully told the man. He wasn't one to taunt and involve himself in feuds. The threat that Hagan meant to kill people he cared about—Indians . . . Cloud Dancing?—if Sully didn't turn Willard's body over to him was more than Sully could stomach.

By the time Hagan got to his feet, Jake and Robert E. stood between him and the clinic. Jake said something to Hagan, and then Robert E. took a step forward, an iron rod in his right hand. Hagan made like he might try to bolt between them, and Robert E. muttered something at him. Hagan finally turned and started off toward the saloon.

Sully wasn't sure his going back there was such a good idea. The whiskey served there could make men mean, if not meaner. Besides, Hagan would have a grudge against Hank now, too, because Hank was guarding Willard's body until Matthew showed up. He might set fire to the saloon, rough up one of Hank's girls. . . .

"Let Robert E. and Jake take care of him right now," Michaela said, and she wasn't making a suggestion. Her expression—drawn, apprehensive, impatient—said she'd had enough of this madness and that she wanted to cut his bandage away and see to his wound. He never had answered her question about what happened to him.

"Where's Katie?" he asked.

"With Grace. Let's go inside, Sully."

This time when she tugged on his arm, he didn't resist. He followed her into the clinic without looking back. He'd worried her more than enough during the last few days.

7

Michaela removed the bloody bandage from Sully's arm, and cleaned and examined the wound. Minutes later, she announced, "I'll have to remove the bullet. It won't be easy—it's deep and fragmented."

"I figured that," he responded. Willard had shot him at pretty close range. A few inches to the left, and the bullet might have killed him.

"I'll set up for surgery. I'll send someone after Andrew to see if he'll assist."

"You ain't puttin' me to sleep."

She stared at him. "Why not?"

"George Hagan's still out there." *And mad as a trapped mountain lion,* Sully thought.

"Sully, you won't be asleep for very long. I—"

"I ain't goin' to sleep at all, Michaela. Hagan's threatenin' my friends. You ain't puttin' me to sleep."

She was angry. Her lips snapped shut in a tight line, her eyes flashed, her hands locked together in front of her. "I've never seen you act the way you've acted lately, since you learned that George Hagan was in town. I've never heard

83

you threaten anyone! I've never heard you want to run anyone out of town. I know there are people you don't care for, Sully, Preston being one of them. But you would never try to—"

"Preston ain't Hagan," Sully snapped. She didn't understand. . . . She hadn't seen George Hagan at work in the mining camps. She hadn't caught him stealing and faced his lack of remorse. Oh, he'd pretended he was sorry, those first two times. By the third time, when he'd tried to make Sully look guilty, Sully had realized he wasn't sorry at all, that he'd let someone else hang in his place. "Preston wouldn't try to frame someone else for accusin' him of stealin' somethin'. Preston's enough of a man, he'd face it. Preston wouldn't steal in the first place."

Frustrated, Michaela shook her head. "Yesterday morning, you wanted to find Levi Willard because you wanted to protect the Cheyenne from what you knew would happen if the army found an outlaw hiding out on their land. Now George Hagan is threatening Cloud Dancing and others. . . . Mr. Willard is dead and Mr. Hagan wants his body, enough that he's making threats against your friends. What's next, Sully—your family? Yet you refuse to turn Willard's body over to George Hagan. Why? The man is dead, and if Mr. Hagan gets the body, he'll leave town. Isn't that what you want, Sully? It's what you wanted when you first realized that George Hagan was in Colorado Springs. It's what 'most everyone wants, actually."

She was sick of the whole business, he could tell. But he wouldn't turn Willard's body over to Hagan. Things went deeper than that now. "Things are different now, Michaela. Willard's dead—after I promised him I wouldn't let Hagan get him."

"But he did, and there's nothing you can do to change that! If he'll shoot a man from a window or wherever he shot Mr. Willard from, what makes you think he won't shoot you from a window? What makes you think he won't shoot someone else?"

84

"Get this bullet out of me an' I'll make sure he doesn't," Sully said.

She turned away. "Oh, Sully."

She stepped outside and he heard her talking to someone, giving instructions, mentioning Andrew's name and then Hank's. She was right—she probably didn't know him too well right now. His protective instincts were standing straight up. He was scared, just like Michaela was. He'd just seen a man shot down right beside him, after he'd promised that man he wouldn't let anything like that happen. He was doubting himself—if he couldn't protect Willard, what made him think he could protect his friends and family from Hagan? Well, he would. *He would.*

Michaela was right—he ought to give Willard's body to Hagan and be done with it.

He wouldn't be able to live with himself. Willard had probably died thinking he—Sully—had taken him within range of Hagan's bullet. That was hard enough to swallow. If Hagan had found Willard and captured him, Sully most likely wouldn't have meddled in their business. But the way Hagan had shot Willard from the saloon—probably from the window of the room Sully had found him in—turned Sully's stomach. Hagan wouldn't collect that bounty. No way. He wouldn't let him.

Michaela came back inside. She cleaned and bandaged the burn on his back, then began arranging her surgical instruments. She went about things pretty slowly. She kept glancing at the window, like she was either nervous or expecting something, or someone. She was real quiet. She was brooding, keeping her anger to herself.

She wasn't acting arrogant or haughty; she wasn't the uppity Boston woman he'd encountered not long after she arrived in Colorado Springs. She didn't tilt her head and look down her nose at him anymore when she was angry. She still did that with other people now and then, but with him she mostly just spoke her mind. They both did, and he liked the openness they had. But, haughtiness or not, she was angry. And no wonder—he'd made it clear to her that he wouldn't budge where Hagan was concerned, that he wouldn't even consider handing over Willard's body.

At her desk, Michaela opened one of her medical books and began reading. When Sully said her name, she looked up, still angry, her delicate jaw still set.

"I watched George Hagan do a lot of things in that minin' camp," Sully said. "Some things, I just knew about or heard about. The men were scared of him. No one did much to stop him, includin' me. I wanted to keep to myself an' have nothin' to do with anythin' that smelled of trouble—that's why I didn't report him those first few times. Things are diff'rent now, Michaela. I've got you, an' I've got a home an' children. It's time I did somethin'. He's got to know he can't bring trouble into Colorado Springs."

From her standpoint, the resolution was simple: "Give him Mr. Willard's body and he'll be gone."

"Until another outlaw decides to hide out around here."

She stared at him. Seconds later she looked back down at her book. "We don't agree on this and probably never will."

God, she could be stubborn! But then, so could he. "We're not gonna agree on everythin', Michaela."

Her gaze met his again. "The little things don't bother me, Sully. The big things do. I don't like the thought that I might have to take our children and hide them somewhere until this is over. Or that I should ride out to the village and warn Cloud Dancing. You went after Willard to protect the Cheyenne. Now Mr. Hagan is threatening to kill some of them." She shook her head. "You're out for revenge, Sully. That's what this is about—revenge. Where will it end? How?"

Michaela didn't mince words when she was angry.

He hadn't considered that, that all the outrage and anger he felt at George Hagan went deeper than just not letting him bring his trouble to Colorado Springs—that he wanted revenge. She was right. He'd saved Hagan's neck twice when he stole gold, and then Hagan had made *him* look guilty of stealing—and Hagan had shot at him as he'd run out of the camp. Then Hagan had tried to help hunt him down. Later, Sully had been proven innocent. But if he really thought about it, he was still angry about Hagan setting him up.

"Maybe I *am* out for revenge," Sully said quietly.

Still, he wouldn't consider turning Willard's body over to Hagan. Some of his stubbornness and outrage stemmed from Hagan's shooting Willard down right in front of the sheriff's office—after Sully had promised Willard he wouldn't let anything like that happen. A lot of good his word had been! That was probably what Willard had thought when he was dying.

Michaela left things at that.

Pretty soon the door to the clinic opened, and in stepped Loren, Andrew, and Robert E.

"Looks like a meeting to me," Sully remarked.

"Since you don't want to be put to sleep, I thought I might need help," Michaela said uncomfortably.

"I brought whiskey," Loren said, holding up a bottle. "Some of Hank's special stuff, sure to deaden any pain."

"I don't drink," Sully informed him.

Loren scrunched up his face. "Well, now, I know that. But you might need to take it up a little, seein's how Dr. Mike's about to start cuttin' you."

Sully shook his head.

"What . . . what d'ya want us ta do, Dr. Mike?" Robert E. asked.

"Hold him," she answered simply. "The bullet is fragmented, and the fragments are in fairly deep."

"Can you do it?" Andrew asked her. He'd drawn close to inspect the wound. He wasn't really asking if she could perform the surgery. It was more like he was asking if she could put the fact that the patient was her husband from her mind and do what needed to be done.

"I think so," she said, but she looked pale, like maybe she

87

was doubting herself. She glanced down at Sully. "Please let me put you to sleep."

He shook his head.

"I'll do the surgery, Michaela," Andrew volunteered. Nice of him to come to the clinic. Sully had gotten the feeling that when Andrew had gone to work at Preston's resort, Preston forbade him to enter Michaela's clinic.

"No, I can do it. But please stay." And she looked like she wanted to add "Just in case."

Sully knew the thought of operating on him without putting him to sleep was hard on her. Actually doing it would be even harder. But he wouldn't risk going off into a deep sleep and having Hagan pull something while he slept. He'd never forgive himself if George hurt someone while he was enjoying the effects of chloroform.

Andrew consented—Michaela didn't have to make the request twice. She washed the skin around the wound, then rubbed the area with antiseptic solution. She instructed Loren to hold Sully's legs still while Robert E. held his arms and chest. She'd have to probe for the fragments, she told them, glancing nervously at Sully, and he couldn't help but move while she probed. Too much movement and she might lose her grip on a fragment or injure him more.

"Where's Hagan?" Sully asked Robert E.

"Still at the saloon."

"Matthew?"

"Still gone. Hank locked the body up. He's watchin' it."

Sully nodded, and then he focused on a spot on the ceiling. Cloud Dancing had taught him to focus his mind and all his strength on one thing. In doing that he could shut out negative things, such as pain. So Sully focused on that spot, and he slowed his breathing, took deeper breaths.

The first touch of the probe inside the wound wasn't bad. It stung and burned, and Sully concentrated more. The second probe went deeper, and it hurt. The third was even deeper, and Sully broke into a sweat. He heard the clang of metal against metal—probably a fragment dropping into a dish—then Michaela began probing again. With the fourth probe, she said something about the remaining fragments being close to the bone, that she'd have to go deeper, and Sully's concentration shattered. He jerked against Robert E., fighting a groan of pain.

"I can't," Michaela gasped, shaking her head. She pulled her bloody hands away and withdrew. "I can't do any more."

Sully had never witnessed or heard of her quitting in the middle of a surgery. She was quitting because it was him, and because she couldn't stand causing him pain.

"Let 'er put you t'sleep, Sully," Robert E. pleaded. "We ain't gonna let Hagan make off with that body, an' we ain't gonna let him hurt nobody, neither. We'll keep 'im holed up in that saloon."

"He's got a gun in there somewhere," Sully whispered hoarsely, licking his lips. They'd gone dry.

"I got guns. They jus' ain't loaded most times. We'll take care of 'im, Sully. Don't you worry."

Andrew twisted around, then twisted back, a bottle of chloroform and a cloth in his hands.

"Don't let him go near the Indian village," Sully told Robert E. He didn't want to be put to sleep, not with Hagan still in town. But having to dig for bullet fragments and worry about how much pain she was causing him was too hard on Michaela. She didn't worry about how much pain she caused when she did surgery while the patient was asleep. Sully had watched her operate and perform procedures enough times to know that.

"I won't," Robert E. promised, and he was one man Sully trusted without doubt.

Sully looked at Michaela. She'd gone white as a ghost. "All right," he said. "Do it."

Relief washed over her face. She nodded her head at Andrew, and he approached Sully's head, prepared to administer the chloroform.

• • •

Matthew had his hands full.

He'd managed to catch the rustlers who had been stealing the Tennesseys' cattle. He'd handcuffed them and brought them to town to lock them up. There, he'd discovered he had a body occupying one of his cells. It was Levi Willard's body, and, as Hank informed him, he was supposed to guard the body to keep George Hagan from stealing it and taking it to Denver to claim the reward money.

Hagan was antsy, or so Hank said. He was holed up in the saloon, probably drinking up all the whiskey behind the bar. He'd told Sully he wanted the body by nightfall—Jake had eagerly related that. And Matthew would bet just about everything he owned that Hagan would be meaner than a rabid coon if he didn't get the body.

"All right, keep an eye out," Matthew told Hank, as he locked the two rustlers inside a cell. "I'm goin' to see Horace. Guess I'd better wire the marshal before Hagan has time to pull anything."

"Gonna deputize me?" Hank asked. He'd taken a comfortable position behind Matthew's desk, his legs up and his boots resting on top of a pile of papers. He was grinning his usual devilish grin, which meant he was up to something.

Matthew thought about saying "Hell, no." Instead, he said, "Well, now, Hank, if I deputize you, you can't lay claim to part of that bounty money."

Hank's grin melted like snow under hot sunshine. Matthew had been joking. But shoo—what he'd stumbled onto! He shook his head in disgust at Hank.

"Hey, don't you think I'm entitled to a cut?" Hank looked insulted. His boots and legs crashed down off of the desk, and he tipped forward in the chair. That chair wasn't real sturdy, and Matthew thought about warning Hank. But he didn't, and Hank suddenly listed hard to the left. His eyes flared and his hand shot out to grab hold of the edge of the desk. He righted himself, and then he flipped his hair back and scowled. He unscrewed his face and sat up straight, in an attempt to gather his dignity.

Matthew restrained himself from busting out laughing. One of the rustlers he'd just locked up hooted, saying, "Did ja see that?" The other one complained that the man in the next cell looked pretty god-awful, like he might be needin' a doctor or somethin'.

"Or somethin'," Hank muttered. "Pine box, maybe."

That drew the rustler up from the cot on which he'd just settled himself. He took up a position at the bars that separated the cells, and he peered at Willard's body, worry making his ruddy face look like a piece of old leather.

"I've stayed here with that damned body all this time," Hank complained.

"From what I hear, it's only been an hour. Where's Hagan's friends?" Matthew asked, trying hard to ignore the frantic rustler who was discovering that Willard was long past needing the help of a doctor. He ignored Hank's grumbling, too.

"I dunno—last I seen 'em, they were bein' entertained, if you know what I mean."

Matthew knew exactly what Hank meant. When he thought of the fact that Emma had once worked for Hank, entertaining men like Hagan and his friends, his stomach turned.

"Course, that was hours ago," Hank added.

"I'm goin' to send that wire," Matthew said, and he headed for the door. He felt dusty and dirty, and Lord only knew, he was starved. He was sure glad those rustlers were locked up. He might be able to sleep tonight. Maybe. Unless Hagan decided to pull something. If he'd told Sully he wanted the body by nightfall, he just might try to get it. But trying to get the body wouldn't do him any good once Matthew wired the marshal that he had Willard's body and that Sully had brought the outlaw in.

"I ain't stayin' much longer," Hank warned.

"Stay 'til I get back," Matthew said.

Hank scowled at him. "I ain't takin' orders from you."

"Looks like ya are," said the rustler who'd hooted at Hank's nearly toppling out of the chair.

"You shut up," Hank said, and he grabbed a tin cup off of the desk and threw it at the cell.

Cold coffee splattered the rustler, who couldn't jump back fast enough. The cup clattered against the cell bars, and Hank was the one hooting this time.

Shaking his head at the two fools, Matthew went outside and headed toward the telegraph office.

8

Dorothy's hands were feeling somewhat better. She suspected that was because of the medicine Michaela had given her, from which she'd brewed a tea several times now. She'd hired a Chinese girl, too, to heat and carry water to a large tub she'd bought from Loren. But she felt sorry for the girl, no matter what she paid her for carrying those heavy buckets upstairs to heat the water, then downstairs (Dorothy lived in the rooms above the newspaper office) to dump the water after her steam bath. Emptying that tub was hard work, though the girl never complained.

Dorothy had been looking over one of the few copies of the *Gazette* this afternoon, and that was when she spotted the advertisement she'd done for Preston about his new resort. He was advertising, among the resort's medical clinic and other things, the new Russo-Turkish bath he'd put in. It was a steam bath, which was exactly what Dorothy needed.

If she took advantage of that newfangled thing he was advertising, no one would have to haul buckets of water upstairs and downstairs for her. And she might get to the point where she could haul the buckets herself, and only

93

when she needed water to drink or to wash herself or for an occasional bath.

That was how she ended up heading toward Preston's resort—and running into Brian along the way.

When she spotted him, she felt guilty that she didn't have a tablet and pencil in hand and that she wasn't gathering information about the trouble that now was stewing between Sully and that bounty hunter. She'd been reluctant to go to the clinic or the saloon with a tablet in hand. And after giving it some thought, she'd realized that she was scared to get in the middle of the trouble, even as a neutral journalist.

Why, that man, that George Hagan . . . he might shoot her dead, just like he'd shot that outlaw dead, and he might not think twice about doing it, either. He might pull his happy trigger and then be on his merry way—probably just so she couldn't report how it had been Sully, not him, who'd tracked and captured that outlaw.

She wasn't sure *why* Sully had trapped and captured the outlaw, and that niggled at her curiosity. She really would like to know why. She didn't for a minute think he'd done it to collect the bounty money. She knew Sully too well. She knew his sense of honor.

In the end, she always made excuses for herself: She wouldn't go bothering Sully right now; he was probably just starting to wake up from his surgery and probably in a lot of pain. That interview could wait until tomorrow, or maybe even the next day. She ought to interview Hank, too, since he was watching over that body in the jail (what a morbid thought!), and Loren and Robert E. because they'd been there during the first part of Sully's surgery. But she made excuses for not conducting those interviews, too, by telling herself that, well, Hank was pretty busy over in the jail, and Loren and Robert E. were busy keeping a good watch to make sure Hagan didn't try anything. So was Jake.

She couldn't believe Sully hadn't wanted to be put to sleep. That he'd faced the pain of having his wound probed for those bullet fragments and had even refused the whiskey

Loren said he'd brought—a bottle, he revealed to Dorothy, he kept secreted in the mercantile. She could have interviewed Loren right then and there. In fact, she'd started to ask him why he did such a thing, but she'd snapped her jaw shut, not wanting Loren to think she was overly concerned about his welfare. She knew he took a fancy to her—he'd made that pretty clear at one time, and she'd put him off. She'd avoid any situation that might lead him to think she was interested in him in a romantic way.

Another excuse.

Nothing had ever kept her from gathering notes for an article.

She glanced down at her swollen fingers. They were the cause of her reluctance; they were the reason for all the excuses. And she was having a hard time admitting that they were.

How could she tell Brian such a thing—that she was letting the problem with her hands get in the way of collecting the information she needed for the next *Gazette*. She'd always told him that a good journalist conducted interviews and gathered information no matter the circumstances. One had to go about things with a certain amount of caution, of course. But a journalist certainly didn't let something like swollen hands stop her.

All of the excuses, and her chastisement of herself, were running circles in her head. She had to clear them out, because Brian was wasting no time coming her way. She had to think of what she was going to say if he asked if she'd interviewed anyone about the bounty business.

If she pretended to be caught up in her thoughts and in a hurry to do something or go somewhere, maybe Brian wouldn't bother to speak to her. But she knew better than that; the friendly Brian spoke to anyone, no matter what kind of hurry they were in. He was a sweet boy, a treasure.

"'ello, Miss 'orothy," he called, and Dorothy knew she was roped into stopping and talking with him for at least a minute or two. His voice sounded funny—all slurred and muffled—and she couldn't figure why.

"Hello, Brian," she said as he neared. "How's your pa?"

One side of his jaw bulged with something, and when he drew closer and shifted the bulge to the other side, Dorothy saw that the bulge was hard candy. No doubt from the jars in the mercantile. "Ma shays 'e'll be jush' fine. 'ow's your 'ands?" His voice became hushed at the question.

"They're a little better." She thought about holding them up to show him that she could bend her fingers more now without having so much pain. But she didn't want everyone to know that she'd been having a problem with them, so she kept them tucked down by her sides. "Thanks for askin'."

"Oh, you're 'elcome." He shifted the candy again.

"That's the biggest piece of candy I've ever seen," she remarked.

He grinned. "I know. Mr. 'ray or'ered the can'y 'alls 'peshal."

"Just for you, I imagine." Loren had taken a shine to the boy several years ago. Oh, he hadn't admitted it at first, because he'd been so caught up in grief and feeling sorry for himself after Maude's death. He didn't admit it much now. Fact was, Dorothy usually had to squeeze the admission out of him.

"Say, Miss 'orothy, I 'as 'inkin' . . ."

Her brow wrinkled. "Yes, Brian?"

"Well. . . ." He bent over suddenly and deposited the candy ball in his hand. He curled his fingers around the candy, then covered that hand with his other hand. When he glanced back up, his ears had gone red, the way they always did when he was embarrassed. "I know what gettin' the paper printed 'n' out means to you. I know it pains you to run the press. I'll help you. You can stand there an' tell me what to do an' make sure I don't do anythin' wrong, you know, to mess it up or anythin'. I mean, I wouldn't do it intent'nal—it'd be an accident—but you could be there to make sure nothin' like that happened. We'd get the *Gazette* out 'n' your hands wouldn't hurt so bad." He shrugged and shuffled his boots in the dirt, acting like he was nervous at even suggesting such a thing. "I have school durin' the day, but I could help durin' the evenin'. I already checked with Dr. Mike, an' she says that's fine, long as I get my studyin' done. What d'ya think, Miss Dorothy?"

He shuffled again, and Dorothy broke out into a smile. "Why, Brian, I think that's the most unselfish thing I've ever heard in my life! Tell you what—in return for your services, I'll help *you* with your studyin'."

That prompted one of his bright grins. "Thanks, Miss Dorothy! Ma says she'll either pack somethin' to eat or she'll send me to Grace's for supper."

"You tell your ma *I'll* take you to Grace's for supper."

"I will!"

He went quiet then, like he was waiting for her to say something more.

"So I guess you haven't written up anythin' 'bout Mr. Hagan an' Sully an' that outlaw. . . ."

It was her turn to shuffle nervously. She did the shuffling with her head, tilting it this way, then that way. Drats! She'd known he might ask if she'd done any work on the bounty business. It was newsworthy information, after all. "Well, I've been thinkin' a whole lot about it . . . I've been watchin'. . . . Got a few angles in my head." She nodded, unconsciously trying to convince him. "I was thinkin' I ought to interview Mr. Hagan—an' Sully, too. But . . . no . . . I haven't written up anythin' yet."

Brian was quiet for about half a minute. "I reckon we've gotta get this paper out 'fore thinkin' of the next one," he remarked.

Dorothy nodded. She caught sight of Preston over in front of Robert E.'s blacksmith shop, his top hat, as always, in place, his clothes immaculate. She couldn't figure how he kept his clothes so clean when there was always dust in the air and the streets were always muddy after rains and snows. But his shirt was always white as snow, and his waistcoat,

97

jacket, and trousers never had a speck of dirt on them. Oh, well, she'd ponder more on that later. Right now, she *did* need to talk to Preston and she *did* need an excuse to put off this questioning by Brian.

"Excuse me," she said, and started past him.

Brian was curious about where she was headed, she could tell; she felt his stare on her back all the way to Robert E.'s shop. She imagined he popped the candy ball back into his mouth about as soon as she walked off.

She didn't want to draw any notice to herself—she didn't want everyone knowing there was anything wrong with her. So she figured she'd try to talk to Preston real quietlike, maybe even take him off somewhere and talk to him.

By the time she reached Robert E.'s shop, Preston was inspecting a horse—and rattling on at Robert E. "I plan to start a 'cab service,' if you will, from town out to the resort. It will run two, oh, perhaps three times a day. I'll order a carriage—one of those fine, lacquered ones. Oh, and I'll design an emblem, a crest, to be painted on both sides of the main body."

"Reckon that sounds like a good idea," Robert E. commented. But, as always when Preston went on and on about his grandiose ideas, Robert E. didn't look him in the eye. Rather, Robert E. was keeping a pretty close eye on the saloon, where things seemed quieter than normal—no men bursting in and out through the swinging doors, no sign of the girls who usually appeared at the doors now and then to lure the men in.

Robert E. commenced to hammering nails into boards—it looked like he was piecing together a wagon—and Preston began talking again, looking off at nothing in particular, no doubt seeing his crested carriage in his overblown mind.

Dorothy drew close to him. "Preston, I need to—"

"I'll need horses, too. Preferably white," he said.

"Preston—"

"No spots, no blemishes," he went on.

98

"Preston, I'd like to speak with you," Dorothy said, affecting an important and firm tone.

"Later. Four of them, Robert E."

"How many people're you plannin' to haul 'round at a time?" Robert E. was having a really hard time with Preston's latest plan, Dorothy could tell. He shook his head and hammered harder on the nails.

"Ride," Preston said, snapping his gaze to Robert E. "They will *ride* out to the resort. They will not be 'hauled.'"

"That kinda horsepower. . . . Sounds like you're haulin' freight or somethin'."

Preston sniffed. "I can get my horses elsewhere."

"Preston, it's imperative that I speak with you." This time Dorothy stepped between Preston and Robert E., and stood facing the banker.

"I'm sure ya can," Robert E. muttered behind her. "Ranchers might set ya up real nice."

"What is it, Dorothy?" Preston demanded, obviously annoyed. "What would possess you to interrupt me this way?"

She squared her shoulders and lifted her chin. He always tried to act superior and holier-than-thou, and like the rich man she knew he was. But she didn't care how much money he had, or how clean he was. Whenever she needed to talk to him—which wasn't often, since she avoided talking to him unless absolutely necessary—she found that persistence worked better than anything else.

"I need to talk to you in private. Follow me," she ordered, and she didn't give him time to decline; she pivoted and headed toward the back of Robert E.'s livery stable.

"What the devil is this about?" Preston demanded moments later, hurrying along behind her. She'd quickened her steps, intentionally forcing him to hurry.

She reached the back of the stable and then pivoted to face him. He halted abruptly—he had to, or he would have collided with her. And my, oh my, wouldn't that have soiled him! Preston A. Lodge, *the third*, didn't like to come into physical contact with many of the people he'd encountered since making his way to the frontier. He'd come here because the American West was the Land of Opportunity, because he was a banker, and because he followed the scent of money; certainly not because he wanted to consort with or even deal with frontier people. He consorted with them because he was forced to, because they were a part of everyday life here.

"I trust you'll be quick and—"

"You're advertisin' a steam bath," Dorothy said, cutting Preston off. Oh, how he detested that—being cut off in midsentence.

He jerked on the hem of his waistcoat, straightening the garment. "Yes. It's part of the medical clinic. People flock to the hot springs, so I thought. . . . Why do you ask?" He'd been about to explain why he'd put the steam bath in, once again getting caught up in his fancy ideas and ways and things. Then he'd remembered whom he was talking to, and he cut off his excited explanation.

Part of the medical clinic? Well, that put a whole new light on things. Dorothy balked at that information. She didn't want Michaela to think she was going to the resort for medical treatment. She was, in a sense, but not really. She didn't mean to let Andrew examine her; she meant to treat herself.

She started to discard the idea of using Preston's steam bath because it was part of the medical clinic. Then she glanced down at her hands, remembered that she could hardly run her press, much less write articles for the paper, and she thought better of it. "I need to visit your steam bath," she announced rather distantly.

Preston's face wrinkled up. "You need to what?"

She scowled. He'd heard her well enough. He was putting on his Boston airs with her, and she wouldn't be dissuaded by his holier-than-thou looks or way of speaking to her. "Oh, stop lookin' like an old monkey. You heard me—I need to visit your steam bath."

"Why?"

He had no right to question her about why. She had money to pay for the time she spent in the bath, and that, along with the fact that she wanted to utilize the steam bath, was all he needed to know. A strong, direct approach worked better with Preston than anything else, she'd found, even better than turning your nose up at him. "Because I need to, that's why. Now what time can I come out?"

"Dorothy, I don't think the Turkish bath is for you," he said real slow as he studied her.

"Why? 'Cause my money ain't as good as other people's money? I've got money same as all those Northerners an' Easterners that've been comin' out to your resort. Oh, but. . . ." She laid her fingers on the side of her nose and opened her mouth in surprise, like she'd just realized something. And indeed she had. "Since I've been sendin' copies of the *Gazette* off to Denver, some merchants there have been wantin' advertisin' space. I told 'em I don't have any more right now. But that ain't right. A new space'll open up soon. Seein's how I won't be able to print your advertisement an' all. There's some resorts goin' up around Denver. The owners want my limited advertisin' space." She said the last with a sly smile and with her head tilted up at him. He wasn't going to treat her like some low-down coyote—she wouldn't allow him to. Her money was just as good as anyone else's, and if she could pay for a visit to his bath, she ought to be able to visit it.

His face fell. If there'd been five hundred feet between his head and the ground, his face would have fallen that far. All he was hearing now was that he had competition, and that that competition was vying with him for the advertising space in the *Gazette*. She was desperate enough that if it came down to it, she'd make up the name of a resort, set it up around Denver, and she'd design an advertisement for it.

Of course, first she had to be able to print the advertisement. Well, no worry—she planned to teach Brian to work her press, and she'd have him print the advertisement for her.

"All right, Dorothy. Four o'clock," Preston said stiffly, jerking on the hem of his waistcoat again. "Don't be late."

He turned and started off, and Dorothy couldn't resist calling, "I won't, Preston! Don't you worry none."

Almost as soon as Dorothy walked off, Brian popped the candy ball back into his mouth. Then he hiked his britches up—they kept wanting to slide down—and stood watching Dorothy, thinking she hadn't interviewed George Hagan or Sully because her fingers were so sore, she couldn't bend them to write notes.

He watched her try to get Preston's attention when Preston was going on about something—some fancy plan of his, probably, judging by the far-off look on his face.

Dorothy was trying real hard to get Preston's attention. Brian knew he shouldn't spy or eavesdrop, but he couldn't help wondering why she was working so hard to try and talk to the banker. She didn't like Preston. Brian had known that for a while. And as far as he could figure, Preston hadn't done anything newsworthy lately that Dorothy might want to interview him about.

When Dorothy started toward the back of the building and Preston followed her, Brian's curiosity got the better of him.

He made a wide arc, traveling clear around some wagons and horses and people, not wanting Dorothy or Preston, or Robert E., to think he was headed their way. He cut around to the other side of the blacksmith shop and livery. When he reached the corner, he peered around.

There were Dorothy and Preston, Dorothy trying to impress something on Preston with her hands still down in the folds of her skirt, and Preston with a put-out look on his face. Brian felt certain Dorothy and Preston didn't see him peek around the corner to watch and listen to them. If they'd spotted him, they would've nabbed him.

Dorothy was saying something about needing to use Preston's steam bath. Preston told her it was part of the medical clinic. At first he didn't want to let her use the steam bath—the expression on his face said he didn't think she was good enough to use it. But Dorothy set him straight about that. Then, when he still seemed reluctant, she said something about advertising space in the *Gazette,* and Preston went all pale.

Why did she need to go to his medical clinic and use a steam bath? Brian wondered. Maybe it was because of her hands—maybe Dr. Mike hadn't helped her much. Maybe that's why she was being secretive about this, taking Preston around to the back of the livery stable to ask him about the steam bath because she didn't want word of her going to his clinic to use his bath leaking out. Ma would hear, and her feelings might be hurt. She might mistake Dorothy going to the clinic as Dorothy looking for other medical attention.

Brian heard Preston mention a time for Dorothy to be at the clinic, and he heard what that time was. Between the steam bath and them printing the *Gazette* this evening, Brian figured she'd have no time to interview Mr. Hagan or Sully today.

Which meant he'd have to do the interviewing. Somehow, some way.

9

Matthew had Horace wire the marshal in Denver, and then he went to relieve Hank.

"Sully oughtta split that money with me," Hank mumbled as he slowly pulled himself up from behind the desk. "Body's startin' to smell."

"It ain't smellin'," said the smart-alec rustler. "That's yer upper lip."

Matthew just about snickered. But then, he figured, why rile Hank more than he already had?

"You shut up," Hank said, spinning around to face the rustler.

Matthew was quick to get between Hank and the cell. "Thanks for your help," he told Hank, and he hoped his look delivered the rest of the message: *"Now be on your way."*

It apparently did. Hank stared at Matthew, tried to stare him down, in fact. Then he backed off, saying, "I'm due part of that bounty money."

"If that's how you feel, see Sully about it once he gets out of the clinic. It'll be comin' to him, I imagine."

That was the end of it. Hank went out the door, slamming it behind him.

Matthew deposited his hat on his desk, then heaved himself into the chair behind the desk. God, he was tired. Rustlers, bounty hunters, bodies. . . . He needed a deputy. Actually, he needed several. He was concerned about who had shot Willard . . . then again, he wasn't. He was almost sure Hagan had shot the outlaw to collect the bounty money. It didn't matter who'd shot Willard, not really. He'd been wanted dead or alive. Just so happened, he'd been turned in dead.

And what if the marshal wired back that he'd send the bounty money and that he wanted Matthew to bury the body instead of bringing it to Denver? That would be good in one sense—Matthew wouldn't have to haul that body to Denver—but in another sense that would be bad. He'd have to figure out where to bury the body. The righteous of Colorado Springs were sure to raise the roof if he buried the body in the town cemetery. But if he buried it in the cemetery, instead of out where he'd buried the outlaw they'd hanged last year, he could keep a better eye on things because he could see the cemetery from his office. He had visions of Hagan, Bodine, and Standly trying to dig up the body and make off with it.

Matthew rubbed his temples and mulled over the dilemma.

Outside the sheriff's office, Hank paused to stretch. He tossed a look at the clinic, thinking he ought to march over there and have a talk with Sully.

He grunted. Michaela would probably meet him at the door. For a little woman, she was formidable. She wasn't someone he wanted to deal with today. Hell, she never was. Michaela was full of fire and spit when somebody angered her or when she felt somebody threatened her friends and family.

A damn shame, being intimidated by a woman.

Hank kicked up a trail of dust as he headed toward the

saloon. If Hagan had bashed up anything or anybody inside the place, he'd have a few words with him. Maybe a few fists *for* him. The man didn't scare him none. After all, it'd been Sully, not Hagan, who'd brought that feared outlaw in. Hagan might've shot him, but Sully had hunted Willard down, taken a bullet from him—and still brought him in.

After Hank had pulled George Hagan off Sully in the street two days ago, he hadn't expected Hagan to frequent his saloon anymore. But Hagan had shown up in the saloon right after the ruckus out in the street, demanding whiskey and a good woman. Hank had warned him then that he was welcome so long as he didn't cause trouble. Hagan had given him a mean look, and then he'd taken his bottle and Sadie Jean, Hank's best girl, and he'd gone upstairs.

Until this afternoon, Hagan had been pretty quiet, from what Hank had seen. But now Hank wondered if Hagan would be back in the saloon, considering that Hank had been guarding Willard's body so Hagan couldn't get it.

Hank was none too sure Hagan had shot Willard; after all, Hagan had looked right leisurely lying back in that bed when Hank came up on the doorway where Sully stood glaring at the man. If Hagan had shot Willard . . . well, he was a coward. If he'd shot him, he had to have done the good deed from that bedroom window, hidden his gun real quick, and jumped back into bed. And—he had to have worked at not being out of breath minutes later when Sully threw open the door. Hank didn't know if that was possible. If it wasn't, that left him with a nagging question: *If Hagan isn't guilty, who shot Willard?*

It might've been Curly Bodine or Kenny Standly, Hagan's buddies. It might've been one of the other men upstairs at the time. It might've been one of the girls—hell, Hank didn't know. He was just guessing. Hagan, Bodine, or Standly was most likely, seein's how they were in Colorado Springs because they'd tracked Willard to this area.

Hank pushed open the saloon doors and walked in. A few customers had come back—three men were gathered around a table playing cards, and several girls hovered behind the men. Ostrich and peacock feathers rose from the girls' hair and fanned the air above their heads. Sequins sparkled on their scanty clothing. Satin and silk rustled when they moved. The man with his ledger was still here. Lately, so many people flocked to Colorado Springs, Hank didn't know half of those who came into the saloon. It wasn't too crowded inside his establishment yet. This evening it would be.

He didn't see Hagan, Bodine, and Standly. Maybe they'd left for good.

Jake stood behind the bar, his shirtsleeves rolled up, his hair slicked back more than usual this afternoon. He slid a glass of whiskey to a customer just as Hank took a seat on a stool at the bar.

"Nice job for a town mayor," Hank remarked, grinning. "Give me a glass of that. I need it."

Jake reached for another glass. "Yeah, well, I didn't know when you'd be along. It was pretty decent of you to mind that body. I didn't have customers anyway."

"Damn sure was," Hank muttered. "Matthew doesn't seem to think I oughtta get a cut of that bounty money."

Jake plopped the glass down on the bar, turned, and picked up a bottle of whiskey. "He's crazy out of his mind," he said, turning back. He popped the cork on the whiskey bottle and filled the glass.

Hank grabbed the glass before Jake had taken the bottle away. He tossed the whiskey back and relished the way it burned the back of his throat and a path all the way down to his stomach. Good stuff. "More," he said, and pushed the glass back to Jake.

"What's wrong with you?" Jake demanded.

Hank glared at him. "What d'you mean? I told you— Matthew doesn't think I ought to get a cut of that bounty money."

"Sully's the one collectin' it, ain't he? Go talk to him." Jake refilled the glass and pushed it toward Hank.

Hank downed that shot of whiskey, too. This time he plopped the glass down on the bar and twirled it around, watching it as he spoke. "Problem is, Michaela's probably guardin' Sully like he's gold."

"She ain't so fierce."

Hank laughed sarcastically. "She can be when she wants to be. Where's Hagan? Gone?"

"Nope. Last I heard, he was upstairs."

Hank snorted. "For a bounty hunter, he doesn't pay much attention to what he's supposed to be huntin'. How d'you reckon Sully found Willard? I thought he'd—"

Jake stared at him, raising his brows, looking expectant, waiting for Hank to finish the sentence.

"God! Pour me some more," Hank said, flipping back his hair. "Matthew set me up."

Jake gave him another funny look. "What are you talkin' about?"

"Pour," Hank ordered. Jake began pouring, and Hank talked more: "He set me up, that's what I'm talkin' about. He came in here, sayin' Willard's tracks led away from the Indian land. I told Hagan, an' I couldn't believe he didn't take off after Willard. He must've thought I was tryin' to lead him off somewhere. Like Matthew was tryin' to lead me off."

"Why would Matthew try to lead you off?"

Hank grabbed the full glass and brought it to his mouth. "'Cause he figured I'd go to Hagan, that I'd be after part of that bounty money." He downed yet another shot of whiskey.

Jake nodded slowly. "Ah. He figured you'd get greedy an' lead Hagan off in one direction while—"

"Sully went off in another. Wouldn't surprise me none if Matthew an' Sully split the bounty."

"Matthew can't collect bounty money," Jake said. "He's a sheriff."

"We'll see if he tries. If he does. . . ." Hank shook a finger at Jake. "If he does, I'll get him."

Brian stuffed his little leather-bound notebook and his pencil in his trouser pocket, then shimmied his way up and over the wooden fence that separated the back of Hank's saloon from the house behind it. The Newtons lived there, and they'd put the fence up to increase the separation between their house and the saloon—leastwise, that's how Matthew had explained the fence to Brian when Brian had asked him about it one day.

Brian was determined to help Miss Dorothy in whatever way he could. She could hardly run her press by herself right now, and after meeting her this afternoon and listening to her and Preston's conversation behind the livery, Brian figured she hadn't interviewed Mr. Hagan or Hank or Sully about that dead outlaw because she couldn't write notes.

So he figured he'd do the interviews for her—and he'd start with Mr. Hagan, since he didn't live in Colorado Springs and might leave anytime. If he left before Brian interviewed him, the *Gazette* couldn't report his side of the story. And how many times had Dorothy told Brian that a reporter tells *all* sides?

Miss Dorothy was at Preston's medical clinic right now, Brian figured. So he had time to interview Mr. Hagan. He was sneaking into the saloon because he didn't reckon anyone would take well to him marching in the front doors and asking for George Hagan.

Sneaking into the saloon scared Brian. The thought of interviewing Mr. Hagan scared him even more. But here he was, despite being scared, tiptoeing up to the back door of the saloon, looking right and left and over his shoulder to make sure nobody was watching. The saloon was where Mr. Hagan could be found. He'd been staying there almost from the day he came to town. From all the talk Brian had heard around town, he was there now.

Brian didn't know how he was gonna find Mr. Hagan once he got inside the saloon. That'd be interesting—and probably a little troublesome. He'd never been inside a saloon; he just knew they weren't places for children and respectable people.

He'd *have* to sneak around once he got inside. He'd have to slink around corners and whatever furniture he came across. He'd have to *peek* around them, too. If somebody saw him right off, before he found Mr. Hagan and told him why he'd come, they might toss him out. Ma and Sully would be angry, and Miss Dorothy might feel bad—she might feel responsible for him getting into trouble.

So he came up on the back door of the saloon real carefully. He reached for the doorknob, and then he pressed his ear to the door to listen for voices on the other side. All was quiet, so he turned the knob and pushed the door open.

There was a dusty, wide hallway, and voices came from somewhere at the end of it. Down there, it looked like the hallway opened out into a hazy room furnished with tables and chairs. And on the right side of the hall, in front of Brian, was a staircase. The steps were partly covered with worn red carpeting, with two inches of wood showing on each side. The whole place smelled like cigar and pipe smoke.

Brian figured he could step real softly on that carpet and go upstairs. But what if Mr. Hagan was in the main room down at the end of the hall? The room where all the tables and chairs were? There might be more people in that main room than upstairs. Brian bet that's where they got their drinks and played cards and did whatever else people did in saloons.

He'd start upstairs. That was really where he'd rather check first. He might luck out and find Mr. Hagan up there, sleeping or something. After that day he'd met him in Mr. Bray's mercantile, Brian sure enough knew what the man looked like.

Brian started up the stairs, taking each step nice and slow, listening for, and dreading the sound of, creaking boards. Five steps up, he hadn't heard any, so he increased his pace.

Pretty soon he was at the top of the staircase, looking up

111

and down another hallway. This one had the same red carpet that was on the stairs. *Yes*. This carpet would muffle the sound of his steps, too.

He didn't think about how to deal with closed doors until one confronted him. Suddenly there it was, and what if Mr. Hagan was on the other side?

Well, Brian figured as his ears heated, he sure wasn't gonna open it. He'd heard enough talk about things that went on with Hank's girls in this saloon to know he shouldn't open any door he came to that was shut.

The next room was empty. So was the one after that.

The next door was cracked a little, and Brian heard women's voices behind the door. He pressed a little closer to try and hear better. They were talking about how many men were downstairs playing cards, and what they thought they'd bring in today.

Brian didn't understand what that last was all about. But he didn't care. He didn't care about anything, really, other than finding Mr. Hagan, or else hearing something about Mr. Hagan that might lead him his way. One woman said she wished Curly Bodine would be on his way. "Why, he's just a overstuffed piece of—"

Someone pushed Brian hard from behind. He hit against the door, and it went flying open. He shot through the doorway and into the room. He tumbled twice, hit his head on a bedpost, then rolled to a stop. His chin grazed a pair of red slippers.

A froth of white petticoats and layers of red satin spilled down on his face.

There was so much material, he thought he might smother before he got his nose and mouth uncovered. And the strong smell of sweet perfume—it was way too much!

He heard giggling and outright laughter; things like "Lookee what I found, pressin' up to the door!", "Spyin' on us, was he?" And, seconds later, "Aunt Ellie! It's just a boy!"

Brian pulled more yards of material away from his face.

112

He found daylight again, at least, and then he uncovered his nose.

"Well, what's he doin' here, Candice? Just lookin' to find out what Hank keeps upstairs? Or is he curious about certain other things at his ripe young age?"

The women giggled more.

Brian shoved the last of the petticoat linen and lace away from his face and stared up at the creatures who surrounded him.

They were all women, and their clothing was all different. What there was of it. They were a sight—one dressed in nothing but her underthings, a camisole and pantellets; two dressed in satin and silk gowns like Brian hadn't seen except in Boston, and one dressed in a white shift. They looked nice enough—fact was, he thought he recognized a few of the women from around town—although their faces were painted and Brian guessed they were employed by Hank to entertain the men, like Myra and Emma had been.

A fifth woman with a heavily painted face and puffy arms bore down on Brian; she wore red satin like that that had covered his face. She made four of a normal-sized woman, and her dress was cut so low in front that when she bent over him, Brian thought her mountains of dough might fall out and suffocate him. He made a noise of terror in the back of his throat, and he'd never been so quick to prop up on his elbows and shimmy backward, trying to get away.

The women giggled, but one of them gasped, "Why, that's Dr. Mike's boy!"

"Oh, Lordy, you're right!" said another.

"If that don't beat all," yet another remarked. "What d'ya suppose he's doin' here?"

The big woman had a scowl on her face and big red lips. Brian couldn't help but watch those lips when she demanded, "So tell us—what *are* you doing in here, boy?"

Brian opened his mouth to answer, but he was cut off by the woman in the camisole and pantalets: "Aunt Ellie . . . Dr. Mike . . . she takes care of us if we need takin' care

113

of—y'know, with personal things—but she's real respectable."

"Dr. *Mike?*" Aunt Ellie blurted. "You called the doc *she.*"

"Well her real name's Michaela. But most ever'one calls
her Dr. Mike."

"A lady doctor. Shoo! Well, I guess a 'respectable' doctor
wouldn't want her boy passing his time in a saloon, particularly not upstairs with the ladies."

"No, ma'am," Brian said, his voice barely eeking out.

"You don't think so, do you?" Ellie demanded, pressing
closer. Her doughy mountains again weren't far away.

Brian's face heated until he was sure it might explode. He
tried to look her in the eye, but couldn't. He finally turned
his head to the right and looked at something besides what
was directly in front of him.

She cackled. "We'll make sure you don't do it again," she
promised.

And then, before Brian could take another breath, she
grabbed his arm and yanked him up to his feet. He didn't
want to annoy this woman too much. One lick and she might
bust his chops.

"W-what're you gonna do?" he sputtered. Now he wished
he'd never gotten the harebrained idea of sneaking in here.
He'd wanted to help Miss Dorothy, but facing "Aunt Ellie,"
a big enough woman that just one of her arms could
probably crush him, was more trouble than he'd bargained
for.

He'd thought about getting tossed out if he got caught.
But he didn't think Aunt Ellie was thinking about tossing
him out. He didn't know what she was thinking of doing.
All he knew was that he didn't much like the gleeful,
devious look on her face.

"Candice . . . 'member what we used to do to those
boys in Denver that sneaked in?" Aunt Ellie asked.

"Oh, you're not thinking of doing *that,* are you?" Candice
asked, a worried look on her face. She had bouncing gold

curls and kind blue eyes that Brian liked to think told him she wouldn't let them do anything to hurt him.

"Oh, I heard about that, Miss Ellie," said the woman in the shift. Her brown hair was freshly brushed, and it spilled over her shoulders and all the way down her back. Her eyes were slanted and green, and Brian didn't trust her an inch. "That's funny!" she told Miss Ellie, and then she clapped her hands and said, "Let's do it!"

"What?" asked one of the women in the gowns.

"Aunt Ellie, it's Dr. Mike's boy!" Candice objected.

Too late. The woman in the shift grabbed him beneath one arm, Miss Ellie grabbed him beneath the other, and they lifted him clean off the floor.

"Clear that dressing table chair!" Miss Ellie commanded. "Rachel, go pick him out a gown. Brings some towels, too. Lord knows, we'll have to stuff this skinny boy to make him look like anything. Angie, you find a piece of rope. He wants to wriggle like a stuck pig. We might have to tie him to that chair."

"Aunt Ellie, I wish you wouldn't do this," Candice pleaded.

"Yeah, Aunt Ellie, I wish you wouldn't either," Brian said.

But Ellie only laughed. "Here I am visiting from Denver and thinking this town's too quiet. You turned up just about the time I was wondering how to liven it up."

Brian twisted and squirmed as they plopped him in the chair and held him there. Miss Ellie probably could have held him in place with one finger. "I just came for an interview with Mr. Hagan!" Brian blurted.

"Mr. Hagan, huh?" she asked.

"Yes. Yes!"

"Well, Dr. Mike's boy. By and by, we'll be glad to take you down to see him."

She laughed even more, and the woman in the shift joined in.

• • •

Over in the clinic, Sully had been awake for a while. At first he'd thought about trying to sit up, but his head felt funny, so he kept it on the pillow. Robert E. and Loren were gone. Now he felt better, and Michaela had gone upstairs.

Which meant there was no one to try and stop him if he got up and left the clinic.

He bet just about anything that Michaela would find him and raise the roof. But right now she wasn't watching over him.

He rose, being as quiet as possible. He found his pants, and he slipped them on—not an easy thing to do with one arm. He pulled them up one side at a time, and managed to hook the buttons through the holes.

He slipped his good arm into the sleeve of his shirt and then draped what remained of the other sleeve over his shoulder. He'd buy a shirt from Loren if he had to; he wasn't leaving town to go out to the homestead until he checked with Robert E. and Matthew and found out what was happening with George Hagan and Willard's body.

Sully had no idea what time it was, but he bet he'd spent hours inside the clinic this afternoon, between the surgery and recovery time. Anything could have happened. Hagan could have made off with the body—or Matthew could have wired Denver by now and told the marshal there that he had Willard, and Willard was dead as a cold doorknob.

He wouldn't waste any more time.

His arm hurt. He tried to ignore the pain, but he couldn't when it decided to tear through him.

He leaned over and braced himself against the examination table for a minute.

He had to get out of here. Michaela might come through that door any minute and see him standing here, ready to go off somewhere. He was, and that's what he'd tell her, and then they'd have words because she'd be determined that he shouldn't go and he'd be determined that he should.

He'd go anyway, despite anything she said and no matter

116

how long she argued. He'd go because he was worried that George Hagan might take out his anger at not getting Willard's body on the town. It never took much to fire up wooden buildings, and a little wind could whip a small flame into a raging blaze in no time at all. The people of Denver knew that.

If Hagan didn't burn buildings, he might do other things—destroy Loren's store or Hank's saloon. Sully wouldn't let that happen. Hagan's anger was aimed at him, and he'd take the force of it. He wouldn't let that anger be unleashed on his friends.

Sully snatched his knife and hatchet from a nearby chair, and he walked as quietly as possible to the front door. He slipped outside and around to the back of the clinic, not wanting Hagan to see him.

He made his way to the jail without being noticed much. He saw Robert E., who looked surprised to see him, then nodded. And he saw Reverend Johnson, who looked alarmed. Trouble was brewing, the reverend's look said. He was right about that—as long as George Hagan remained in town, the reverend had reason to worry. There was no avoiding trouble. Hagan *was* trouble.

When Sully entered the sheriff's office, Matthew leaned back in his chair. He'd already made up his mind how he was going to handle the situation if Sully showed up in his office. He sure hoped the marshal wired him back soon. Then he could either deputize someone and head to Denver with Willard's body, or he could bury the thing. He already had someone digging a grave in the cemetery.

"I'm takin' Willard's body to Denver," Sully said. "I'm gettin' it out of here." It was the best way he could think of to get Hagan out of Colorado Springs. His timing was off—it was a little late to be thinking he shouldn't have brought Willard into town. But late or not, he'd done it, and now he felt he had to get the body out of here. Hagan would follow the body, because the body was worth money to him.

Sully reached for the keys to the cell—they were lying in

117

plain sight on Matthew's desk. Matthew slapped his hand down over Sully's, stopping him from making off with the keys.

Sully locked eyes with Matthew, and Matthew shook his head.

"I ain't lettin' you do that," Matthew said. "You'll get yourself killed."

"How long do you reckon it'll take Hagan to start killin' people around here?" Sully demanded, not believing that Matthew would try and stop him. "He'll follow me if I have the body."

Matthew grabbed the keys with his other hand. He opened a drawer and dropped the keys in it. Then he closed the drawer and sat back, fixing his gaze on Sully. "The body ain't goin' anywhere except to the cemetery or to Denver with me. I wired the marshal. I'm waitin' to hear from him. If he wants proof that it's Willard, I'll deputize someone who'll mind things here, and I'll take the body to Denver."

The office door opened behind Sully. He didn't turn around to see who it was. He wanted Willard's body, and he wished he could figure a good way to convince Matthew to let him take it. He hadn't expected this kind of resistance.

"Then I don't have a choice," Sully said.

"What does that mean?" Matthew demanded.

"It means I'll have to take care of Hagan myself."

Shaking his head, Matthew stood up behind the desk. "Sully, you're—"

"Got a telegram," Horace said behind Sully. "For you, Matthew." He hadn't bothered to close the door, and the noise from the street—lumbering and rattling wagons, people talking and shouting—drifted into the office.

"From the marshal, I bet," Matthew said, coming around the desk.

Reverend Johnson burst into the office, his face a wrinkled mess of worry and alarm. "Why is that man digging a new grave in the cemetery? The only person who's died is—"

"Willard," Matthew finished for him.

"You can't bury that man in our cemetery."

"Why not? A body's a body. If the marshal says 'bury him,' I aim to bury him."

"*Not* in our cemetery," the reverend pressed.

"One's as good as another," Matthew said, reaching for the telegram Horace held out to him.

"Respectable people won't want an outlaw buried near their kin. Maude Bray is buried there—and a lot of other beloved people, too. Loren won't want that outlaw buried near his dear wife."

"I want that body," Sully said from behind Matthew.

"Do ya mind, Matthew?" Horace said, casting a meaningful look at the telegram. "I gotta get back to the telegraph office. Didn't have nobody else to deliver that. I'd like to stay an' see if ya want me to send anything back, but—"

"Wait, Horace. Please." Matthew started to unfold the paper.

"I want that body," Sully said again.

"You can't bury that man in our cemetery," huffed Reverend Johnson. "You *can't.*"

Michaela pushed into the office. She focused on Sully, thank God. Matthew was about ready to boot them all out. Maybe she'd convince Sully to leave—before he had to.

"What are you doing?" she demanded of Sully. "It will take very little movement to make the bleeding start up again. You should be lying down." Her gaze darted to his wounded arm and the bandages beneath his draped shirt. "It already has," she said.

"I'm takin' Willard's body to Denver," he said, and Matthew knew the two of them had a standoff going. Dr. Mike didn't back down where her patients were concerned, especially not when the patient happened to be her husband. And Sully didn't intend to back down where Willard's body was concerned.

"Thank God," the reverend said. "Now then, Sully.

119

Something else . . . about that bounty money. You can't mean to accept it. It's blood money."

"Matthew, should I send somethin' back?" Horace pressed. "I gotta go."

Matthew had had enough of the confusion. "Horace, wire back and tell the marshal it might be better to bury Willard here—Hagan's camped in town an' we've got feudin' goin' on over the body."

"It's leavin'," Sully said, and this time he took a step forward, like he might go for the desk drawer that held the keys.

Matthew stepped between Sully and the desk. "We've never had differences, Sully," he said, his voice low. "But we will if you go for those keys. Hagan'll kill you over that body. He'll wait for you somewhere an' he'll cut you down. I'll lock you in with those rustlers if you keep this up. Go back to the clinic with Dr. Mike. That's the best place for you right now."

Sully studied him, like maybe he'd finally made a difference, gotten through to him.

"I'm goin'," Horace said, and he excused his way past Dr. Mike.

"I'll take you home, Sully," she said. "I'll take care of you there."

"Lawd knows we could use some comp'ny in here," said the smart-alec rustler.

"That bounty money . . . ," said the reverend.

Matthew had had enough of him, too. "Reverend Johnson, doesn't the Bible say something about not judgin'? Ain't that the Lord's job?"

The rustler hooted, and the reverend turned red. "Well, I . . . I really *don't* think Loren will take kindly to that man being buried near Maude. And—and that bounty money. . . ."

"I'm about to arrest you for disturbin' the peace, or obstructin' justice—or somethin'!" Matthew exploded.

Reverend Johnson didn't waste too much time in shrinking back through the doorway. He backed onto the walkway, then turned and disappeared. The thudding of his boots on the planks was the only indication that he was not completely gone. And even those sounds faded directly.

"Sully, what about letting Mr. Hagan collect the money?" Dr. Mike suggested. "He'll leave then—isn't that what you want?"

Sully stared at her for a minute, his jaw fixed, his gaze cool. Then he walked toward the doorway, obviously meaning to leave. Once outside, he cut to the left—in the direction of Hank's saloon.

Dr. Mike started after him, and Matthew grabbed her arm and shook his head. "Don't get in the middle of it, Dr. Mike," he advised. "I don't know what's gonna happen. But I do know I wouldn't be too good at raisin' Brian an' Katie by myself. Think about them."

That stopped her. She held back, and when she did leave the office, she went right, toward the medical clinic.

Matthew locked the drawer he'd dropped the cell keys in. Then he pocketed the key, grabbed a chair, and carried it outside. He plopped it down in front of his office window, and sat down. If troubled started. . . . Well, he couldn't see anything from inside his office. But from right here, he could look toward the church and cemetery. He saw the reverend hurrying that way; he even thought the reverend was *stomping* that way. He also could see Dr. Mike's clinic and Hank's saloon.

If trouble started, as long as he was sitting here, he'd know.

10

Michaela had told Brian he could stay in town and help Dorothy this evening. But she had expected to see him after school. She hadn't seen him, and she'd been too busy to worry about him. She'd had Sully to worry about, his surgery and recovery, and now she had Sully to worry about again, it seemed. Katie was with Grace, and Brian was with Dorothy, or so Michaela hoped.

Matthew had made her realize that she wasn't reaching Sully, that she couldn't make a difference in his determination to do something about George Hagan and Mr. Willard's body and that bounty money. Take the outlaw's body to Denver himself? What was Sully thinking? George Hagan might tag along behind him and—

That was what Sully wanted, Michaela realized.

Sully wanted Mr. Hagan to leave Colorado Springs, and he meant to use the body as bait. Only Matthew wouldn't let Sully have the body.

Good for Matthew.

She was perspiring, and this was anything but a hot day.

It was mild, and every now and then a breeze kicked up and made the air feel cold on the face and hands.

She wasn't getting through to Sully. She couldn't seem to influence him at all in this matter—she couldn't convince him to leave George Hagan alone; she couldn't convince him to return to the clinic and rest his arm; and she couldn't convince him to give Mr. Hagan the body. If he did that, this would all be behind them, surely. Mr. Hagan would take the body and leave town.

She walked toward the *Gazette* office. She would check on Brian, then she'd get Katie.

Of late, she hit a stone wall when she tried to talk to Sully. He was consumed with George Hagan and Mr. Willard's body; with worry over Mr. Hagan possibly hurting his friends and family; and with not wanting Mr. Hagan to have the bounty money. So she would check on Brian, then collect Katie and maybe return to the clinic. With more trouble threatening right now, she didn't know if she wanted to go home just yet.

She was approximately a hundred yards from the *Gazette* office when a thought struck her, a new idea for dealing with the threatening trouble. She'd check on Brian and Katie, then collect her medical bag from the clinic and go to the saloon. There, she would pretend to call on "Hank's girls," as the townspeople called them, to make certain they were having no problems. Then she would approach George Hagan and see if she could convince him to leave town. Sully had tried, and Sully had failed. But maybe Mr. Hagan would listen to her.

Maybe he would listen if she promised him an amount of money equal to the bounty.

At the saloon, Hank and Jake saw Sully coming, and they moved quickly to head him off before he could stir up trouble.

Right after Sully pushed open the swinging doors, Hank grabbed him by one arm and Jake grabbed him by the other.

Hank guessed Sully was in pain; he stiffened up, and that stiffening wasn't just because their stopping him made him angry. It was because Michaela had cut him just hours ago, and now they jolted the wound.

They swung Sully around and walked straight back outside with him. Hagan was seated at one of the saloon tables, back against the far wall. Maybe he hadn't noticed Sully trying to enter. But maybe he had.

Hank couldn't believe Hagan had come back in here after Hank had guarded Willard's body. But Hagan liked Sadie Jean a whole lot, and he was buying drinks for her right and left. He'd paid for her, too—for the whole night.

"He's all settled down," Hank told Sully. "You don't drink. You don't hardly ever come into my saloon. That leaves me thinkin' you're here to stir things up."

Sully stared at him.

"Leave it alone, Sully," Jake advised. "Hagan'll be gone pretty soon—soon as that body's out of here."

"We've gotta talk about my cut of the bounty money," Hank said. "Seein's how I kept watch over the body 'n' all."

Sully shook free of their hold. "I ain't takin' bounty money."

"You're crazy," Jake said flatly.

Hank, and almost everyone around these parts, had thought Sully was mad when he started hanging around the Cheyenne camps so much. Since then, Hank had learned to appreciate certain things about Sully. Now he, like Jake, was back to thinking Sully was mad.

Sully set off, and they watched him go. Jake rubbed his jaw. "Can't believe that. Who'd turn down that kind of money? Especially after takin' a bullet to bring Willard in."

"He'll end up takin' another one from Hagan," Hank grumbled.

"Yep—and that one just might kill him."

Hank glanced at Jake. He was right—it might. And where would that leave Michaela and Brian and Katie?

He shouldn't care. He didn't, not really, he told himself as he watched Sully walk toward the mercantile. And there was Michaela, down the road a ways, going toward the *Gazette* office, determination in her steps. Hell, Michaela A. Quinn could take care of herself. If Sully got himself killed, she'd probably walk to the graveyard for the service with her head held just as high.

But what about Brian and Katie? Brian had already lost his pa to San Francisco and his ma to a rattlesnake bite. And Katie. . . . Hank would never admit it to anyone, but she was about the cutest baby he'd ever seen. She shouldn't lose her pa before she could even run around good.

"Matthew still set on takin' that body up t'Denver?" Jake asked.

"I don't know," Hank said.

He really didn't. He glanced across the street at Matthew, who'd pulled a chair onto the walkway in front of his office. It looked like he was camped there. He was kicked back in the chair, his hat shading most of his face. At first glance, someone might think Matthew was sleeping. But no way— Hank knew better.

As much as he hadn't exactly liked the idea in the beginning of Matthew being sheriff, Hank had to admit that he had turned out to be a pretty fine law officer. Aw hell, he was still irritated that Matthew hadn't wanted to deputize him earlier. But he couldn't help but admire the fact that Matthew was watching everything real close right now: Sully making his way to the mercantile; him and Jake as they stood here; Michaela as she opened the door to the *Gazette* office and stepped inside. Matthew was keeping an eye out for trouble. And after tracking those rustlers for days and finally bringing them in. After that alone, Matthew had to be dog-tired.

All things considered, Matthew was probably the best damn sheriff this town could have.

Hank pulled a cigar out of his vest pocket, bit off the end, and had the cigar clenched between his teeth and lit in no time.

"I'm goin' to get some supper," Jake said, rubbing his belly.

Hank inhaled cigar smoke. "You do that."

Michaela came out of the newspaper office, looking mystified. Hank wondered why. She headed toward Grace's Café, just beyond the *Gazette* office.

Jake stepped off the walkway and headed the same way. He turned briefly to ask, "Ain't you hungry?"

Hank nodded. "You could bring me somethin' back. I ain't leavin' right now."

"I will," Jake said, and then he was off, jerking on the bottom of his vest to make sure he was unrumpled and respectable-looking. Hell, he'd just come out of a saloon, Hank thought, laughing to himself. And everyone knew he still had a drinking binge every now and then.

Sully had settled himself on the mercantile steps and leaned back against a post. Blood had soaked through his bandages and splotched his shirt in places. Fool! He oughtta go back to the clinic and rest. He just might sit there and bleed to death, trying to keep an eye on Hagan or wait until Hank turned his back.

This situation was getting out of hand, Hank thought, taking another draw from the cigar. Hagan set up nice and pretty in the saloon. Sully watching to make sure he didn't come out—or to grab a chance to go in and rough Hagan up. Matthew camped out on the walkway in front of his office, ready to bolt at the first sign of trouble.

Hank couldn't believe Michaela was going about her business, not fussing over Sully. But then, if Sully had gotten up and walked out of her clinic, Hank bet Michaela and Sully had had words before Sully left.

A crazy thought began jumping around in Hank's head. No way. *He'd* be the fool if he let it take off running.

All the same, it *was* about to take off running.

He watched Grace hand Katie over to Michaela. Katie wrapped her arms around her mother's neck, and Michaela rubbed the baby's back. Then mother and daughter parted to look at each other. Michaela beamed at Katie, and Katie clapped her hands together.

The scene dripped with sweetness, almost to the point of making Hank sick at his stomach.

He was getting too soft about things.

Minutes later, he turned away. He couldn't watch Michaela and Katie anymore. The thought that might just make him do something crazy was running wild in his head. It didn't disappear, no matter that he turned his back on the mother-child scene.

A good five minutes later, he kicked in frustration at the molding around the edge of his bar. *Damn.* He'd be having another conversation with Matthew real soon.

Dorothy nestled down into the steaming water and sighed with pleasure. This was almost sinful, this bath that felt so good. The water seemed to go right through her skin down into her bones, particularly to her joints, and soothe them. This was much better than watching someone carry in water for her and then carry it out when she was done. That poor Chinese girl had sweated at times! All so that Dorothy could enjoy the benefits of a bath!

Smiling, Dorothy leaned her head back against the wooden support. Poor Preston. She'd thought he might have a heart attack when she put the idea of her using the resort's steam bath to him. She'd thought he might fall through the wall of Robert E.'s stable and go crashing into a stall with a horse. Then he might've had to scramble back to keep from being kicked or stepped on!

She giggled at the thought of Preston with straw in his hair, scrambling around on a stable floor, his clothes all rumpled and perhaps even a little smudged in places. Oh, that would be a sight to see! A regular—

A rapping came on the door. "Time up, Mrs. Jenning," called the Swedish girl who had shown Dorothy the way in.

"Already?" Dorothy grumbled. Why, it seemed like she

hadn't been in here but five minutes. That was probably because the bath felt so good.

The door eased open, and in came the girl, carrying an open towel to greet Dorothy when she stepped out of the bath. "I help you dry and dress," the girl said.

"Oh, for heaven's sake," Dorothy said, embarrassed. "I can dry an' dress myself. I've been doin' it for. . . ." She let it go. Considering all the aches and pains she'd had in her hands lately, and the fact that drying herself and dressing herself *had* been rather difficult for some time now, she ought to hush and let the girl help her.

Which is exactly what she did.

"The doc-tor vill see you now," the girl said as she fastened the last button on Dorothy's dress.

Dorothy stared at her. "Oh, no. There's no need for me to see the doctor," she said, walking toward the door. "I'm sure Andrew has other things to do. Besides, I—"

She bumped into Andrew at the door.

"Oh, hello," she said. "I was just leavin'."

"Hi, Dorothy," Andrew greeted her with a big smile. "Preston told me you were coming. He said he thought something might be bothering you. He said you were very insistent about using the steam bath."

Out of habit, Dorothy had buried her hands in the folds of her skirt. She'd taken to doing that lately, not wanting people to notice how red and swollen her hands were. Of course, since she'd begun taking the medicine Michaela had given her, and now with the steam bath, her hands didn't look so bad. Still, Andrew might notice. And then, Andrew might want to examine them.

"Well, I . . . I printed his advertisement an' . . . an' I thought the bath sounded wonderful," Dorothy stammered. "Yes . . . I thought the bath sounded wonderful. Like somethin' I needed . . . *wanted*. An' it was wonderful!"

Andrew tilted his head. "Dorothy, what's the matter?"

"Nothing. Really."

She eased around him, going for the door.

"Do you need a ride back to town?" he asked, apparently giving up trying to convince her to let him examine her.

"No, no. I can walk," she said. "The walk'll do me good. I'd like to use the bath again in a few days. You'll tell Preston, won't you?"

"Yes, certainly."

After that, Andrew didn't try anymore to find out what was wrong with her or why she'd come to use the steam bath. He let her go, saying, "Have a nice evening."

Dorothy wished him the same, and then she escaped. Michaela was her friend and her doctor, after all, and letting Andrew examine her would be like betraying Michaela. If she did let him examine her and word of that got back to Michaela, Michaela might feel awful. Dorothy would have no part in that.

At Grace's Café, supper was just getting under way. Katie had slept for the last hour, Grace told Michaela, who knew that that was doubtless the only way Grace had managed supper preparations and Katie's care at the same time.

"Have you seen Dorothy and Brian?" Michaela asked, letting her gaze skim the people seated at the checker-covered tables. She knew almost everyone. A few people waved, and she waved back. Jake dipped his head in silent greeting, and she returned that gesture, too. "The newspaper office is dark and empty—there's no sign of either of them. I know they were planning to eat supper here."

"Dorothy's gonna have a late evenin' with the paper?" Grace responded.

"That's what I thought. She and Brian were going to print."

"Haven't seen 'em yet."

"I wonder where they could be," Michaela said.

Grace shook her head.

Michaela let the subject drop. She was sure Dorothy and Brian were together somewhere and that they'd be back in the *Gazette* office before long.

"Thank you for keeping Katie," Michaela told Grace, prying Katie's fingers loose from her hair. Katie laughed, and Michaela couldn't help but smile at the baby. "I know it wasn't the best time of day to ask you to take care of a baby."

"Oh, don't you be fussin' 'bout that," Grace scolded, stirring a huge kettle of chicken soup. "What were you gonna do? Try an' take care o' her an' get that bullet out o' Sully at the same time? I don't think so. How is Sully, anyway?"

"Stubborn." In one word, Michaela had described exactly how he was today.

Grace gave her a worried look, then she cast a look at the clinic. "He's ain't there anymore, is he? At the clinic, I mean."

Michaela shook her head. "Look down at the mercantile."

Grace glanced that way. "Lord! What's he tryin' to do? Bleed to death?"

"He seems to think he can't," Michaela said. She finally pried Katie's fingers free of her hair. Katie fussed about that. She flailed her arms and howled an objection. She was probably hungry as well as frustrated that her mother wouldn't let her play with her hair. "Oh, Grace, what can I do?" Michaela blurted.

Grace twisted her mouth. "Feedin' her might help. She can eat some soup, can't she?"

"Yes, but . . . I didn't mean about Katie. I meant about Sully. He's determined to run that man out of town. I think he may be determined to do more." Michaela lowered her voice to a whisper with the last sentence.

Grace flinched. "Sully?"

"I know. . . . It doesn't seem like him at all. It's *not* him. He hasn't acted like himself since George Hagan showed up in Loren's store that day. I'm contemplating a certain way of dealing with the problem."

"It ain't gonna end you up in trouble, is it?"

131

Michaela shifted her gaze to the pot of soup, then back to Grace, as she bounced Katie a little on her hip. "It could."

"Dr. Mike . . . what're you plannin'?" Grace asked apprehensively.

"I'm thinking of talking to Mr. Hagan myself." Michaela waited a few seconds for that information to be absorbed, then she went on: "Sully could, conceivably, collect the bounty money because he brought Mr. Willard in to Matthew. I'm thinking of offering that same amount to Mr. Hagan."

A few more seconds passed while Grace absorbed that even more important information. She seemed to have to work at digesting what it all meant. Her face twisted, then untwisted; her eyes flared, her mouth opened and snapped shut, then opened again. "You're thinkin' . . . you're thinkin' o' *bribin'* him?"

Michaela took a deep breath. That was exactly what she was thinking of doing—she was thinking of bribing Mr. Hagan into leaving Colorado Springs.

She, who normally would be the last person to try and force anyone out of town, was contemplating forcing someone out of town.

Well, not really forcing him. Mr. Hagan would have a decision to make. If he decided to take her money and leave, that would be wonderful; it would be the decision she wanted him to make. He wanted money—he stayed to try and collect the bounty money—so she would give him money. And she hoped he would take it and leave soon. In fact, if he took the money, she would insist that he leave within the hour.

Mr. Hagan's leaving town surely would bring Sully back to his senses. He would stop watching the saloon, and he would lie down and concentrate on recovering.

"You're thinkin' o' collectin' the bounty money?" Grace queried slowly, studying Michaela.

Michaela blanched. She shook her head. "No. I wouldn't touch the reward money. I would simply offer Mr. Hagan

132

the same amount. He'll think it's the reward money and that we're simply handing it over to him. He considers it rightfully his anyway."

Grace nodded. "Yep, he sure does. But Dr. Mike, can you do that? What I mean is . . . y'know—is it worth it? Ain't the reward a lot o' money?"

"It's a lot of money, yes. Is *Sully* worth it? Yes. He's my husband, Grace, and although he wouldn't admit it, he's in trouble. I have to do what I can to help."

It didn't take Grace long to agree with that. She smiled sympathetically and stirred the soup. "Put that way, I can't argue. When're you goin' to talk to him? Y'know—Mr. Hagan. You'll have to go to the saloon. He's pretty well camped in there, from what I hear."

"I thought I would go now," Michaela said. "Considering Sully's medical condition, I don't think I should wait."

"No, I don't think you should either. Leave Katie, y'hear?"

"During supper, Grace? I could take her to Reverend Johnson. He's offered to keep her anytime I need help."

"Oh, no. Don't you worry none. I'll manage. I don't think I'll be real busy for a while. B'sides, you go ask Rev'rend Johnson an' you're sure to get an earful 'bout the grave Matthew's havin' dug for Mr. Willard in the cemetery. Rev'rend was here earlier, sayin' he didn't know where Matthew ought to bury the man but that he shouldn't bury him in the cemetery 'longside respectable people. I'm tellin' you, Dr. Mike, the rev'rand's in a temper 'bout it all."

The news worried Michaela. Yet, whether they should bury an outlaw in the town cemetery seemed trivial compared to the fact that Sully was sitting on the mercantile steps with fresh blood on his shirt, staring at the saloon and contemplating only God knew what. "I'll talk to the reverend later," Michaela said, and then she thought a little more. While she'd like to think she wouldn't mind Mr. Willard being buried next to her relatives if she had relatives buried in the town cemetery, the truth was, she *didn't* have a single relative buried there and she didn't really know how she would react if she did. "Perhaps that's a question to put to the council and to the general population," she suggested. "Whether or not to bury an outlaw in the town cemetery."

"That's a good thought," Grace said. "But right now that body's sat long enough in the jail. It ought to be buried now. It can't wait for a vote."

Michaela agreed.

She put Katie in the high chair that Grace kept at the restaurant for her, and she broke up pieces of bread for Katie to eat while Grace waited for a bowl of soup to cool.

Gwennie came along and offered to take care of Katie, to feed her and play with her, while Michaela went off and did whatever she had to do. (She didn't tell Gwennie she planned to go talk to Mr. Hagan. Her bribery of Mr. Hagan was not something she wanted everyone to know about.) Michaela was grateful, and Grace had to be somewhat relieved, although she said nothing. She'd said she wouldn't get busy for a while, but the tables were beginning to fill with people. Some would want only coffee, Michaela knew; still, having to wait on at least ten people and take care of a baby might quickly overwhelm a person. Grace was organized and efficient, but Michaela didn't want to heap that much responsibility on anyone.

Gwennie pulled a chair alongside Katie's high chair and settled herself on it. Michaela kissed Katie on the top of the head. Then she took a deep breath, lifted the hem of her skirt slightly to protect it from dirt, and set off.

She collected her medical bag from the clinic, and then she exited the clinic through the back door. She walked down the street a little ways, past a few houses and businesses, a bookstore that had recently gone in, far enough that when she cut up to the street on which the saloon sat, Sully was less likely to see her.

Before turning toward the saloon, she walked by more homes and businesses, the backs of them. Finally, she approached the rear of the saloon, as Brian had done hours before.

As she walked by the staircase that led to the second floor of Hank's establishment and approached the smoky main room of the saloon, Michaela had no idea that a number of "Hank's girls" were upstairs having the time of their life—and that Brian was their subject.

Ellie had painted his face, and the girls had put just about every dress they owned on him, one at a time, pushing them over his head and fastening all the laces and clasps, then stepping back to see what they thought. They'd laced a "corset" on him over his shirt and over some balled-up stockings. They'd put perfume on him, several different kinds from several different bottles.

Brian didn't yell or try to bolt because he was scared that shouts from him might bring Mr. Hagan upstairs and blow what he'd come here to do. Bolting was out of the question because twice Miss Ellie had seen him looking at the door and she'd plopped herself, all of herself, right in front of it. The window was the only other option, and the ground was a long way down.

He reckoned he'd never go into a saloon again. Heck, he wouldn't even think of going into a saloon again.

Miss Ellie drew near him with a wig in her hands, and that was the last straw. The dresses and the paint—they were bad enough. A wig was too much. And she was talking about putting it on him, then taking him downstairs to meet Mr. Hagan.

That wasn't going to happen.

From the corner of his eye, Brian caught sight of the unprotected door. He didn't dare make like he was looking at it. Miss Ellie would see him and go off to guard it again. She'd leave the wig for one of the women to put on him, he was pretty sure.

All of the women but one were digging through the trunks they'd pulled into the room and opened. The trunks were full of lacy, frilly women's underwear and dresses.

Other clothes were scattered all over the room—across the spread, on bedposts, thrown on chairs, and tossed on the floor. Brian smelled like a whole flower garden or something, and he didn't even want to think about what his face looked like.

He'd had enough, and when he shot out of the chair and toward the door, he didn't think about not getting the interview with Mr. Hagan, or whether he'd make it to the door and downstairs. He thought about what the fresh air would smell like when he got outside, and he thought about how good it would feel to tear off the lacy red velvet dress the women had put on him. Then he'd jerk off the corset and be down to his own clothes. If they'd tried to undress him before putting their clothes on him, he *might've* commenced to shouting, Mr. Hagan or no Mr. Hagan.

He made it to the door and he threw it open. One of the women shouted that he was getting away.

Instead of barreling after him the way he expected, Miss Ellie hooted and said, "Aw, let him go. He's had enough. He won't be back. I don't imagine he'll darken the door of a saloon for the rest of his life."

He heard the last just as he reached the top of the staircase. "Pick up your skirt now, boy!" Miss Ellie hollered. "Wouldn't want you tumbling down those stairs!"

He yanked the skirt up and tore down the steps. The back door was open. He shot through it, forgetting about the three steps that led up to the door. He flew past them, landing facedown in the dirt.

Gritty dirt stuck to the face paint. But Brian didn't worry about that. He was finally out in the fresh air, and he was free, and he meant to make like a swift-footed deer being chased by a pack of wolves.

He found his feet, and he bolted, rounding the saloon, forgetting to cut a wide path down a ways before turning back up. If he'd done that, he could have avoided the main part of town, as Michaela had. But he didn't, and he ended up in front of the barbershop.

Brian was so shocked by the sight of Jake walking out of the shop, slowly wiping his hands on a white towel and staring like he'd never seen such a sight in his life, all he could think of was getting away from there. He spun around, his feet tangling in the skirt of the dress, and he set off again, heading straight for the sheriff's office without realizing it. He ran blind, not paying attention to where he was going.

A hand reached out and snagged him. It yanked him onto a walkway and then pulled him into a building.

Brian felt a new wave of panic as he glanced around the room. The desk, the wall of papers, the cells . . . he knew where he was. His face burned red under the paint.

"Brian?" asked Matthew as he hunched in front of his brother and squinted at him. "What are you *doin'?"*

"I'm—I'm playin'," Brian stammered quickly.

Yeah, that was it—that's what he'd tell anyone who asked why he was wearing women's clothes and why his face was painted. He was just playing.

11

When Michaela walked into the main room of Hank's saloon, several familiar men at the tables spotted her right away. Their eyes flared, and they drew themselves up straight from their former positions of hovering over the glasses, cards, chips, and money that littered their tables. Their expressions changed, from the tenseness of concentration to a flicker of recognition, then to an attempt to look respectable. Zachary Trevors even scooted his chair back several inches from the table, no doubt wondering if Michaela meant to tell his wife she had seen him here.

She'd seen him in here before, of course, when she came to treat the women for various ailments, and she had never said a word to Martha, Zachary's wife. He had a problem with gambling and drinking, as did many other men who frequented Hank's saloon. His skin showed evidence of numerous broken capillaries just beneath the epidermis, and it had a yellowish hue. This was not the first time Michaela had seen him at a saloon table where a pile of money made her wonder if Mr. Trevors was gambling away what little his family had. The Trevorses had young children, and they lived on a modest homestead not far from town. Zachary was in his mid-forties, and Martha was in her early thirties.

Too many men became caught up in the drinking and gambling and rough, dangerous lifestyle that dominated not just Colorado Territory, but all the Western states and territories. Saloons—and there were plenty of them—offered raw whiskey and amusements that made men—and women, for that matter—mean and ill. The whiskey was served by bartenders like Hank, proprietors who, from their standpoint, were just people trying to make a living.

Men like Hank—*opportunists,* as Michaela thought of them—didn't consider the fact that their whiskey slowly but surely killed people. She'd become less quick to point that out to Hank; after all, she was an opportunist, too. She, too, had traveled west and settled here to take advantage of the freedoms offered by the more liberal communities. Her intentions were more honorable than those of men like Hank, however. She didn't prey on people's weaknesses, hoping to make a quick dollar, hoping to get rich.

The sight of Hank's gambling tables always made her tremble a little inside. They brought back memories of Charles, Claudette's husband, Michaela's brother-in-law. His gambling problem, his drinking problem, his weakness for women . . . those things, illnesses in their own way, had ruined his life and turned his wife's and children's lives upside down for years. The weaknesses had destroyed Charles financially, and they had eventually helped kill him. Claudette and the children had had to piece their lives back together, struggling to find sanity and normalcy again.

Whenever Michaela glanced at the gambling tables, an image of Charles's face flashed in her mind, and she always hesitated before walking on. She always spent a few seconds gathering her breath and composure. Then she marched forward, nearing the tables and asking Hank's girls how they felt and if they needed her services this week.

Music tinkled from the piano directly to Michaela's right.

Mr. Britton sat there, wearing a striped shirt and stiff black tie, his dark, bushy mustache wriggling as he twisted his mouth in concentration. He glanced at Michaela, smiled, and dipped his head to her. She smiled back. She liked him; she found him a calming catharsis in an environment that made her tense and uneasy. Mr. Britton was the only good thing in this wretched place.

He had played Hank's piano ever since Michaela had been in Colorado Springs. He was not a drinking man, nor a rough man, nor even the sort of scurrilous man who normally frequented Western saloons. He was a pleasant, almost timid man who simply entertained Hank's customers with his piano playing. When his time was up, Mr. Britton rose, jerked on the ends of his sleeves a few times to straighten them, gathered the coins patrons had dropped on the top of the piano, and went on his way.

Mr. Britton lived in a small whitewashed house on the northern outskirts of town, and no one heard much from him. Michaela saw him in the mercantile now and then, and she'd seen him recently in the new bookstore. A few months ago he'd played a harmonica and then an accordion outside of Loren's store. He'd turned his top hat upside down and placed it on the ground beside him. People had wandered along to listen to him, and they had dropped coins in his hat. Days later, Michaela heard from Loren that Mr. Britton had used the coins he gathered from that performance to help purchase a round-trip train ticket from Pennsylvania to Colorado for his mother. Mrs. Britton had arrived weeks later and had visited for nearly a month.

Clutching her bag in front of her, Michaela drew a breath of unclean air, filled with the heaviness of cigar smoke, sour-smelling whiskey, and human sweat. She forced her gaze away from Zachary Trevors, making herself glance around the saloon.

Mr. Hagan was here, she noted quickly. He sat at a far table, playing cards and drinking straight from a bottle, not bothering with a glass. Very likely he was inebriated. Not so

141

much so, she hoped, that her words would make no sense to him.

One of Hank's girls hung on Mr. Hagan's right shoulder. It was Sadie Jean, whom Michaela had treated just last week for soreness and occasional pains in her right lower abdominal quadrant. Sadie Jean had an ovarian cyst that would eventually need to be drained. The thought of having a needle stuck in her had so scared Sadie Jean that she had run out of the clinic and had not been back since. When she collapsed from pain, Michaela would become involved again. She hoped Sadie Jean would not let the cyst go that long and that far—if it burst, she could die from peritoneal poisoning.

"Michaela," Hank said, and Michaela jumped slightly. He stood just to her right. When she'd first paused in the doorway, he'd been behind the bar. "Since when did you start comin' in the back way?"

"It was closer," she lied. She wasn't beyond a little deception if it was for a good cause. And she wasn't beyond a big deception if it would save her husband's life.

"Really?" His half-grin and the way he looked at her from under his dark brows told her he didn't believe her.

"Really," she said. "I'm here to check on Sadie Jean."

"Well, as you can see"—he glanced toward the back table—"she's busy right now."

"It will take only a moment."

"She's busy right now," he said again, with force this time.

Michaela tipped her head. She knew how to deal with Hank—she'd certainly dealt with him enough times when he was being intentionally obstinate. "She has a medical condition that could worsen at any time. It could kill her if it does."

That information made his eyes narrow a little and his grin slump. She wasn't in the habit of revealing her patients' medical conditions, and she wouldn't reveal very much about Sadie Jean's, not even for the sake of deceiving Hank

142

and saving Sully's life. But she was not beyond elaborating some if Hank tried to stand his ground.

"What's she got?" he demanded, looking rather worried suddenly. "Has she got one of those sexual things? 'Cause if she does, I need to know. I can't have her givin' it to customers."

"I would think that her life being in danger would concern you more." Michaela couldn't help the comment. The coldness of some people never ceased to amaze, and shock, her.

"Why would you think that?" Hank asked, producing a cigar from a vest pocket.

Michaela gave him a look of cool tolerance. "You don't fool me, Hank. I've seen evidence that you have a heart. You're not as selfish and self-interested as you would like everyone to believe."

He let her last remarks go by without responding to them. "You don't fool me either," he said, biting off the end of the cigar and spitting it on the floor. He stuck the cigar between his teeth. "I know why you're here. Michaela's always gotta be in the middle of things, one way or another. This—this bounty business—it's man's business, Michaela." He scratched a match on the door frame. The stick fizzed and flamed, and he lit his cigar, squinting at her around the cloud of smoke he exhaled.

"I can't tell you how many times I was told that doctoring was a man's business," she retorted.

He shook his head. "Leave it alone."

She squared her shoulders, and increased her resolve. "If you'll excuse me . . . I need to talk to Sadie Jean."

She didn't trick him, not for a second—she could tell. But she could also tell that he knew he couldn't stop her unless he dragged her out of the saloon by her boots. She might be the most freethinking, most independent woman he had ever known, and at times he became more irritated with her than any woman he'd ever known. But he would never lay a hand on her *because* she was a woman.

He propped himself against the door frame, and she walked off.

She approached the table around which Mr. Hagan, Sadie Jean, and George Hagan's two allies in his quest for the bounty money were gathered.

"Look who's here," George Hagan said in a gravelly voice when Michaela was several feet from the table. His eyes were still focused on the fanned cards he held. He clenched the stump of a cigar in one corner of his mouth. "It's Dr. Quinn." He reached for the blackened cigar and flicked it at a spittoon in the corner to his left. "Come to play cards with us, Dr. Quinn?"

"I'm afraid I don't play cards, Mr. Hagan. I'm here to see Sadie Jean."

Sadie Jean flinched. She was no more ready to talk about Michaela draining that ovarian cyst than she had been last week. She was still just as frightened. "I'm workin', Dr. Mike," Sadie Jean said quietly.

Michaela tried to catch Sadie Jean's gaze. But it skittered around everywhere—to the table, to Mr. Britton as he played a lively tune, to the front doors, to the table again. She was so young; Michaela wouldn't guess Sadie Jean to be a day over seventeen. To die at such a young age would be a waste. And she *would* die, and die in a most agonizing way, if that cyst burst and poisoned her abdominal cavity.

Michaela sometimes wondered where Hank acquired these girls—if they came to him or if he went looking for them. Regardless, as soon as a young girl signed on with a saloon proprietor, she often doomed herself. Because of her many sexual associations, she could acquire any number of diseases and illnesses. Not to mention how such a profession affected a woman's opinion of herself. Michaela had seen too many cases in which the woman's low opinion of herself made her sink deep into depression.

"Sadie Jean, it's very important," Michaela said. "Please, we need to talk."

"I'm workin', Dr. Mike," the girl said again.

144

Although Michaela's main goal in coming to the saloon today was to talk to George Hagan, she couldn't help feeling frustrated with Sadie Jean. The girl was killing herself, simply because she was afraid of needles and surgical procedures.

For a moment Michaela focused on Sadie Jean, wanting to plead with her, wanting to explain to her, even if she had to explain in front of everyone, that the draining of that cyst periodically would save her life. And yet Michaela bit her tongue and held back. How well she knew that when a patient refused medical attention, there was nothing she could do.

She detested the feeling of having her hands tied. She'd been such a headstrong, obstinate, temperamental child; self-restraint was something she had forced herself to learn and exercise. Around the age of twelve, she had finally realized how much trouble her rebellious temper got her into, and that it very often made a bad situation worse.

She was still rebellious and her temper still flared at times. But those traits were nothing like they had been when she was a child. Years in Boston spent trying to gain respect from fellow physicians and to treat patients as a licensed doctor but being turned away at numerous bedsides had taught her the value of self-restraint. She had learned when to walk quietly away from a troubling situation. Although . . . since coming to Colorado Springs, she *had* jumped headfirst into several situations.

"All right, Sadie Jean," she said quietly. And then she couldn't bite back the words. "Another time."

She shifted her attention to George Hagan. He still refused to look at her.

"Curly here . . . he'd teach you to play cards, Dr. Quinn," Mr. Hagan said. "He thinks you're real pretty."

Curly glared at George Hagan. Mr. Standly and the other man laughed. Curly smacked Kenny in the chest with the back of his hand. "That ain't funny," he said. "Ain't intendin' no disrespect by it, Dr. Quinn."

145

"If your husband and that sheriff would hand over that body, they'd make things easier on theirselves, Doc," said Mr. Hagan. "I'm gettin' real short on patience. Ain't no tellin' what might happen when the well runs dry. It's just about dry right now."

Michaela inhaled deeply, trying to draw in courage. Inside, she felt like a quivering mound of calf's-foot jelly. People often admired her courage and her resolve. Little did they realize that she was as frightened as anyone might be when faced with a problem, especially one involving life or death.

Boldly she said, "I would like to talk to you about that situation, Mr. Hagan."

That made him look at her. He studied her for several seconds. She forced herself to maintain eye contact with him. Looking away would tell him that she was afraid of him, that she doubted herself and even the solidness of the floor on which she stood.

"So talk," he said.

"Privately," she responded.

He laughed, the evil sound rising from the back of his throat as he leaned back in his chair and placed his cards facedown on the table. "I reckon we could go upstairs."

She didn't flinch. He was trying to shock the Eastern lady in her. She held his gaze. "A table across the room will do nicely."

A few more seconds passed.

"You ain't gonna let her talk us into leavin' town without Willard's body, now are ya, Hagan?" Kenny asked worriedly.

"I ain't leavin' without it," Curly said. "We've been here longer'n I wanna be, but I ain't leavin' without that body. I'm runnin' low on money, myself."

"Long as we collect, that body don't matter to me. But I hear Sully ain't meanin' to let us collect a dollar," Mr. Hagan said. "An' that makes me want to get ugly, real ugly."

146

"Ya already are," Curly said, and laughter cut loose from him.

Michaela heard the smack Curly took on the chest before her eyes registered seeing Mr. Hagan's arm fly out. Curly yelped and slammed back in his chair. The chair toppled backward, and Curly landed on the floor, yelping again when his head thumped against the puncheons.

Mr. Hagan rose and walked off, saying, "Come on, Dr. Quinn."

She hesitated only a moment, and then only to see if Curly was all right, not because she was afraid to follow George Hagan. That thump could have caused a concussion. Curly rose, shaking off the blows and suddenly looking meek. But Michaela did not miss the look of absolute hatred that Curly cast at Hagan's back. He might work with the man for the sake of obtaining money, but he didn't like him.

Michaela followed George Hagan to a table at the opposite side of the room. He was seated before she reached the table, seated and leaning back, looking at her with smug impatience.

"I get bored real easy," he said.

She ignored the comment. Better to get this over with and be done with it. She went right to the reason she'd come: "The reward is five hundred dollars. I'll write you a draft for that amount—provided you leave Colorado Springs."

She'd caught him by surprise, something she thought not many people did. The smug look disappeared from his face. He went still, so still she wondered if he even breathed. His eyes narrowed and flickered.

"Eight hundred an' you've got a deal."

Michaela caught her breath. *Eight hundred dollars.* She had it, but that was about all she had. She'd have to work more to recoup some of the money. She had jewelry she could sell and some other belongings that were precious to her—china and other things. Normally she wouldn't consider parting with them. But her jewelry and china were worth far less, even in sentimental value, than Sully's life.

"Mr. Willard's body stays here," Michaela told George Hagan.

"All right. It's got to be cash."

"Eight hundred then," she said. "Cash. There's an abandoned miner's shack a mile east of town. I'll meet you there in one hour. Before then, I want you to make Sully think you've given up on getting the money. As soon as you have the money, I want you to leave town."

He grinned, a lecherous, greedy grin. The most evil grin she had ever seen. "Yes, *ma'am.*"

She couldn't stand the sight of him. She turned away to walk off, feeling nauseated. She was shaking—she couldn't seem to hold her medical bag still against the front of her skirt.

"Hey."

Michaela didn't want to turn back. But she did, for Sully's sake. She stared in silence at Mr. Hagan.

"Sully gets in my way again, I'll kill him," George Hagan said. His grin was gone. His words were a promise, not a threat.

Michaela didn't respond. She walked across the room, forcing herself to go at a slow, steady pace. She wanted to run; she wanted to get as far away from the horrible man as possible. She reached the doorway and then the hall just beyond it and the back staircase. Then she broke into a run.

Once outside, she stopped. She leaned against the wall to one side of the door, tipped her head back, closed her eyes, and fought to catch her breath. The full impact of what she had just done hit her.

She had made a deal with the devil. And if Sully ever learned of what she'd done, she would have to pray that he would forgive her.

Curly watched Dr. Quinn until he couldn't see her any more, until she'd disappeared past the back doorway of the main room. He'd watched George and Dr. Quinn talking at that table—he'd watched them from the corner of his eye so

148

George wouldn't notice. He'd seen George lose his grin for a minute, and that made him suspicious.

Curly wasn't real bright, but he had enough smarts, and he knew George well enough to know that something was up. The talk between George and Dr. Quinn was real short, and that was strange, too.

Something had happened. Maybe the doc had some dirt on George and had threatened to use it. But then, George must've found a way out 'cause he'd started grinning again.

"What was that about?" Curly asked when George sauntered back to their card game.

"Nothin'," George said. He glanced at Sadie Jean. "C'mon back over here, darlin'. Ooh-ee. You're pretty enough to take to Californy."

The way George didn't look Curly in the eye when he talked to him made Curly even more suspicious. George looked people in the eye except when he wanted to make a person feel real small—or when he was cheating someone or had plans to cheat someone.

"What'd she want?" Curly pressed. "What'd you talk about?"

"Nothin'," George said again.

"California?" Sadie Jean said in a real excited voice as she nuzzled George's neck.

"Yep—California." George kissed her neck, then her mouth.

Sadie Jean had been friendly with him before. Now that George was talking about taking her to California, Curly bet she'd become a lot friendlier. That's the way most saloon girls were. They were looking for a rich man to come along, or at least one who'd take them away from their troubles. George loved saloon girls. Hell, George loved *saloons*. But he didn't love this saloon so much since that Hank had taken him down a time or two. Curly figured George was sitting tight here until he had the opportunity for some revenge on Hank. And maybe Sadie Jean had a little something to do with that revenge. Yep, George loved saloon girls, but he never talked about taking them away with him.

Curly got bored with saloon girls pretty quick. Hell, he'd been bored with Sadie Jean all day, and antsy, knowing George might have more planned for her than she bargained for. Curly didn't have any special connection to the girl, he just didn't especially want to see her get hurt.

Curly wasn't used to sitting in one place for days at a time. The three of them—him, George, and Kenny—usually did their business, spent maybe a day and a night in a saloon in whatever town they were in, then moved on. Why the hell they didn't just storm that jail and take that body—they could do it after dark, could have done it last night—Curly couldn't figure. He was sick of waiting around.

"C'mon, George, you talked about somethin'," Kenny said, shifting his hand of cards around. He was interested, but only a little, and maybe only because Curly was. If Curly hadn't started asking questions, Kenny wouldn't have asked even the one. Mostly he just followed along behind George and Curly in whatever they did.

"Nothin', I said." George's temper was running short. He glared at Curly, then Kenny, who lowered his hand and paled like he always did when George lost his temper. Then George looked back at Curly. "Nothin'."

Curly might've believed him if George had offered some kind of explanation, like maybe the doc had asked him to leave town and he'd refused. Or like maybe she'd asked him to leave that Sully alone and he'd refused. They'd talked about something, and George had no reason for not telling what they'd talked about—unless he was hiding something.

"Bounty money in yet?" Curly asked. He took a swig from his whiskey bottle, watching George all the while.

"How the hell am I s'posed to know?" George growled.

"Her—the doc."

If George reached out and smacked him again, Curly would take his head off. He'd already decided that. George

150

wasn't going to knock him to the floor again—not now, not ever.

"You think she'd tell me if it was?" George demanded.

"Well, what'd she say then?"

"Nothin'," George growled again. This time, he stood up, so fast that his chair screeched across the floor and toppled. Sadie Jean yelped and jumped back. George caught her by the hand and told her to come on, they were going over to the bar to get something else to drink.

Curly let George go without any more questions. But once George was safely at the bar, he said to Kenny, "He's hidin' somethin'. I don't trust 'im. I ain't much good at cipherin' an' you can't cipher at all. But you listen. Near's I can figure, he skimmed off more'n his share of the last bounty. I ain't gonna let 'im do that again. He's bein' secret 'cause he's thinkin' of cheatin' us, Kenny."

Kenny squinted at Curly, disbelieving. "If he ain't got no bounty money, how's he gonna cheat us?"

"Mebbe he just got offered bounty money."

Kenny's squint increased. "What're you talkin' about?"

"Well, the doc didn't come to see him about nothin' medical, that's for damn sure! What d'ya wanna bet they just cut some kinda deal?"

Kenny studied him. "Naw," he said finally. "George wouldn't cut no deal with her an' not include us in it."

Curly shoved a full glass of whiskey at Kenny. It landed in his lap. Kenny jumped up, trying to brush the whiskey off. "Why'd ya go an' do that?"

"Don't be stupid," Curly said. "If he cheated us once, he'll cheat us agin. Once a cheat, always a cheat—that's what my mammy said. She was right, too. Sit down, now, 'fore he gets to suspectin' somethin'. I aim to keep a real close eye on George. If I find out he's cheatin' me . . . I'll send 'im straight to hell."

Kenny gulped. "You mean kill him?"

"Yeah, just like I killed that Levi Willard—an' ever'one's been thinkin' George did it. Sit down," Curly snapped.

"What'd you think I meant? George'll die just like anybody else. Just wait 'an' see."

Kenny sat down. He was real nervous, though. Twice he dribbled whiskey down his whiskered chin when he was trying to drink, and he kept looking all around and at Curly. Like he was wondering if Curly would really do it, really kill George if he found out George was cheating them.

12

While Loren was worrying himself sick over Sully sitting on his walkway with fresh blood on his shirt, Horace received another telegraphed response from the marshal in Denver. He hastened to deliver it to Matthew.

"Why don't you go home?" Loren asked Sully as Horace cut a path across town. He normally paid a boy to deliver messages for him. But these messages back and forth between Matthew and the marshal . . . they were too important to put into anyone's hands but his and Matthew's. Horace had a horrible fear—always had, since he'd taken on the job of telegraph operator—of losing or misplacing the messages that were entrusted to him to send or deliver. In his early days on the job, he actually *had* misplaced a few messages. He'd been real careful ever since.

"I've gotta watch for Hagan," Sully told Loren. "He's gonna try for Willard's body."

"Well, what if he does?" Loren grumbled. "You ain't in no condition to do nothin' about it."

He watched Sully shift himself around, and he shook his

153

head and drew his mouth up real tight. There'd been a time when he hadn't liked Sully much, when just the sight of Sully made him angry. He'd blamed Sully for his daughter's death, and wished Sully would just disappear. He'd regarded Sully as a strange character, dressing in those Cheyenne buckskins and believing in all that Indian stuff—in smoking this and burning that and chanting over everything.

In recent years, Sully had changed; or maybe *he'd* changed—Loren wasn't sure. The passage of time had helped both of their dispositions, that was the one thing Loren was certain of. He and Sully had both gotten over Abigail's death. Then Maude had died, and Loren had felt a loneliness that reminded him of a deep black hole, one that wanted to swallow him up at times. He'd never thought he could feel so lonely, especially at night. A boy became a man, and he slept alone just fine until he married and had the companionship of a woman. It never occurred to him that sleeping alone again would be difficult—until he had to do it.

So he'd had to adjust to that, and he'd had to admit that he'd never have any grandchildren. He didn't especially like having children underfoot anyway. But grandchildren . . . they might've been different. They might've been something to him—he might've felt different about them.

But that was all useless thinking. With Abigail dead, he'd never know what having grandchildren was like. That baby girl—hers and Sully's—had died with her. That had been a hard thing to take, too.

Loren had finally settled down to all that, telling himself that's how things were—Abigail and the baby and Maude were all dead and buried, and for some reason, the Lord had decided he should go on living. *Why?* he'd wondered at times. Maybe there were reasons. Maybe for Brian, because for some reason the boy had taken to him. Loren often pondered that, too—why Brian had taken to him when he'd been nothing but a grouchy old man.

And maybe he'd lived for Dorothy, too, because she'd needed help getting through her bad situation with her husband beating her. Lord knew she'd needed to feel like she was worth something to someone, if only to herself.

Loren was real proud of Dorothy these days. He loved her from a distance. Although, like he'd told her, he wasn't going to say that again and again and ask her to marry him. That was all. He wasn't going to make a fool of himself by interfering in her life. Dorothy needed her own section of the world, and she needed something like the *Gazette* to make her feel real proud of herself and like she was leaving her mark on the world. So Loren pretty much left her alone, in her own section of the world, or at least in her own section of Colorado Springs.

"You're bein' a fool," Loren told Sully. "I ain't gonna let you sit here an' bleed to death."

"I ain't gonna bleed to death," Sully responded, and his voice sounded weak to Loren.

"Well, you might."

Loren received a cold look, one that reeked of stubbornness. Loren felt panicky inside. Sully had a lot to be thankful for these days, and he was gonna throw it all away because of his feud with that George Hagan?

Loren sat down beside Sully and glanced at nothing in particular. Matthew had disappeared from his walkway. Hank kept peeking over the saloon doors every once in a while, probably to see if Sully was still sitting on the mercantile steps. Every now and then Jake walked out of the barbershop and looked up and down the street, like he, too, expected trouble. Loren watched people walk back and forth and up and down the street, some of them hurrying along like they had business to take care of and wanted to get it done before the trouble started.

Things weren't usually like this. Citizens usually went about their business at a leisurely pace. Why, even the wagons and horses clipped along quicker than normal today. Loren wondered if he was just imagining things.

He scowled at Sully. Sully needed to go home. That would help. Things might calm down then. Of course, George Hagan was still sitting in the saloon, waiting. . . .

"We didn't have Abigail for very long," Loren said slowly, sadly. The subject always made a little pain tweak through his chest. "I had her for longer than you did, but I still didn't have her for very long. When a man lives to be my age, twenty years don't seem like much anymore. A drop in the bucket maybe." He shook his head. "Aw, Sully, you're bein' stubborn an' foolish. You had Abigail for just part of that drop, and you had that baby girl for even less. Now you've got another wife—a real good one—and another baby girl. But you're gonna sit here an' bleed to death, or you're gonna start somethin' with George Hagan that could end you up in the cemetery."

Sully sat in silence. But he'd tipped his head a little, and Loren wanted to believe that some of what he was saying was sinking in.

"I didn't always like you," Loren said, drawing out the *I*. "Lord knows there was a day when I didn't want you buried by Abigail if somethin' happened to you. Now I don't want you buried by Abigail 'cause you don't belong there. You belong here, with Dr. Mike an' Brian an' that baby girl. Get yourself killed an'—"

"I ain't tryin' to get myself killed," Sully said.

"Yeah, you are," Loren said. "You know that man's dangerous." He waited a minute, then went on. "It don't bother me the way he acted that day in the mercantile. Don't worry about that. Don't be stickin' up for me. Remember all the times I didn't stick up for you."

"I won't let him terrorize my friends an' family."

Friends? Sully was referring to him as a friend. . . .

Loren puffed up. *Of all the crazy.* . . . "I ain't no friend of yours," he snapped. "Don't be thinkin' that."

Sully stared at him, and Loren could tell he didn't believe him.

Loren jumped up. Well, as quickly as a man his age and

with as many creaks and aches could jump up. "I can see there's no talkin' to you," he snapped. "No gettin' you to understand you're gonna hurt people if you sit here an' die, or if you go off an' get into a ruckus with George Hagan an' die that way. It ain't gonna do nobody no good."

He dusted off his trousers, then he walked back into the mercantile, shaking his head and thinking Sully was acting like the biggest fool he'd encountered in all his days.

Inside the sheriff's office, Matthew blinked hard several times and peered down at Brian. After snatching him off the street, Matthew had pulled Brian into his office and started questioning him. And he wasn't done. Brian had clammed up. But Matthew meant to get some answers, and his questions wouldn't stop until he did. It was the damnedest thing he'd ever seen, Brian all dressed up in women's clothes—clothes that were a mile too big and his face painted like a saloon girl's.

What was going on?

Brian had never had any interest in women's clothes, or in painting his face. Not that Matthew recalled, anyway. Oh, there'd been the one year that Brian and Mr. Bray had dressed up like clowns, and they'd painted their faces for that, sure. But Brian was dressed up like a girl right now, like a *saloon* girl. And he'd been out in the open where everyone could see him. Hurrying along at a pretty good clip. He'd been out in *public* dressed and painted like this. He'd had a pretty god-awful look on his face, too, like he'd been running scared from something.

"Brian, what . . . ?"

"Woo-hoo, look at that perty girl," hooted the rustler, for about the tenth time.

Matthew was tired of that man. Fed up to the eyeballs with him. He turned slowly, pronouncing every word real clear. "Shut—your—mouth." He glared at the man, whose face was pressed up against the cell bars.

"Got stuff to do. Gotta go," Brian said, real quicklike.

Before Matthew could turn back completely, Brian shot off, scrambling toward the door, jerking it open, and dashing outside.

He plowed into Horace, who'd just stepped onto the walkway, and he and Horace tumbled backward. Horace did a perfect backward roll—Matthew would never have guessed Horace was so limber. And Brian . . . well, he flipped over in the dirt a couple of times but never lost his pace. Not a second passed between his flipping and getting back on his feet, despite the skirt he wore. By the time Matthew got outside, Brian was scooting down the road faster than Matthew had ever seen him go.

Horace was sitting about five feet from the walkway, spitting out dirt and staring in bewilderment at the pint-sized figure tearing down the street. Horace's eyes had a way of taking on a glazed-over, wide look when something amazed, shocked, or baffled him. His mouth sometimes dropped open, too.

Matthew bet Horace wished he'd have snapped his mouth closed this time. He might be eating dirt for a while. Hell, he might have already swallowed a cupful. But he damn sure still had a telegram in his hand that he'd obviously been about to deliver to Matthew.

"Got somethin' from the marshal, Horace?" Matthew asked, stepping off the walkway. He wanted to know what was going on in Brian's head, but he reckoned a telegram from the marshal was more important right now. He'd like to get that body out of that cell before it started stinking.

Matthew offered Horace a hand, but Horace just sat there staring at him.

"The marshall—yes!" Horace said suddenly, and with such force Matthew almost jumped back.

Horace spit out dirt. Then he fluttered the telegram, shifting it from hand to hand as he fumbled around, trying to get back onto his spindly legs. He held the telegram out, then spotted the dirt on it and snatched it back. He brushed at it, still looking dazed, baffled.

Matthew reached out and grabbed the telegram, losing his patience again. He shook his head. Some pretty crazy things had gone on around here lately, and he'd be real glad when everything settled down. "A little dirt don't matter, Horace," he snapped.

At first, Horace's eyes flared in surprise. Then he looked wounded. "I'd have given it to you real soon. I never misplace a telegram. Or—or forget to deliver one."

Matthew scowled. "I know." Horace took his job real serious, too serious sometimes. Sometimes he slept on a cot by his telegraph machine instead of hiring someone to take his place from time to time.

"What was that?" Horace blurted as Matthew unfolded the message. Horace was looking down the street, in the direction Brian had gone. Poor man was probably thinking he'd imagined Brian in that dress with his face all painted. Or maybe he didn't realize it was Brian.

Matthew wasn't eager for anyone else to discover Brian in that dress, so he shrugged and pretended to focus on the telegram. Matthew's ears felt hot suddenly. His brother wasn't going to run around town dressed like that with his face painted. He'd catch Brian and tan him good.

The telegram was from the marshal. It read: BURY BODY. STOP. WILL SEND REWARD MONEY. STOP.

Well, thank God. Matthew had never had to lock up a body before. And he hoped he'd never have to again.

He'd take care of that body—it wouldn't take much to bury it because the grave was already dug—then he'd deal with Brian.

When he looked up from the telegram, Matthew glanced at the saloon. He reckoned he'd better find himself some deputies. When he went to move that body, he could just about count on Hagan causing trouble.

Right about that time, Hank came out of the saloon, an intent look on his face, and moved toward Matthew. *Hagan's making trouble,* was Matthew's first thought. And then his second thought was that if Hagan had decided to

159

make trouble in Hank's saloon, Hank probably would have dealt with the man himself, then *maybe* explained everything to Matthew later.

"I'll send the marshal another wire later," Matthew told Horace. Then Horace went off, shaking his head, probably still wondering what in the world had plowed him down.

Matthew had just stepped back onto the walkway in front of his office when Hank reached him. Hank moved beside him, and he leaned in real close.

"I'll take that body to Denver," Hank said. "No strings attached. I'm not lookin' to be no deputy, an' I'm not lookin' to make money by takin' the body neither. I'm just offerin', if you need someone to go."

Matthew's brows shot up. Hank didn't do much out of the goodness of his heart. In fact, some people would question whether Hank had a heart.

"What's your motive?" Matthew asked.

Hank scowled. "Do I have to have a *motive?*"

"You usually do."

"Yeah, well, this time I don't. 'Cept maybe I don't want any more trouble. Sully's gonna sit there an' bleed to death, an' Michaela's gonna get in over her head."

Matthew's interest perked up. "Why do you think Dr. Mike's gonna get in over her head?"

Hank ran a hand over his mouth, like he wasn't sure how much he should say, or if he was even sure of what he was about to say. "I think she worked somethin' out with Hagan. She was in the saloon. Made like she wanted to check on Sadie Jean, but she ended up takin' Hagan off to a corner an' talkin' to him."

"Maybe she just asked him to leave town."

"Maybe. Maybe not," Hank said. "She came in the back way, and she left the back way. Now, Michaela's never come in the back way. She just marches in, bold as brass, 'cause that's the kind of woman she is. She didn't come to talk to Sadie Jean—hell, she didn't spend five minutes talkin' to her. She came to cut a deal with Hagan. Tell you

160

somethin' else . . . Bodine an' Standly are worried about Michaela cuttin' a deal with Hagan an' about Hagan maybe cuttin' them out of their share of bounty money. Henry Hughes was sittin' pretty close, an' he heard them discussin' things. We've gotta do somethin' with that body 'fore there's more trouble, 'fore somebody else gets killed."

"I'm gonna bury it," Matthew said. Surely Dr. Mike hadn't done anything but ask Hagan to leave town. Surely she knew better than that, though—surely she knew that just asking the man to leave wouldn't get the job done. And if she did know better than that, what had she and Hagan talked about?

"She's tryin' to protect Sully," Hank said, shaking his head.

"Find her an' keep an eye on her, would you?" Matthew requested. "I just got a wire from the marshal. He wants me to bury the body, an' that's what I plan to do. There might be trouble from Hagan when I take the body to the cemetery. I don't want Dr. Mike in the middle of it."

Hank nodded, and for once, Matthew felt he could depend on him.

Dorothy hadn't seen hide nor hair of Brian since she'd returned from the resort.

She was sitting in front of her press, shooing Mouse away from tussling with her skirt and contemplating trying to print copies of the *Gazette* by herself. Between the medicine Michaela had given her and the steam baths she'd been taking, particularly the one this afternoon at Preston's resort, she was feeling better, and she reckoned she'd get quite a few copies of the *Gazette* printed before her hands started paining her again so bad that she had to stop. Ten or twenty copies were better than one or two, and maybe, just for this week, townspeople could share their copies with others who didn't have one because there weren't enough to go around.

That thought was like her giving up. Why, she'd never—

"Stop it, y'hear?" she scolded Mouse. She and the puppy

161

still weren't getting along, although she had to admit he'd been a little quieter lately. Right now he had the hem of her skirt between his teeth, and he was growling and backing up. He'd have the hem ripped in a minute. "Not if I can help it," Dorothy said, and she kicked at him. There was no contact, but Mouse jumped back and yelped like there was.

The *Gazette* office door banged open, and Dorothy didn't know what to think—if someone was angry at her about something, or if someone was barging in to rob her in broad daylight.

She swung around and saw the little person standing there. A little girl, Dorothy thought at first.

But then she noted the short hair that stood up in spikes all over the little person's head. And when the little person spoke, Brian's voice came out of the mouth: "Miss Dorothy, you gotta help me. You gotta! I can't have Ma seein' me like this. I can't have *anyone* seein' me like this. You . . . you gotta help me!"

Dorothy had never cared much for heavy perfumes, and now was no different. She sat back on her stool, leaned back really, because Brian—if the little person really *was* Brian—smelled like about ten different sweet perfumes. All the smells together would give her a headache. And a headache on top of aching hands would be no fun.

She crinkled her eyes, squinting, trying to make sure of what she was seeing. Nope, her eyes weren't playing tricks on her. It was Brian standing in front of her, the blue and black paint all smeared around his eyes and down onto his cheeks. There, the blue and black met red—rouge. Further down, his lips were painted a pretty rose color.

"Heavens, Brian!" Dorothy gasped. "What've you done? I gotta *help* you . . . ? What kind of mess have you gotten yourself into?"

"All these clothes. . . ." He started peeling the dress off, shoving it off his shoulders. He was wearing a corset over his shirt, laced up tight and stuffed with something to make

162

it look like he had breasts! The sight made Dorothy nearly fall off her stool.

"Where'd you get those clothes?" she asked, coming off the stool. "An' that paint? Loren didn't sell it to you, did he?"

Brian shook his head, real hard and real fast. The dress spilled in a heap around his feet. He started working at the front corset lacings. They were done up real tight, though, and she saw that he'd have no luck at all.

"Wouldn't your ma be appalled?" Dorothy went on. "Brian, what were you thinkin', dressin' up like some— some *floozy*? An' then runnin' in here?"

He groaned and shook his hands, having a time with those corset lacings. "Is that what you called Myra an' Emma?" he demanded, sparks of frustration in his eyes.

Dorothy winced. No, that was not what she'd called Myra and Emma, former saloon girls—and she shouldn't have called those other saloon girls that either.

"I went . . . I went lookin' for a story," he informed her as he recommenced trying to untie the corset strings. "I met up with you this afternoon an' then I was thinkin' *Miss Dorothy hasn't interviewed Sully or Mr. Hagan or anyone else involved in the bounty an' outlaw bus'ness 'cause her hands are hurtin' her so bad she can't take notes.* So I figured I'd take notes for you. Figured I'd start with Mr. Hagan, seein's how he'd surely be leavin' town soon. So I went to Hank's saloon, only I didn't want nobody to see me . . . Sully's sittin' on the mercantile steps, so I went 'round to the back. I went upstairs an'—"

"Brian!" Dorothy blurted. "In the saloon?"

He glanced up from the corset strings. He nodded. "Don't tell, Miss Dorothy. Don't tell Ma or Pa. Those women grabbed me an' put all these clothes an' paint on me."

"'Those women'? You mean *Hank's* girls?"

Brian nodded again.

Dorothy didn't like what was going through her head, but

163

she had to ask Brian, just to be sure: "They didn't do anything more'n put the clothes on you and paint you?"

He shook his head. He went back to working on the corset strings, and after a few seconds, the knot came loose and he pulled the lacings apart. "Said they were gonna teach me a lesson I wouldn't forget."

Dorothy arched a brow at that information. "An' did you learn anythin'?"

"I don't wanna go in a saloon ever again in my life!" Brian said as a balled-up stocking spilled out from the top of the corset. It rolled like a tiny tumbleweed across the wooden floor, collecting dust, finally colliding with the corner baseboards and stopping. Mouse chased after it. Other balled-up stockings spilled out, too, and they rolled all over the *Gazette* office floor. Mouse didn't know which way to go.

More tumbleweeds gathering dust, Dorothy thought, and she hurried over to the windows to pull the curtains shut. Hank's girls had padded Brian up mighty good. When he turned slightly, trying to maneuver the boned corset around, she saw that they'd padded his backside, too. They must've packed more balled-up stockings inside of the drawers they'd put on him.

"Well, maybe that's what they intended," Dorothy said in response to his remark about never again wanting to go into a saloon. She uncrooked her fingers—they didn't hurt so bad right now—and worked at pulling the corset lacings free.

"Hold still now, Brian," she grumbled. "You've . . . you've gone an' twisted this thing around." He had, too. He'd frantically been trying to get it off, and in doing so, he'd twisted it around so the front was in the back and the back was in the front. The lacings were jumbled up underneath the encased whalebones and. . . . "What a mess."

"I was just tryin' to help, Miss Dorothy," Brian said.

Lord! How humble and sorry he sounded! She'd find this

164

all mighty funny—definitely would later, in fact—if he didn't look so pitiful.

She pulled back and gave him a soft smile. "No story's so important that I want you to risk gettin' hurt, Brian. That Mr. Hagan . . . he's in such a temper right now at Sully, there's no tellin' what he might've done if you'd gotten to him. He wants somethin' he thinks Sully's got, an' he just might be mean enough to take somethin' that means a whole lot to Sully—*you*—an' try an' use it against Sully. What you did, or tried to do . . . that was real sweet, Brian. Tryin' to help me that way, with the story an' all . . . that's sweet. But I don't ever want you puttin' yourself in danger to try an' get a story for the *Gazette*."

Brian's eyes had widened again. "I didn't think about that—that Mr. Hagan might use me to hurt Sully more."

Dorothy nodded. "I know. That's why it's important to talk to adults most times before you decide to go off 'n' do somethin'. You know I wouldn't have told you to sneak into the saloon an' try to interview Mr. Hagan."

She shook her head. Brian *was* sweet, and his unselfish motive was the only thing that prevented her from becoming angry with him. How could she, when he'd gone into the saloon to try and help her with a story?

She couldn't breathe a word of this to anyone, and neither could he. Well, she didn't think he was eager to share his experiences this evening with anyone. Between the two of them, they had to keep this situation real quiet. She knew Michaela, and if Michaela thought that Brian would put himself in danger for a *Gazette* story, she might not let Brian help Dorothy with stories anymore. And that would be a tragic thing, because Brian showed promise as a writer and as a journalist.

"Let me help you out of these clothes, Brian," Dorothy said gently. "I'll put 'em in with my laundry an' return 'em to those girls. I'll even thank 'em for occupyin' you so you couldn't get to Mr. Hagan. An' I'll be sure an' tell 'em you won't be goin' into another saloon."

165

She fought to keep from laughing a little. Those girls dressing and painting Brian so he'd learn a lesson and not enter another saloon was something to laugh about! It sure was.

Hank's girls liked Michaela, and they knew Brian was her son. So Dorothy didn't really think they had done anything more with Brian than dress him and paint him; she didn't really think they'd treated him like any other male who entered the saloon. But, all the same, she'd had to ask him if dressing him and painting him was all they'd done. She'd had to be absolutely certain. And now that she was, and now that she felt relieved that he hadn't gotten to Mr. Hagan . . . well, what those girls had done with Brian was actually comical.

"Shoo!" she said. "We'll have to get you washed up, too. All that perfume'll give me a headache!"

Brian looked so pathetic, hanging his head, sulking, his shoulders slumped. Because he looked so beat, Dorothy didn't say much more about the predicament he'd gotten himself into. She went about helping him clean up.

She took him upstairs—Mouse tagged along behind, of course—where they washed his face and hair. She had a little vinegar in a jar, and she rinsed his hair in that to help rid it of all the perfume smells. She took a towel and dried his hair a little for him, too. All the mothering seemed to help. When she lowered the towel, he gave her a sheepish smile and thanked her. She found a comb, and he stood in front of her looking glass and combed his hair.

By the time it was all done, her hands and fingers were smarting pretty good again.

She fixed herself some tea brewed from the powder Michaela had given her. And while she drank the tea, she and Brian talked about how deceit wasn't a good thing and how neither one of them should lie if anyone asked them questions about what happened this afternoon; all the same, in this case, Dorothy said, clamming up was probably the best way to go. Telling Dr. Mike and Sully outright about what had happened to Brian probably wouldn't be a good idea. They might not appreciate the saloon girls' lesson, and Brian might not be able to write stories for the *Gazette* anymore.

Brian agreed, as Dorothy had thought he would—he surely didn't want to have to tell his ma and pa what had happened, so he'd sooner just avoid the subject.

"Well, we'd best get to work," Dorothy said, and she rose from her chair.

Brian rose, too, and rushed to her and hugged her tightly around the waist. So tightly, Dorothy wondered if she'd ever get loose. He told her he loved her, and he thanked her for helping him.

She smiled down at him and gave him a pat on the head. Then they went downstairs to print the *Gazette*.

13

"I don't intend to inform you of why I need the money, Preston," Michaela told the banker irritably as they walked up Main Street, heading toward the bank.

"Eight hundred dollars, Dr. Quinn. . . ." He shook his head, obviously wishing she would explain why she needed so much money, and in cash.

Michaela snapped her lips together. She would not explain herself to him, why she needed to withdraw her own money from her own bank account. "I need to withdraw the money, Preston. That is all you need to know."

He tipped his head and peered down his nose at her.

The arrogant man! He had nothing on her—and she had no patience at the moment. At least not where he was concerned. She had been born and raised in Boston, too, in a household where upper-class snobbery prevailed. Elizabeth Quinn had perfected the art of arrogance and haughtiness. Michaela might be smaller than Preston in stature, but she certainly could affect upper-class snobbery. When she tipped *her* head and peered *up* her nose at him, Preston was no match for her. And he knew it; they had clashed before.

His eyes narrowed worriedly, his brows drawing together in a frown. He smoothed his coat sleeves, as if she had rumpled them, and then he straightened the collar at the back of his neck and jerked his head around a little, as if he had suddenly grown uncomfortable.

Ridiculous man! He should have known better than to challenge her with snobbish arrogance. It wasn't very Christian of her to act the same in return, and she felt a twinge of guilt that she had. But she suppressed the twinge and walked on. How dare he question why she wanted to withdraw her money! How dare he act as if the money were his!

She had ridden out to the resort, knowing she'd find Preston there. She had told him privately that she needed to withdraw eight hundred dollars from her account, and, of course, Preston had reacted horribly. He'd stiffened, drawing himself more upright than ever, and then he'd demanded to know why she wanted to withdraw the money. He had made the demand again, and finally she'd lost her patience. Why she needed her money was none of his concern, and she'd told him exactly that. In response, he'd stiffened more, and then he'd taken his time about finishing up a few things at the resort. Finally, reluctantly, he'd gathered his coat and top hat and he'd followed her into town—where he'd asked twice more why she needed eight hundred dollars.

By the time they reached the bank, Preston was pouting. Michaela didn't care. Soon she would have the money—she'd brought along a haversack in which to put it—and then she would ride as fast as possible to the old mining shack just east of town.

When they exited the bank, they spotted Matthew and a number of other men in front of the sheriff's office. A wagon sat there, and the men carried Willard's body, now covered and bound inside a sheet, out to the wagon.

"I hope Sheriff Cooper plans to bury that body finally,"

Preston said. "He'll have quite a time doing it. He'll have to get by the reverend and the group of citizens he'll undoubtedly gather to meet them at the cemetery. Reverend Johnson doesn't want the outlaw buried in the town cemetery."

"I know," Michaela said, and suddenly she was glad the reverend didn't want Mr. Willard's body buried in the town cemetery. If Matthew was about to take the body out there—and she hoped he was, that he wasn't heading for Denver—the scene Reverend Johnson might cause would distract people from her leaving town to meet Mr. Hagan at the miner's shack.

She started off with her haversack of money, and she met Hank as she approached the clinic.

"Where's your doctor's bag, Michaela?" he asked, tossing down a cigar and extinguishing it with his boot.

"Is someone hurt? I mean, besides Sully." She couldn't help but wonder. Why else would he ask her such a question? But he didn't look distressed, as most people did when they came after her because someone was ill or injured.

"Just askin'. Ain't used to seein' you with a different kind of bag."

"I . . . my medical bag is in the clinic."

"You just came from the bank," Hank remarked. "Now ain't that suspicious, seein's how you just met with Hagan not too long ago and took him off in a corner to talk to him."

Michaela bristled with nervousness. She couldn't let Hank know what she was up to. She couldn't let anyone know what she was up to. "My business is not your business," she said.

"Business, huh? Did you work somethin' out with Hagan, Michaela? Offer him the bounty money or somethin'? To protect Sully, right?"

She bristled more. "I asked him to leave, and he refused."

Hank grinned. "You ain't in Boston anymore, an' I ain't stupid. You plannin' on meetin' Hagan somewhere?"

171

Michaela was silent. She felt backed into a corner.

"You are, aren't you?"

"No," she said quickly, then mounted the steps leading up to the clinic.

In a flash, Hank was beside her. His voice was much lower this time. "You're thinkin' about payin' him off, an' I ain't sayin' that's wrong. But I ain't lettin' you go off alone to meet with Hagan. Not when Hagan would love to get revenge on Sully for all the trouble Sully's caused him these last few days. Let me take the money."

Let him take the money? She didn't know if she trusted him with the money. Sometimes she trusted Hank and other times she didn't.

"Think about it, Michaela."

"Excuse me," she said, her voice sounding weak and cracked. "I—I have some things to record and instruments to clean."

He nodded slowly, as if not believing her, and he watched her walk into the clinic.

Once inside, with the door shut behind her, she wrung her hands in nervousness. She had to go meet Mr. Hagan at the miner's shack—before Sully bled to death on the mercantile steps. But if Hank was standing guard—and she had a feeling he was. . . .

She'd leave through the back door.

Matthew had deputized four men who weren't directly involved in town business. He didn't know whether or not to expect trouble from Hagan on his way to the cemetery, but he wanted to be ready just in case.

One deputy had brought a buckboard up to the office steps, and Matthew carried Willard's body out and let it drop into the bed of the wagon. Robert E. had built a pine box lickety-split, just like Matthew had asked him to, and they were headed to the blacksmith shop with the body.

The deputies were mounted and ready to go. Matthew

172

glanced around at them as he stepped up onto the wagon and settled himself on the seat. They'd better watch his back, his look said. When Hagan got wind that Matthew was moving the body, he'd most likely appear. And while Matthew hoped he'd gathered all the firearms Hagan, Bodine, and Standly had carried into town, he couldn't be sure. Rough men often had backups, just in case they met with trouble.

Matthew took the reins and shook them. The harnesses creaked as the horses set off in the direction of Robert E.'s blacksmith and livery.

From where he sat on the mercantile steps, Sully watched Matthew and his group of deputies take Willard's body away. The sun was lowering in the western sky, turning reddish-orange and casting different colors on the mountain slopes and peaks. Flanked by the mounted deputies, the wagon went down Main Street while Sully shifted his gaze between it, the doors of Hank's saloon, and the position Hank had taken up on the clinic steps.

Why would Hank be sitting there? Why wasn't he in the saloon? Sully wondered if someone was sick or injured. Hank got up, paced the porch area directly in front of the clinic door, then he grabbed the doorknob, opened the door, and disappeared inside the clinic.

Sully glanced at the saloon again. More and more men were drifting into the establishment. Sully expected Hagan to appear at the doors anytime, and Hagan didn't disappoint him.

The doors pushed open and Hagan walked outside and leaned against a support beam. He made no move to follow the wagon—he just watched it go—and he wasn't carrying weapons, at least none that Sully saw.

Curly Bodine and Kenny Standly came out behind Hagan, and they watched the wagon, too.

Curly said something to George. Hagan didn't respond. Curly said something else, and George shot him a deadly look. But Curly didn't back down. He shifted his boots—

173

even from this distance, Sully heard them shuffling back and forth on the walkway—and he got right in Hagan's face and said something else. He was agitated. It didn't take a genius to figure that out. Hagan was letting Matthew and his deputies take Willard's body away, and Curly didn't like that; he thought they ought to be doing something.

George balled up a fist and caught Curly in the gut with it so fast, Curly didn't have time to anticipate the move. He doubled over, while Kenny jumped back out of the way. Hagan shook open his fist and stepped off the walkway.

He was going after Willard's body.

Sully pushed himself up from the step, thinking of nothing but stopping George. He was shaky on his feet. But only he knew that, and he didn't dwell on the fact, didn't let it stop him. He leaped from the first step down to the dirt street, and from there, he walked toward Hagan. People had emerged from shops and businesses, and they watched from safe distances, near shelter.

George spotted him and smirked, shaking his head. "You don't know when you're beat, do you, Sully?"

"You ain't gettin' that body," Sully said.

"I don't need that body," Hagan responded. "I'm not such a fool that I'd go after it when there's four armed deputies guardin' it."

"You ain't never given up before," Curly shouted from near the saloon. "You ain't never let anyone stop you 'fore."

"That's right, except for Sully here," George said. "He's always gettin' in my way. There's other bounties." With that, he turned and started back toward the saloon.

Curly couldn't stand it. "You yeller-bellied, no-good . . . ! We tracked Willard 'cross two territories! If you ain't gonna collect that money, I am!"

Curly was right. George didn't just give up. Something wasn't right. Sully watched George walk off, and he felt a growing frustration.

Hagan shot Sully a grin over his shoulder, and that didn't

174

sit right with Sully either. The man was acting smug about something. "I don't need that bounty," George said.

Sully couldn't figure what he meant, why he felt that way. Hagan was a greedy man. If a man could be evil to the core, George was. He was up to something. Sully didn't know what—but he knew Hagan was up to something.

Curly must have glanced at the deputies, the wagon, and Matthew half a dozen times before he decided to make a move. Why he even considered taking on four armed deputies and the sheriff by himself, Sully wasn't sure. Greed did crazy things to people, made them act like they didn't normally act. It sure made Bodine mad right then—Curly bolted after the wagon, determined to stop it and take Willard's body.

"Look out!" someone shouted, and Sully, crouching instinctively, realized the voice belonged to Jake. "Matthew— he's comin'!"

The deputies' horses reared as their reins were jerked. The horses turned, rifles came up.

Curly Bodine pulled his brake handle. He saw four rifle barrels aimed at him, and he skidded to a stop so fast, he left tracks several feet long in the dirt. "Doan . . . don't shoot!" Curly shouted, his arms darting straight up into the air. "I ain't doin' nothin'! Nothin! I ain't doin' *nothin'!*"

Matthew had reined the horses that were hitched to the wagon, and he'd twisted around on the buckboard seat. Sully figured Matthew expected to see George Hagan chasing after them, and Matthew looked surprised when he spotted Curly Bodine instead.

"Get back, Curly," Matthew warned, stone-faced. "The marshal said to bury Willard's body, an' that's what I aim to do. If you get in the way, you'll get hurt."

Sully had backed up to the mercantile steps when the deputies' horses turned and the rifles took aim. From behind him, Loren said, "He's gonna *bury* that body? Bury it where? In our cemetery? Where Maude's buried? An outlaw?"

And where Abigail was buried. But Willard being buried out there didn't bother Sully. It wasn't like Maude or Abigail or even Charlotte Cooper could object. Or would. Maude and Charlotte would have wanted to put a stop to all the trouble by simply burying the man, and Abigail . . . Abigail had disliked any kind of prejudice. She wouldn't have objected.

Kenny Standly still stood in the street, worrying himself to death over Curly, shouting that Curly oughtta get back— he was gonna get himself shot and killed. But George Hagan had disappeared.

Sully glanced around, looking for Hagan. He had given up too easily. And Curly chasing off after the wagon carrying Willard's body had been crazy. Sully had thought Bodine had gone mad for a minute or two. But maybe he hadn't. Maybe Curly chasing after the wagon was a diversion. Maybe Hagan was planning to cut wide around town and ambush Matthew and the deputies at the graveyard.

"Sully!"

Hank was running toward him from the clinic. He'd just taken a step, meaning to search the saloon for Hagan, but he stopped when he saw Hank. Hank running out of the clinic like that, and Michaela being nowhere in sight, meant something was wrong over there.

Hank slid to a stop in front of Sully. "Let's follow Hagan," he said, real low, so that no one else could hear. "Michaela's meetin' him. She's gone."

Michaela was meeting Hagan?

"Where?" Sully blurted.

"I don't know," Hank said, turning off toward the saloon. "C'mon."

Sully tore toward the saloon. All he could think of was that maybe Hagan had tricked Michaela into meeting him.

Sully didn't notice that Curly had disappeared, slipping between buildings, intent on getting back to the saloon as quietly as possible. Curly had suspected that Hagan was up to something with Dr. Quinn, that maybe they'd worked out some kind of financial solution, and he had made some plans of his own. No way in hell was he gonna let Hagan make off with any money.

Sully caught up to Hank, then both of them burst into the saloon and took a quick look around.

"I'll search upstairs. You look out back!" Hank told Sully from across the saloon. Behind the bar, Jake was serving customers.

Sully shot down the hallway that led to the back door. Outside, he spotted George and Sadie Jean mounting horses that looked ready for travel; they carried bulging saddlebags, several canteens, and bedrolls tied to the saddles.

Hagan spotted Sully and jerked the horse around by the reins. "That woman of yours—she made it so I didn't have to worry about that bounty," he said. He laughed, then he and Sadie Jean kicked their horses into action. They raced off, soon disappearing up the street.

Sully didn't have a horse handy to leap onto. He couldn't chase after George, catch him, and ask him what he'd meant by Michaela making it so he didn't have to worry about the bounty.

"Michaela worked somethin' out with him," Hank said, rushing out the back door. "Can't say what, 'cause I wasn't privy to the conversation. She came here, though. Said she wanted to check on Sadie Jean . . . somethin' medical. C'mon, let's find horses."

He rushed up the backstreet, and Sully followed. They swung onto two saddled horses that stood at a hitching post in front of a house. The horses didn't belong to Sully or Hank. Neither man was a horse thief, but neither had an attack of conscience over temporarily borrowing the horses. They'd risk being accused of stealing later. To Hank's way of thinking, an extreme situation called for extreme action. Sully and Hank rode off, hoping to pick up Hagan's trail.

"My bet is, Michaela worked out a money deal with

Hagan," Hank said. "I bet he's cuttin' Bodine an' Standly out. Hagan an' Bodine ain't exactly gotten along well since they've been here."

A money deal? Sully stiffened. Michaela wouldn't go behind his back, work out something with Hagan—*pay him off . . . ?*

The eastern road out of town wasn't frequently traveled, and Hank and Sully picked up Hagan's trail easily enough.

"Maybe he wants us to pick up his trail," Hank suggested. "He's bein' too obvious."

Maybe Hagan did want them to pick up his trail easily, Sully thought.

The trail dropped off the road after a while, and Sully tracked it up into the forest. He and Hank slipped off their horses and walked, carefully following the trail. The forest was quiet today, serene until a woman's scream echoed in the distance.

Sully snapped his jaw shut, going rigid. To his right, Hank cursed. A rifle shot cracked through the forest. Another followed, then another.

Sully leaped onto the horse he'd been leading. He didn't need to track Hagan anymore. He'd ride toward the sound of the rifle shots.

Michaela paced outside the miner's shack. The haversack strap cut between her breasts and the bag rested on her hip. She couldn't seem to stop her hands from twisting together nervously. When Mr. Hagan arrived, she planned to force her hands down to her sides and put on a brave front.

Perhaps she shouldn't have come here alone. Perhaps, since Hank already suspected what she was up to, she should have asked him to come with her.

But she hadn't, and there was no sense fretting about that now. She would face Mr. Hagan, give him the money, then watch him ride off. And she would hope never to see him again.

That was, if he ever arrived.

She'd been waiting for him for some time, for too long. She rubbed her hands together to warm them; as much as she had twisted her fingers, one would think they would be warm already. The sun had lowered a considerable amount since her arrival, and the air had grown cooler. She didn't want to be caught here after dark, still waiting on Mr. Hagan, and that sentiment had nothing to do with being afraid of the dark.

She paced more, back and forth, crunching twigs and scrub in front of the shack.

Oh, where was he? Mr. Hagan wanted the money, and she had it for him. Now he just needed to collect it. The sooner he took it and rode off, the sooner she could go back to town and tend to Sully.

She was simply nervous, or so she told herself; she really hadn't waited long at all.

She wondered how matters had gone, or were still going, in town. She'd told George Hagan to make Sully believe he was giving up on collecting the bounty money. Surely he'd done that by now, and surely he was on his way here.

Surely . . . barring any problems.

Provided Sully hadn't tried to stop Mr. Hagan.

She was doing her best to protect Sully. She prayed that he hadn't discovered why Mr. Hagan was leaving, and that he hadn't put himself in George Hagan's way. Mr. Hagan was a hard man. He wanted this money, and it made no difference to him whether that money was hers and Sully's or Colorado Territory's. He'd made a deal with her—to leave town and to leave Sully alone in exchange for her money. He was so close to getting the money, Michaela was certain he could smell it. Being so close, he surely would kill Sully at this point rather than tolerate Sully's further standing in his way.

Michaela paced more. She wrung her hands more. She jumped at every noise—at the sound of small animals scurrying through the forest and birds fluttering in the trees.

She sat. She stood. She prayed. She waited.

She had just walked into the crumbled old shack when she heard a scream in the distance. Michaela whipped around.

Seconds later, a rifle shot cracked the crisp air. Michaela jumped, clenching the haversack strap. She made some sort of sound, too—a squeak, she thought.

She stepped back outside, glancing all around, just as another shot went off, echoing through the trees. Another followed, then another. Her horse, tethered to a nearby log, skittered and tossed its head, its eyes wide and fearful.

Michaela's stomach turned over. Her heart hammered. Her legs felt soft and weak.

She soothed the horse, running her hand along its neck. "Ssh. It's all right. Everything is all right."

She hoped. A hunter might have fired the shots.

But so many?

Another one split the forest.

After that shot, Michaela couldn't stop herself from mounting her horse and riding off to see who was firing—and at what, or whom.

She was aware of trees flying by her, of branches catching at her coat, poking through the material of her skirt and scratching her legs. She listened for more shots, her senses alert as she crouched over the horse's neck. She heard nothing but the crashing of the horse's hooves on the undergrowth.

She spotted a riderless horse ahead, saddled and equipped as if for travel, and she slowed her horse. She glanced around, wondering if anyone was still there, if anyone was injured. A few minutes and a short distance later she caught sight of a man's body lying facedown and twisted in a tangle of bushes.

She approached slowly, cautiously, still glancing around, feeling almost certain the man had been shot.

She halted her horse, then dismounted and neared the man.

Michaela stared down at him, her mouth falling open slightly. She knew who the man was before she turned him over: George Hagan. She also knew there was no chance of saving him, that he was most likely dead. A bullet hole marked the back of his bloody duster.

14

S he was right—he was already dead. He had been shot through the forehead and the neck, too.

Michaela sat back on her heels. She knew of only one person who had motive enough to want Mr. Hagan dead.

Sully hadn't killed George Hagan, surely. Sully hated guns and rarely had anything to do with them. Besides, running a man out of town was one thing. Sully would *not* kill him.

But other people in Colorado Springs . . . what would they believe?

Michaela turned to mount her horse, preparing to ride back to town. She'd bring a wagon out here and someone to help her collect the body, then she'd deliver the body to Jake, the town undertaker.

On second thought, instead of taking matters into her own hands, as she usually had an inclination to do, she ought to ride back into Colorado Springs and notify Matthew that someone had shot Mr. Hagan and that he was dead. Murder was a matter for the sheriff, after all.

She had just mounted when she spotted Sully cutting through the trees up ahead. She closed her eyes for several seconds, thanking God he was safe.

A moment later, she caught herself looking to see if he had a rifle, and she immediately felt guilty. Sully wouldn't do such a thing. He wouldn't kill someone—at least not for revenge.

Hank rode up behind Sully. Michaela watched them. They dismounted, and walked over to look at the body.

"Someone cut him down good," Hank remarked, shaking his head. "He's deader'n a doorknob."

Sully said nothing. He glanced around, and Michaela could tell he was listening, trying to hear anything that might tell him the murderer was still close by.

He obviously heard nothing unusual; he looked back at Hank. "Sadie Jean was with him."

Hank was silent for a few seconds. "Where is she now? You ain't gonna tell me you're thinkin' it was her that screamed?"

"Or Michaela," Sully said, and his voice dropped so low Michaela barely heard him.

She stepped out into the open. "No, it wasn't me. I didn't scream."

"Michaela!" Sully breathed, and he ran toward her. He wasn't far away, but even if he had been, he wouldn't have taken long to reach her.

Mindless of his injured arm, he grabbed her in an embrace and held her tight. "Thank God . . . thank God you're all right." Then he pulled back and looked at her. "What happened? What did you do, Michaela? You've gotta tell me." His face was more drawn with worry and concern than she'd ever seen it.

She realized what he must be thinking, and she shook her head. "I didn't . . . Sully, I didn't kill him. I don't have a rifle or a gun. I was supposed to meet him, but I didn't kill him. Sadie Jean was with him? It must have been her who screamed."

Surely he didn't think that she'd killed George Hagan. He knew her too well to believe such a thing. He knew she was a healer, that she was respectful of human life, that she wouldn't dream of taking a life.

But maybe, just maybe, he'd thought she had been desperate enough to take George Hagan's life. He knew she'd feared the threat Hagan was to him.

"I know," Sully said, and then the suspicion, the question, was gone from his eyes.

Relief swept through Michaela, relief that he was alive and unharmed—and that he didn't believe she had killed Mr. Hagan.

She laid her head on his shoulder, relishing the warmth of him and the strength of his arms as they held her.

"We've gotta find Sadie Jean," Hank said.

Michaela and Sully agreed.

"She couldn't be far from here," Sully remarked.

Hank suggested, "Let's scatter."

Sully shook his head. "Stay with me," he told Michaela. It wasn't an order—he knew she wouldn't respect an order. It was more of a plea because he wasn't over the fear that she might have been shot.

She touched his arm. "Please, Sully. Let me tend your wound first."

He studied her. She wondered if he knew she had been about to pay George Hagan to leave town. He didn't act like he knew. But perhaps he was waiting for a more appropriate time to mention it—when they were alone.

He agreed to let her tend his wound. Hank said he was going to look for Sadie Jean. He'd fire a shot if he found her, he told them, then mounted his horse and tore off.

Sully sank onto a nearby log and let Michaela pull off his shirt. She removed the soiled dressing, tore away most of her cotton chemise and shredded it, then poured water from canteens over several of the strips of material.

She washed his wound, finishing just as a gunshot disturbed the stillness and serenity of the forest. Although

185

Hank had told her and Sully that he'd fire a shot if he found Sadie Jean, Michaela jumped. Then she gathered her wits and wrapped the other strips of cotton around Sully's arm and tied them off.

Hank soon returned with a weak, beaten Sadie Jean. He said the other horse, apparently the one Sadie Jean had ridden, had run off. Both of the young woman's eyes were swollen, and they were rapidly turning blue and purple. A cut along her jaw would require stitching, Michaela observed. She meant to exam Sadie Jean more once they took her back to town.

Sadie Jean was crying, and Hank said, "She told me she shot Hagan 'cause he was beatin' her. That cut . . . it's from a knife. He told her he was gonna scar her up so she couldn't work for me no more. She tripped him, then got her hands on his rifle."

Never in her life had Michaela been glad that anyone was dead, but right now, at least for the moment, she was glad that George Hagan was dead. She said so aloud and impulsively—and then she couldn't look Sully or Hank in the eye, she was so ashamed.

"I reckon that's a pretty normal thought," Hank said in a low voice after a moment of awkward silence. He helped Sadie Jean up onto one of the horses. "Be much longer, Michaela?"

"No," she said curtly, working at another tie.

Sully put his hand over hers, forcing her to look at him. She was tired of everything that had happened these past few days, and she fought tears of frustration at the situation, and shame over what she had just blurted out.

"I'm sorry," she said. "I didn't mean that. I—"

"Yes, you did," Sully told her. "It's all right—you're human, Michaela. Like Hank said, it's pretty normal."

Michaela loved Sully more than ever during those moments. She loved him for not judging her, for loving her despite her faults and weaknesses, for assuring her that succumbing to human emotions now and then was all right.

186

She kissed him. Then she finished tying off the last knot, and she helped him onto one of the horses. Hank had draped Hagan's body over the other horse.

Once Michaela was mounted and ready, Hank took the reins of the horses carrying Sadie Jean and Hagan's body. He led the way back to town, and no one said a word on the way.

Earlier, after the trouble on Main Street had cleared—after George Hagan and his men disappeared—citizens realized that Matthew and the deputies were headed for the cemetery with Levi Willard's body. Some people had gone on about their business, mostly that of finishing supper and settling their families for the evening. But a small group of townspeople, inspired by Reverend Johnson, had formed to follow Matthew to the cemetery and object to the burying of the outlaw's body there.

With dusk closing in, Preston Lodge wasted no time taking up a lantern and joining the protesters, seeing it as an opportunity to increase his popularity. "Are we going to stand idly by while our sacred cemetery is soiled by the flesh of such a man?" he shouted to the people. "I say 'no!'"

Preston thought he was being clever, Loren felt certain. But the overblown man sounded ridiculous, as usual, taking up a cause for his personal benefit. Which was exactly why he hadn't been elected mayor.

Loren trailed the crowd, mostly to see exactly where the grave had been dug. Not too close to Maude and Abigail, he hoped. It better not be. Matthew had buried that other fellow, that man they'd hanged last year, somewhere outside of town because the reverend had objected to that criminal being buried in the town cemetery. Why couldn't Matthew bury Willard's body wherever he'd buried that other criminal's? Maybe because he could keep a better eye on the cemetery from his office and make sure Hagan didn't dig up the body or something. That was a gruesome thought, but

Loren couldn't figure what else might be going through Matthew's head.

Loren caught up with the group that followed the reverend. Not because he especially wanted to be a part of it, but because he had to see for himself if Willard's body was going to be buried near Maude and Abigail. If it was, Loren just might have to say something.

The group passed the *Gazette* office, and just as Loren expected, Dorothy wandered out. Brian was with her, that feisty puppy chewing at his trouser legs. Dorothy didn't have a notebook in her hands, and Loren found that odd. Usually if she thought there was information to be gathered for the newspaper, she was scribbling in a notebook. Brian was, too, sometimes. But neither one of them held a notebook right now. Brian picked up the puppy and petted it, trying to calm it down. Then he and Dorothy started walking behind Loren, following the small crowd that trailed Matthew, the deputies, and the wagon.

Soon Jake joined Dorothy and Brian. Robert E. put down his tools and followed them. Grace left her café in the care of the two girls she'd hired to help her, and she and Gwen soon caught up with Robert E. Grace bounced Katie Sully on her hip to try and quiet the baby.

Hank and Sully were absent, along with Dr. Mike. She might be in her clinic, absorbed in something, but where were Hank and Sully? They'd torn into the saloon a while ago after that trouble on Main Street, and Loren wondered if they were trying to convince George Hagan and his two buddies to leave town—Colorado Springs had had enough of them. *I sure hope there's no more trouble out of those men,* Loren thought. If there was, the trouble would probably be *between* them. That Curly Bodine fellow hadn't been too happy that George Hagan had decided to give up on getting the body and the bounty. Loren hoped Hagan and Bodine waited to settle their differences until after Matthew finished at the cemetery. Matthew couldn't deal with trouble in the saloon while he was across town trying to bury an outlaw.

"Matthew, what about this . . . ?" the reverend was saying, drawing up alongside the wagon and the deputies. Matthew didn't look at Reverend Johnson. He kept his eyes on the path ahead. "What about a separate cemetery for outlaws and renegades?"

"For anyone of questionable character," said the stuffy Mrs. Margaret Ogleby. She was a stout woman, more woman than Loren thought he could ever handle or tolerate. She huffed and puffed, but she managed to keep up with the wagon.

"A separate cemetery!" Preston said. "A wonderful idea!"

"We don't want no outlaw buried in our cemetery!" shouted Evelyn Hughes, the always vocal wife of Henry Hughes, a local rancher who spent a great deal of time in Hank's saloon. Henry was probably there right now, absorbing a few glasses of whiskey, if not a bottleful.

Matthew ignored the objections and shouts. He kept his eyes straight ahead. The deputies he'd hired, mostly quiet men around town, kept riding alongside the wagon.

The procession crossed the bridge spanning the creek that zigzagged its way around this part of town, and the protesting people followed, holding lanterns in case night closed in while they were still busy doing their civic duty. The gathering was made up mostly of men and women who wanted to drive things like drinking and loose women out of town—things Loren felt were needed. To his way of thinking, saloons provided advantages not just for the lonely man, but for the prostitutes, too. Like Emma, many of the girls who ended up working in saloons needed money, and the men who frequented the saloons provided that money. Why, if drinking and prostitution were driven out of Colorado Springs . . . that would shut Hank's business down and take away places where a man could go now and then—that's how it ought to be, just a now-and-then thing, not an every day occurrence—to relax and have himself a

189

drink and a woman if he wanted those things and if he had
the right amount of money in his pocket.

"Sheriff Cooper, please reconsider," said Martha Trevors.
Lord Almighty! She had her brood in tow, all four of her
white-haired, stair-step children. Martha had been like a
daughter to Maude, so in a way Loren understood why she
objected to Willard's body being buried in the cemetery.
Zachary, Martha's husband, was probably in the saloon
alongside Henry Hughes; Zachary was a mighty heavy-
handed drinker. A frequent drinker, too. It was a wonder he
managed to provide for his family.

"Take that body somewheres else!" shouted John Perkins.
"There's a heav'n an' there's a hell, an' that man's burnin'
right now. He ain't goin' in our cemetery."

The spindly-legged fool was well over six feet tall, and he
rushed alongside one of the deputies, reached up with his
long arms, and tried to yank the deputy off his horse.

"Let go," the deputy—Bud Starns—ordered, wriggling
around on the saddle. The horse snorted, then whinnied and
tossed its head. In a minute or two, it might rear and dump
Bud!

John pulled on Bud some more, and Bud finally brought
the butt of his rifle up and whacked John on the shoulder.
John let go.

"Gettin' out o' hand, ain't it?" Robert E. asked, walking
up beside Loren. They'd gone beyond the bridge now. They
weren't far from the cemetery.

Margaret Ogleby had commenced to arguing with one of
the other women, Mrs. Wainwright. What that was about,
Loren couldn't figure. He strained to hear.

One of Mrs. Wainwright's son's—the oldest, if Loren
remembered right—had been accused some time ago of
being involved in a train robbery over in Missouri. He'd
been found not guilty, but that didn't matter to Mrs. Ogleby,
who voiced her disapproval at Mrs. Wainwright's participa-
tion in such a gathering of protestation—considering, after
all, that her son was a "robber." Mrs. Wainwright defended

her son, saying he'd been found not guilty. When Mrs. Ogleby tossed her head and said he'd have to find another place to be buried, too, Mrs. Wainwright screeched.

Just as the procession entered the cemetery and began passing headstones, Mrs. Wainwright went after Mrs. Ogleby's perfectly curled and pinned hair and commenced to tear it apart. Evelyn Hughes, Preston, and John Perkins rushed forward, planting themselves some ten feet in front of the wagon, refusing to budge. Martha Trevors scooped two of her children onto her hips, told the other two to hurry, and they joined Mrs. Hughes, Preston, and John Perkins in blocking the way.

Matthew was forced to stop, and Loren had to wonder what would have happened had Matthew gone on. Would Evelyn, Preston, John, and Martha Trevors and her children have moved? Or would they have been plowed down by the horses and wagon because of their stubbornness and righteousness?

Loren spotted the grave up ahead, a big brown hole with a large mound of dirt beside it, waiting to be piled on top of the coffin in which Matthew and the deputies had placed Willard's body. It looked like the grave wasn't far from Maude's and Abigail's, maybe twenty feet.

Suddenly, Mrs. Ogleby tussled Mrs. Wainwright to the ground off to the left. The two women had forgotten about protesting the burial; they were more interested in tearing each other's eyes out right now. When Loren glanced again at Martha Trevors standing there with her young 'uns, he suddenly didn't care how far the fresh grave was from Maude's and Abigail's. It didn't matter. Maude and Abigail were dead, and they didn't give a hoot who got buried beside them. Loren cared—but he didn't want to see the living go at each other this way.

"Oh, stop it!" he shouted at Mrs. Wainwright and Mrs. Ogleby.

He marched over and tried to untangle the women. They snatched at him, too, and suddenly Jake was there to help him. The two men managed to untwist limbs and separate the fighting women.

Mrs. Wainwright and Mrs. Ogleby looked like they had just gotten out of bed. Their hair was a fuzzed, tangled mess, rambling around their faces. Their faces were scratched, and their dresses were torn.

"Just look at you two!" Loren scolded. "I ain't never seen two women go at it like that! All over where a body's gonna get buried!"

"She said my Abe ain't good enough to be buried here!" Mrs. Wainwright cried.

"Lettie, we'll bury him right next to my Maude," Loren said. "It's taken all sorts to make this town, an' all sorts can be buried in our cemetery."

"Not the likes of Levi Willard!" John Perkins shouted.

"We'll reserve this cemetery for upstanding citizens," Preston said, swelling his chest. "We'll put up iron gates!"

"You can't mean that, Loren," Reverend Johnson said.

"It ain't like *you've* never done anythin' wrong," Loren said to the reverend. "Remember when you mortgaged the church an' almost lost it? An' John Perkins, you might not take a likin' to Hank's saloon, but I've seen you up in Denver." John knew what he was talking about—Loren had run into him in more than one Denver saloon.

John didn't say another word in protest. He sank back into the crowd, and Loren didn't see hide nor hair of him for a good week, until the next time he came into the mercantile.

Mrs. Wainwright and Mrs. Ogleby were straightening their clothes and hair. Mrs. Wainwright was crying quietly. Her tears got to Loren.

"I didn't say a word at the time," he told Mrs. Ogleby. "But that youngest daughter of yours . . . I caught her stealin' candy in my store one day. All the young 'uns do it a time or two. There ain't one that's perfect."

Mrs. Ogleby flinched. She said, "Well!" then pivoted and

stomped off. The sight of her heading across the bridge was a good one.

"Get out of the way, or I'll lock you up," Matthew promised Mrs. Hughes, Mrs. Trevors, and Preston.

"You wouldn't!" Preston said.

Matthew gave him a stone-cold look. "I would."

"Maude wouldn't object to anyone bein' buried here," Loren said, looking straight at Martha Trevors. "She always found somethin' good in people when I couldn't. She probably would've found somethin' good in Levi Willard, too. She's gone, anyway. It ain't like she cares whose body ends up bein' put in the ground around here. The body . . . ," Loren turned to Reverend Johnson, ". . . ain't it just the house we live in for a while? Maude ain't really in hers anymore, just like Willard's not really in his anymore.

"We've had enough trouble lately," Loren told the entire gathering. "People threatenin' an' shootin'. . . . People attackin' other people. . . . People judgin' when there's really only one judge. I wouldn't have said that a few years ago. A lot of things have changed since then. A lot of people have come to Colorado Springs. I ain't no better than any of 'em. Neither are any of you. We've all got to learn to get along. If we can't get along, well, there's gonna be more threatenin' an' shootin'."

He scowled. He didn't normally give speeches. He didn't have a whole lot to say most of the time. But the sight of everyone fighting and arguing had bothered him more than he could really express.

"I say we let Matthew bury that body. Then we can get on with things. That's it," Loren said, and turned away.

He passed Gwennie and Grace with baby Katie on her hip. He grumbled his way by Reverend Johnson, and then by Robert E. and Jake, who reached out and slapped him on the shoulder, as if saying he'd done a good thing. But he was done with the business. If the townspeople wanted to stay in the cemetery all night and argue about whether or not to bury Willard's body out here . . . well, Loren wasn't going to be part of such a needless mess. He was going back to the mercantile. There, he'd make his way upstairs and make sure the curtains were drawn tight. He'd boil some potatoes and make himself a nice bowl of hot soup.

Dorothy smiled at him as he went by. He heard her say, "Loren, you're a good man," but he didn't put much store in that. He missed Dorothy's company, too much to dare look at her. Used to, she would have sat and had a bowl of soup with him. They would have shared conversation and each other's company, and then they would have parted for the night.

As Loren trudged off, he missed seeing the way Martha Trevors hung her head. She again gathered her children together—several had wandered off a few feet—and quietly headed for home. Preston rattled off a few more plans for the cemetery for Upstanding Citizens, then, when it appeared no one was interested in listening, he, too, walked off, raising his hands several times as he went. Other people who had come to object to the burial in the town cemetery mumbled and talked low among themselves, then began to disperse.

The reverend's shoulders slumped, and he quietly went over the words he recited at almost every deathbed and funeral service, words of which Loren had just reminded him: *This body was the temporary house.* . . . Like Maude, the Lord God probably found a bit of good in everyone, even in men like Levi Willard and George Hagan. Reverend Johnson, seized by a fear of the recent events involving Mr. Willard and Mr. Hagan, had paid more attention to his own voice—the voice of panic and worry (and righteousness)—than to the voice of the Almighty. Thank goodness he'd been struck down, albeit in a gentle fashion. At least he hadn't been turned to stone. He walked toward the church, a meek minister intent on spending time in solitary silence.

Seeing that the tension had ended and that all was well, Grace turned away with Katie and Gwen, and the three of them returned to the café.

194

"Brian, go fetch my Bible, would you please?" Dorothy requested. "It's upstairs on the table b'side the bed. The reverend ain't in no condition to say anything over the grave. Somebody ought to."

Jake agreed. So while Brian went to fetch Dorothy's Bible, Jake followed the wagon to where the grave had been dug. He'd stick around for the burial and reading, he figured. He was town mayor, after all.

15

Michaela, Sully, and Hank arrived back in town just as Dorothy closed her Bible over Willard's grave and said, "Amen." Brian, Jake, Matthew, and the deputies echoed her word, then they turned away as the gravedigger took up his shovel and started filling the hole. *This is a story unto itself,* Dorothy thought. An outlaw buried in the Colorado Springs cemetery.

Her hands were feeling much better, she realized as she, Jake, and Brian walked toward the bridge that led into the main part of town. She spotted Sully on horseback, his chest bare and a thick bandage covering his arm. Michaela rode alongside a horse carrying a slumped-over woman, and Hank followed beside a horse over which a man was draped.

"Oh, Lord," Dorothy breathed, putting a hand to her throat. "What's happened now?" She hadn't realized that Michaela, Sully, and Hank had ridden off. But apparently they had. One didn't take four horses just to go across town.

"I don't know," Jake said. "Let's go see." He rushed off to find out what was happening.

"C'mon, Miss Dorothy!" Brian urged, tugging on her arm.

She shook her head. "I'm afraid I don't have the energy you do. Go on ahead if you want." After the unpleasant excitement out at the cemetery, Dorothy wasn't in a rush to find out who else had been injured or killed, and why. Of late, life had been a little too exciting in the normally calm town of Colorado Springs.

Brian hurried off.

Minutes later, he rushed up to Michaela and began rattling off questions. When Dorothy had just about reached the front of the clinic, Brian called to her, "It's Mr. Hagan! He's dead!"

"Oh, dear," Dorothy said. Another dead person. And who had killed Mr. Hagan? She didn't think Matthew had learned yet who had killed *Mr. Willard*. Now this. Dorothy quickened her steps, suddenly feeling more curious.

After dismounting, Michaela went to Sully to help him down. Then she followed Hank, who was carrying Sadie Jean, into the clinic.

Once inside the clinic, Hank laid the unconscious Sadie Jean on the examination table and Sully fended off curious people at the door. He finally shut the door and bolted it, and Michaela urged him to go upstairs and lie down, which he did without objection. Then she turned her attention to examining Sadie Jean while Hank went outside.

He was met immediately by questions—*What happened to Hagan? Who shot 'im? Was it Sully or you?* Michaela heard the questions through the door. She also heard Hank growling at people to get back before he leveled them, that it hadn't been him or Sully who'd shot Hagan.

Besides her facial injuries, Sadie Jean had a few broken ribs, Michaela soon learned. The young woman had lost consciousness when Hank pulled her off the horse to carry her into the clinic, probably because of her pain. She wasn't having trouble breathing, so Michaela wasn't worried about the broken ribs having punctured a lung.

However, the possibility that that could have happened during the ride here made Michaela doubt her objectivity where her patients were concerned, when Sully was one of those patients. Back in the forest, she should have sent Hank for a wagon to transport Sadie Jean to town. But she had wanted to get Sully to a bed where he could rest comfortably as quickly as possible. So far, she had given him more medical attention than she'd given this girl, and she knew that was because he was her husband and she loved him so much. Another weakness, this time one that had made her place a patient in jeopardy.

Michaela bound Sadie Jean's ribs tightly. She put ice packs on Sadie Jean's eyes, then washed the cut on the young woman's chin and settled on a stool beside the examination table and prepared to stitch the cut. It was a good four inches long and laid open to the jawbone. At least Mr. Hagan had used a very sharp knife.

Small stitches might not leave such a terrible scar. Michaela wanted to stitch the slash so carefully that the scar would be barely noticeable, not because she cared whether or not Sadie Jean was of any use to Hank in his saloon. She wanted to do it for Sadie Jean, because she was so young—and because vanity in a young woman could be a fragile thing. Hank had helped Michaela considerably today, but to her way of thinking, he was of no help to the women he employed. It was difficult for such women to rise above employment as prostitutes.

"Dr. Mike," Sadie Jean whispered, regaining consciousness. Tears slipped down her temples and into her hair.

"Don't talk," Michaela said softly. "He cut your jaw."

Sadie Jean nodded.

"I'll fix it using tiny stitches. They'll leave less of a scar. It will take longer, but the results will be better."

The young woman nodded again.

Michaela applied antiseptic solution to the wound. "George

Hagan is dead," she whispered to Sadie Jean. "There's no need to fear him anymore.

Sadie Jean cried more.

Matthew wasn't too happy about having to bury another body, but at least he didn't have to guard this one. It could be buried right away. But first, Matthew had to investigate this murder. He needed some answers from Dr. Mike, Sully, Hank, and that girl—Sadie Jean. The most important questions were *who killed Hagan?* and *why?* If someone had killed him just to kill him, Sully was the most likely candidate, since he and Hagan had had a spat going—that meant trouble, and then more trouble to follow.

Matthew took a quick look at the body, leaving it draped over the horse's back. Three shots, one to the head, which meant somebody sure intended to kill the man. You didn't shoot someone in the head by accident, not to Matthew's way of thinking. And you damn sure didn't shoot them three times. There were no rifles on the other horses tethered in front of the clinic, horses, Sully, Dr. Mike, and Sadie Jean had ridden in on, according to the people still hanging around. That was good. But on second thought, Matthew wasn't so sure about that—a weapon could have been dumped somewhere.

Matthew didn't like to think Sully might have killed Hagan. He'd known Sully for a long time, and as much as he knew Sully hadn't liked Hagan, he'd never known Sully to kill anyone. Sully didn't like guns, so it didn't make sense that he might have shot Hagan. But then, Sully had acted strange for days now.

Several people who were still around Hagan's body told Matthew that Sully, Dr. Mike, and Sadie Jean had gone into the clinic, and that Hank had gone over to the saloon.

Matthew knocked on the door of the clinic, and when no one answered, he tried opening the door. It was bolted.

"Dr. Mike?"

As he waited for an answer, Matthew glanced at the body

draped over the horse. Hagan . . . dead. Good riddance. Still, it was Matthew's job to find out how this had happened. He sure didn't want to arrest anyone for getting rid of such scum, but he'd have to if he found out that Sully had killed the man just to make sure he didn't bother anyone anymore. He couldn't let even Sully go around doing that. *He* couldn't shoot people just to make sure they didn't bother people anymore, and he was the sheriff.

Matthew knocked again. "Dr. Mike?"

"Wait, please," she finally answered, calling out instead of opening the door. "I'm tending a patient."

"It's Matthew. I need to talk to you an' Sully as soon as possible."

"You'll have to wait," she said.

"For how long?" He hated to keep pestering her, but he had a murder on his hands.

"An hour. Perhaps several."

He shook his head. "Where's Sully?"

"Upstairs, resting."

"He's gotta stay there until he answers some questions about Hagan bein' dead."

Silence followed for a minute. Then Dr. Mike called, "He'll stay."

He wondered who she was treating—Sully or Sadie Jean. A few people had told him that Sadie Jean looked like she'd been roughed up. He figured he'd go over to the saloon and ask Hank a few questions until Dr. Mike could talk to him. He might even find Jake there, and he'd ask Jake to take care of the body until it could be buried. At the saloon, he meant to find Bodine and Standly, too, if they were still around. Considering the way Hagan had taken Bodine down on Main Street earlier, Bodine might have shot Hagan.

Matthew started off the walkway, feeling more tired than he'd felt in a long time. And it might be a while before he got any sleep. These last few days, Gwennie had given up on spending any time with him. He'd seen her around town, but that was about all.

The saloon was packed, alive with men, music, cards, and whiskey. Bodine and Standly were nowhere in sight. Matthew cut through the crowd and the smoky air and made his way to the bar, where Hank was serving drinks and Jake was settled on a stool, a cup of coffee in front of him. Jake pretty much stayed away from alcohol unless he was on a drunk. Then he holed up in his barbershop with the curtains pulled.

"Got a body for you," Matthew told Jake. There wasn't an empty stool in sight. In a far corner some men started roughing it up. Matthew turned away from the sight. Whenever there was trouble in here, Hank handled things pretty well most of the time.

"I figured that," Jake said. "I didn't want to touch it until you said, considerin' the circumstances an' all."

Matthew nodded.

Hank wandered their way.

"What happened with Hagan?" Matthew asked him.

"He hightailed it out of town while Curly was chasin' after you an' Willard's body. Took Sadie Jean with him and tried to cut her up so she couldn't work for me no more. He beat her up some, but he only got one cut in. She got hold of his rifle an' shot him."

Matthew considered the explanation. Part of it didn't make sense. "So you're tellin' me Hagan just left town, that he didn't care about the bounty money anymore? He just gave it up an' rode off?"

Shrugging, Hank wiped his hands on a towel. "Seems like he did." Hank's eyes skittered away for a second or two, then returned to Matthew.

"How'd you know?"

"Me 'n' Sully noticed he was gone. When Curly went after the wagon, Hagan disappeared. We followed him."

"Why?"

"'Cause he had Sadie Jean, that's why," Hank said sarcastically. "Man takes off with one of my girls, I'm goin' after him."

"That doesn't explain why Sully went after him."

Hank's eyes flashed with anger. He leaned toward the bar. "Look—I know he didn't kill Hagan, 'cause he was with me when I heard the shots. I found Sadie Jean an' she said she'd shot Hagan. Take a look at her face an' you'll know why. I'm glad she did, if you wanna know the truth. I'm losin' a bundle of money t'night. Sadie Jean brings it in like no other girl I've had, not even. . . ."

He pulled back and looked away. *Not even Emma.* That's what he'd been about to say. Anger sparked in Matthew. He squashed it by reminding himself that Emma had been one of Hank's girls by choice, not because he'd held her to a contract she'd signed when she maybe needed a little money, as many of Hank's girls did.

If Sadie Jean admitted to shooting Hagan in self defense, Matthew figured he wouldn't bother to question Sully. But something else troubled him: Dr. Mike riding into town with Hank, Sully, and Sadie Jean.

"How'd Dr. Mike get involved?" Matthew asked as Hank started to turn away.

Hank turned back with a bottle of whiskey in his hand. "We met her coming back into town," he said, refilling the glass of the man who sat to Jake's right. He watched the whiskey trickle into the glass.

"Where was she headed?"

Hank shrugged. "Don't know. Doctor call, maybe?" He finished filling the glass, then plopped the bottle on the bar and leveled a hard look at Matthew. "All I know is, she wasn't there when the shots went off."

She wasn't there . . . ? Like she had arrived on the scene later? But Hank had just told him they'd met Dr. Mike on their way back into town.

Hank was looking him in the eye, but Hank was lying.

"How long has Sadie Jean worked for you now?" Matthew asked.

"Two months."

"Did you know her before that, or did she just wander in?"

"She wandered in."

"So you haven't had time to get attached to her. . . ."

"Only to the money she brings in."

"Better than Emma's?"

"No."

"You didn't give Emma a bad time about leavin'."

"I didn't like it."

"You go through girls pretty fast sometimes," Matthew remarked, shoving his hands into his pockets.

"That's my business." Hank was getting more agitated. His eyes flashed again, and he looked at Matthew from underneath his brows.

"Like maybe it's nothin' to get rid of one an' get another one in."

"If a girl ain't makin' money, she goes," Hank said flatly.

"What the hell are you drivin' at?" Jake demanded of Matthew.

"You sure Sadie Jean was makin' good money?" Matthew asked Hank.

"He's sayin' that maybe I'm sacrificin' my girl for Dr. Mike. That maybe *Dr. Mike* killed Hagan an' I'm usin' Sadie Jean to cover for Michaela," Hank growled, tipping his head back and looking Matthew straight in the eye. "I wouldn't do that for no one." He jerked the towel from his shoulder and slapped it on the bar. "If you've got more questions, Matthew, they'll have to wait 'til tomorrow. I'm *busy* here, as you can see."

He walked off, shutting off the interrogation.

Jake shook his head at Matthew. "You think that? That he's makin' it all up about Sadie Jean and Hagan to cover for Dr. Mike? You think maybe Dr. Mike killed Hagan?"

Matthew scowled at Jake. "I didn't say that." He wouldn't either.

But he had to know where Dr. Mike had been during the shooting. Hank said Sadie Jean had confessed to shooting Hagan—but then he'd lied and said that he and Sully had met Dr. Mike coming back into town.

Hank was covering something up for Dr. Mike. And Matthew wanted to know why.

"Bodine an' Standly are gone," Jake said. *"Gone,* as in no longer in Colorado Springs."

"I figured that." Matthew shook his head. He hoped they were really gone. Just in case they weren't, he meant to keep a watch over Willard's grave.

"Thanks," Matthew said to Jake, then he slid off the stool and made his way to the door, hoping Dr. Mike finished soon so he could question her and Sully.

Less than an hour later, Michaela finished stitching the skin on Sadie Jean's jaw. She had given Sadie Jean laudanum before she began stitching, and now she gave her another dose, a smaller one, to help the young woman rest. Michaela washed her hands and the instruments she'd used, and Sadie Jean dropped off to sleep.

Grace still had Katie, and Brian was still with Dorothy. Michaela thought she ought to collect her children. But she had no one to sit with Sully and Sadie Jean, and she didn't want to leave them alone, particularly not Sadie Jean. She hoped that since Dorothy and Grace had Brian and Katie, they would come and check on things here soon. When they did, maybe they would bring the children, and then they could leave them with her.

Michaela went upstairs to look in on Sully, and found him sleeping peacefully. A quick look at his bandage brought her almost instant relief. The bleeding had stopped. Rest and good food were the best things for him right now.

Back downstairs, she examined Sadie Jean's abdomen while the girl slept. The ovarian cyst was the same size as the last examination, and that relieved Michaela, too.

She pulled the sheet back up over the young woman, then she walked outside for a breath of fresh air. She left the door open so she could hear her patients if they woke and called, and she sat on the porch settle. Michaela didn't mean to fall asleep. But she was exhausted, and soon her eyelids shut and her head listed to one side.

Upstairs, Sully awoke. The clinic was quiet. Through the open windows he heard noises on the street—horses snorting and whinnying, people talking, wagons creaking. Not as many people were out as during the daytime; still, there was more traffic than normal for this time of evening. Laughter and music drifted from the saloon.

He pulled on his pants and fastened them. His arm felt achy, and the muscles spasmed and stiffened as he worked.

He walked downstairs, wondering how Michaela and Sadie Jean were doing. He wanted to talk to Michaela about his suspicion that she'd meant to offer Hagan money to leave Colorado Springs, but he didn't want to talk to her about that until they were alone.

Things were quiet downstairs. Sadie Jean was fast asleep on the examination table. Her face was bruised pretty bad, and her eyes were purple and swollen. Her jaw was stitched up nice and clean now.

The front door stood open, and Sully wondered if Michaela had stepped outside. He walked toward the door, passing a chair on which rested the haversack Michaela had been carrying in the forest. Sully paused when he reached the chair, and he stared at the haversack. In the forest, she'd had nothing but the haversack, and he'd never known her to carry one. If she *had* been in the forest to meet Hagan and offer him money to leave town, maybe the money was in that haversack.

He walked on, and when he reached the front door, he saw Michaela sitting up, asleep, on the settle. He leaned against the door frame, hesitating again. Then he went back for a look in the haversack.

Hundred dollar bills. Eight of them.

Sully clenched his jaw. Where had she gotten the money? From their savings, or had she borrowed it from Preston? It didn't matter. What mattered was that she'd been about to

206

put their money in Hagan's hot and greedy hands—when she knew how he felt about George Hagan.

Sully was pretty glad that Hagan wouldn't be around to bother anyone anymore.

Michaela was usually more careful with money. She didn't usually keep it out in the open. But she hadn't exactly had her mind on being careful with this money when he and Sadie Jean had come in here. Michaela had pulled the haversack strap off over her head, and she'd tossed the haversack aside and gone right to work on him and Sadie Jean.

"Sully," Michaela said softly from the doorway. She sounded startled. She probably was, seeing him hunched beside the chair, the haversack in one hand, the bills in the other hand. She stepped inside the clinic.

"We should have talked about this, Michaela," he said softly. He didn't want to wake Sadie Jean. He figured she needed her rest. He didn't want anyone else to know that Michaela had meant to pay Hagan to leave town.

Michaela obviously didn't know what to say. She hadn't counted on him finding the money. She brought her lips together, thinning them, then parting them again like she always did when she was upset or nervous. "It—it was for Mr. Hagan."

"I know who it was for. Where did you get it?"

"Savings," she answered in a small voice.

"You were gonna pay Hagan off when I didn't want him to get his hands on that bounty money?" Sully shook his head. "You were gonna give him our savings? An'—an' Colleen's college money?"

She flinched. "I didn't think about that. About some of it being Colleen's college money. You know I wouldn't jeopardize Colleen's college."

He thrust the money into the bag and sat back on his heels. He couldn't believe she'd been about to give Hagan almost their entire savings and Colleen's college money, too. It wasn't like Michaela to act without thinking. She was the most levelheaded woman he knew. She didn't do rash things.

Someone knocked on the door frame behind Michaela. She jumped.

Andrew poked his head into the clinic just as Michaela spun around. "Oh, Andrew!" she gasped.

"I—I know there's been all kinds of excitement today. I heard about Sadie Jean, and I thought I could sit with her for the night so you can go home and rest."

"I don't know. . . ." Michaela glanced at her patient, who was still sleeping soundly. "I would hate for her to wake and I not be here."

"I'll explain that you needed to go home and rest."

"I think you oughtta take Andrew up on that offer," Sully said. He lifted the haversack and placed its strap on his uninjured shoulder. Tomorrow he'd put the money back in the bank.

Michaela glanced at him, at first like she was offended that he would try and force her into making a professional decision. Then she seemed to settle down, maybe realizing that he had her best interest in mind.

"Thank you. You can sleep on the cot," she told Andrew, motioning to the cot set up against the far wall. She glanced at Sadie Jean. "She may need more laudanum in a little while. Tell her I'll be back in the morning."

"Of course," Andrew said, approaching the girl. He assessed the stitched wound on her jaw. "Wonderful work," he remarked.

Michaela joined her hands in front of her. "I'm hoping the scar will be minimal."

"It may well be," Andrew said, looking at the wound more closely.

Michaela crossed the room to her desk. She busied herself putting things in her medical bag: bottles, instruments, the pieces of her stethoscope. From a nearby cabinet with clear glass doors she took several small brown packages that Sully knew contained cleaned bandages. She put them in her

208

medical bag, too, then she snapped the bag shut. She gathered a folded blanket from the bottom shelf of the cabinet, and she approached Sully, unfolding the blanket as she walked. She draped it over his shoulders, meeting his gaze briefly.

She was uncertain of how things stood between them, he could tell. He was upset that she'd gone behind his back and made a deal with Hagan. But that didn't mean he loved her less.

He dipped his head and kissed her. He let his mouth linger on hers, then kissed her again. Tears slipped from her eyes, and he brushed them away.

She gave him a faint smile just before she crossed the room to collect her cape from a hook on the wall behind the desk.

"Thank you," she said to Andrew again as she fastened the cape at her neck.

He nodded and said he was glad to help.

"I'll see you in the morning, then." She picked up her bag and met Sully at the door. They slipped outside.

Matthew sat on the settle now, his eyes glinting in the faint light of a post lamp. "Thought I might have a word with Sadie Jean," he said as Michaela pulled the clinic door shut.

"She's resting," Michaela said. "She killed Mr. Hagan in self-defense. I'll be glad to let you talk to her in the morning, when she's stronger and not quite as traumatized."

"Hank says you met up with him and Sully on their way back into town with Hagan's body an' Sadie Jean. That right?"

Sully and Michaela exchanged cautious glances. Hank had lied for her? Sully couldn't believe what he'd just heard. Why would Hank lie for her? So people wouldn't know she'd been out in the woods waiting to pay off Hagan? If so, Sully owed Hank. He'd rather people not know that Michaela had worked out a deal with Hagan.

Michaela started to open her mouth and say something. She probably meant to tell Matthew the truth—that she'd been waiting for Hagan in the woods because she'd worked out a financial deal with him, that she hadn't met Sully and Hank on their way back into town. Sully didn't like lying, but not answering the question wouldn't be lying. He shook his head at Michaela, and she shut her mouth.

"Sadie Jean admitted to killin' Hagan," Sully said. "That's all anyone needs to know."

Matthew stood up and heaved a big breath. "Dr. Mike, I'm your son. Unfortunately, if somethin' different happened today than what you, Hank, an' Sully are sayin', I need to know. I don't wanna think you had anything to do with Hagan gettin' killed, but——"

"She didn't," Sully said. "You know she'd never do that—she'd never have a hand in murder."

That silenced Matthew. But only for now, Sully had a feeling. Matthew stared at him, looking determined to get answers somehow.

"We're goin' home," Sully told Matthew, and he placed his hand on Michaela's lower back and urged her off the porch. She always left their wagon at the livery stable when she brought it to town for the day. They'd go see Robert E., get the wagon, collect their children, and go home.

Sully took the reins of Michaela's horse just as Matthew stepped forward on the porch.

"Two of the horses that were out here . . . the ones you an' Sadie Jean came in on . . . ," Matthew said, looking Sully in the eye. "They belong to Jedediah Hawkes. He reported them stolen. That's a hangin' offense."

Michaela gasped. "Matthew, I'm sure the horses can be explained!"

Sully glanced around for the two horses. He didn't see them.

"I returned them," Matthew said. "Hank said he 'borrowed' them. Seems he's got an explanation for 'most

everything, except where Dr. Mike was when the shootin'
happened."

"We'll talk to you tomorrow," Sully said. Then he and
Michaela headed toward Robert E.'s house, Sully leaading
her horse.

"I'll be waitin'," Matthew called.

16

Michaela picked Katie up from Grace while Sully and Robert E. went to the livery stable. There, the two men hitched the horses to the wagon.

Grace and Robert E. told Michaela and Sully what had happened at the cemetery: the reverend and other citizens trying to prevent Matthew from burying Willard's body; Preston's attempt to fire up people to reserve the town cemetery for "upstanding citizens"; Loren's speech that finally made most of the protesters go off looking meek and humble. Reverend Johnson had looked ashamed of himself, Grace said, to which Michaela replied, "I think he *should* feel ashamed of himself."

Grace had food for Michaela and Sully (she always had food); neither of them had eaten since this morning. She had a kettle of lamb stew on the stove, and she dipped out steaming bowls of it for Michaela and Sully. After they had eaten and thanked Grace and Robert E., they set off in the wagon, heading for the *Gazette* office, where they hoped to find Brian.

At the newspaper office, Brian and Dorothy had a few

more copies of the paper to print. They had been taking turns printing, Brian said proudly. Dorothy smiled and said he was a marvelous assistant.

Dorothy was pleased and relieved to see Michaela and Sully. They both looked so tired that she didn't even consider asking them exactly what had happened this afternoon—how Hank's girl had been injured and who had killed Mr. Hagan.

Sully rested in a chair in a corner. Michaela pulled a stool near him and cradled a sleeping Katie in her arms while Dorothy and Brian finished printing. Michaela watched them, marveling at how proud and professional Brian seemed. The puppy Dorothy had acquired from one of Hank's girls was tired, for once, sleeping on a rag rug with his head on his paws. Michaela was amazed. Every time she saw that puppy, he was gnawing and growling and running around. She had never seen him quiet and still.

"Without Brian, I wouldn't be gettin' the *Gazette* out this week," Dorothy remarked. Brian was rather quiet this evening, Michaela noticed. But maybe he was simply tired. After attending school all morning and all afternoon, he didn't normally help Dorothy print the paper all evening.

"My hands're better," Dorothy added, working the press.

Michaela had not intended to mention Dorothy's rheumatism with Sully and Brian present; she valued patient–doctor confidentiality. But since Dorothy didn't seem to mind discussing her medical problem in front of Brian and Sully, Michaela didn't mind, either. "They do seem better. Yesterday you could barely use them."

"An' not without pain," Dorothy said. "Oh, they're still painin' me a little, but they're not so swollen an' red, an' the pain is nothin' like it was."

"That's wonderful. How have you managed the baths?"

Dorothy looked startled for a few seconds. Michaela wondered if she imagined the look. Why would Dorothy be startled?

"Oh, I've—I've had some girls helpin' me. One more,

Brian, an' that'll be enough," Dorothy said as Brian stepped beside the rollers and began turning them. She laid aside the paper she had just printed. "Sorry we're runnin' so late," she told Michaela. "We got a late start, an' then all that trouble happened out at the cemetery. . . . I was real proud of Loren, sayin' Maude an' Abigail wouldn't mind Mr. Willard bein' buried out there. Why, a few years ago, Loren wouldn't have said somethin' like that! He was just as prejudiced as some townsfolk still are."

Michaela agreed. Loren had been very prejudiced when she first came to Colorado Springs.

Brian finished the last paper.

Dorothy went to a nearby shelf, picked up a vase, and dumped coins into her hand. She tried to give Brian several of the coins—to pay him for helping her, she said.

But Brian shook his head. "I *wanted* to help you, Miss Dorothy. Besides, I reckon this means we're even."

Michaela couldn't imagine what he was talking about. Dorothy hesitated, then she smiled gently at Brian and dropped the coins into the vase. Neither Brian nor Dorothy said anything about *why* they were even. Michaela didn't ask. If they wanted her to know, they would tell her.

Brian's clothes were smudged with ink, and so was his face. But he looked content and proud of himself when Dorothy handed him several copies of the *Gazette*. "Since it's the first paper you've printed," she said.

A little later, Brian was the first one in the wagon. He laid his papers down neatly and with great care, then took Katie as Michaela handed her up to him. Michaela and Sully climbed onto the wagon seat, and everyone said good night to Dorothy.

Michaela took up the reins and shook them lightly to set the horses in motion. In a little while, Sully would be home and in bed, resting comfortably. Michaela meant to make certain of that.

• • •

At home, Sully said nothing to Michaela about the money she had withdrawn from the bank. Brian looked very tired by the time they reached the homestead, and he washed and went to bed right away.

Michaela bathed Katie while Sully watched in silence, sometimes looking deep in thought. Michaela dressed Katie in a soft cotton shift and brushed her hair, then she settled in the rocker with the baby and Katie began nursing contentedly.

Was Sully thinking about the money? Michaela wondered.

The fact that she had been meaning to give the money to George Hagan had certainly angered Sully. Back in the clinic, when she stepped inside and saw him with the money in his hand, she also saw hurt and disbelief in his eyes. She'd worked out a deal with a man he'd regarded as an enemy. *Why would you do that?* his look had said, and Michaela felt small and ashamed. Then she remembered exactly why she'd done it—to save his life—and her shame had dissipated. He wouldn't understand her motive as long as he was angry, she'd told herself, and she had stifled her words and her plea that he try to understand why she had intended to spend the money without talking to him first.

She thought about trying to talk to him about the money before they fell asleep. But they were both tired; the day had been long and trying, and she'd learned that they shouldn't try to solve problems when they were tired. A good night's sleep and a new day might bring different thoughts and perspectives.

She wondered if Sully thought she would withdraw money from the bank under normal circumstances without consulting him first. If he did, he was wrong.

Sooner or later they would have to talk about the money, and she hoped that eventually he would understand that the circumstances she'd faced *hadn't* been normal. Under normal circumstances, she wanted them to decide together how their money should be spent.

216

"Loren said somethin' to me this afternoon that didn't sink in until a few hours ago," Sully said from the bed.

"What was it?" Michaela asked.

"That I had Abigail an' our baby girl for such a short time. He told me that I wasn't thinkin' of what I have now—you an' Katie an' Brian . . . Colleen an' Matthew . . . this home."

"I understand your feeling that you weren't able to give Mr. Willard the protection you promised him," Michaela said softly as Katie tugged at her breast. "I understand the rage you must have felt when he was killed."

He slipped into silence again. Michaela rocked and nursed Katie some more. Then, when she was sure the baby was sleeping soundly, she put her in the cradle and covered her with blankets.

After extinguishing the lamps, Michaela joined Sully in their bed and snuggled close to him. He whispered that he loved her, and she fought tears as she caressed his hip. He molded his body against hers, and soon they fell asleep.

Michaela woke before he did the next morning. In fact, she had Katie and Brian up and Katie fed and dressed before Sully opened one eye.

Michaela redressed the wounds on his back and arm. He felt stiff and sore today, and he elected to stay close to the homestead rather than go into town, as he'd planned. Michaela had to look in on Sadie Jean, however, so she had Brian help her harness the horses and hitch them to the wagon. Katie was bubbly and playful, as she was every morning. Brian, however, still looked tired.

Once in town, Michaela left Brian at school and the wagon and horses at the livery. She took Katie with her to the clinic, where she found Sadie Jean resting quietly.

Andrew sat behind Michaela's desk reading *The Art of Surgery*.

When Michaela entered the office, Andrew fumbled his way up from the chair, knocking a notebook and several pens off the desk and trying to grab them as they went flying. He was sometimes self-conscious and nervous to the point of causing small calamities, and Michaela always felt sorry for him at those times. She hurried over to pick up one of the pens as he dropped behind the desk to reach for the notebook.

"The—the patient is well," he said, poking his head up over the desk. "I gave her laudanum twice during the night. No fever, no restlessness." He placed the notebook on the desk exactly where he'd found it.

"Thank you for staying with her," Michaela said as Andrew headed for the rack on which he'd hung his coat last night.

"Certainly. I knew it had been a long day for you." Andrew shrugged his way into the coat. "How's Sully today?"

"Sore," Michaela said, prying Katie's fingers from her hair. "I believe he's finally realized that he needs to rest." Now that George Hagan was gone, Sully would think clearly again, she hoped. He would be himself again.

"Send for me if you need me," Andrew said.

Michaela smiled and nodded. Andrew slipped out the front door.

Months ago, when Katie had begun scooting around and pulling herself up on tables, chairs, and other furniture, Sully had built a little wooden fence in one corner of the clinic's main room. The fence did a nice job of containing Katie, who had since learned to crawl quite fast and was now trying to walk.

Michaela had put a number of wooden toys and other objects—a little brush, several spoons, and a wooden box—inside the fence. Katie liked the box most of all. She frequently filled it with her toys and other items, then dumped it, then filled it and dumped it again. She did that over and over, almost every time Michaela put her inside the fence.

This morning, almost as soon as Michaela lowered the baby behind the fence, Katie reached for her box. She held it up and grinned at Michaela, as if showing it off. Michaela smiled, and Katie began filling the box with her belongings.

Michaela began her day in the clinic by examining the stitched wound on Sadie Jean's jaw. It was clean and dry, and Michaela turned away satisfied. She brought a basin of water closer so she could clean the young woman's other wounds again.

Besides her blackened eyes and the cut on her jaw, Sadie Jean had a number of small facial abrasions and cuts. She woke as Michaela was cleaning the wounds, and she quietly thanked Michaela for taking care of her. When she mentioned that she was having more pain in her stomach—pain like what she had had when Michaela diagnosed her ovarian cyst—Michaela asked Sadie Jean if she could examine her abdomen. Sadie Jean agreed, and Michaela lifted the sheet that covered the young woman.

The cyst was no larger than it had been yesterday, but Michaela still recommended aspiration.

"I guess needles aren't as bad as I thought," Sadie Jean said rather meekly. "You stitched my jaw, an' that wasn't so bad."

"True."

"Will it hurt, Dr. Mike?"

"You'll be asleep during the procedure. There might be a little discomfort afterward, but certainly no more than you're experiencing right now. It will be gone within a day or two."

Sadie Jean gave that some thought. She didn't take long to make a decision. "All right."

"I'll arrange to do the procedure this afternoon," Michaela said. "I'll take Katie to Grace and arrange for Andrew to assist."

"Dr. Mike, when will my eyes get better?"

Michaela drew a deep breath. "Like the cut on your jaw,

219

your eyes may take as long as several weeks to heal. The swelling will ease within the next three or four days, probably. But the discoloration will worsen before getting better."

"Is it really bad?" Sadie Jean asked. "Do I look awful? I do, don't I?"

Michaela couldn't tell the young woman that she didn't. That would be a lie. Her eyes did look awful. "It's not permanent," she said softly. "The swelling and discoloration will go away in time."

Sadie Jean turned her face away from Michaela, who pulled the sheet back into place.

Later that morning, Michaela spotted Reverend Johnson near the mercantile, and she snatched from her desk the message she had written out for Andrew, asking if he would assist her with a surgical procedure this afternoon. Katie was sleeping on a blanket inside her fence, and Sadie Jean was resting comfortably and quietly.

Michaela ran across the street and asked the reverend if he would mind taking the message to Andrew. She half expected to hear an account from him of yesterday's events out at the cemetery. But Reverend Johnson appeared reserved and quiet today, not at all eager to talk about the business that had had the town in an uproar for days. Michaela thanked him for agreeing to take the note, then returned to the clinic.

Not long afterward, Matthew appeared at the clinic, wanting to question Michaela and Sadie Jean. Sadie Jean was awake, and a fearful look entered her eyes as soon as she saw Matthew.

"I need to know what happened," he said, and the young woman glanced at Michaela as if asking for advice.

"It's all right," Michaela assured the girl. "It was self-defense. Nothing will happen to you."

"He said . . . he said we were going away together," Sadie Jean told Matthew. She moved her painful jaw as little as possible, slurring her words slightly. "That's all I've wanted for years now—to go away from this area. I've got a lot of bad family mem'ries . . . my ma dyin' when I was little, my pa drinkin' and beatin' me if I didn't do things just right at the house—the cookin' and cleanin'. If he ever found out where I was, he'd be after me. George said he'd take me to California, to San Francisco. But—but he had it planned. We got out of town—he said we were goin' to meet Dr. Mike 'cause she had money for him—and he started talkin' crazy about Hank."

Sadie Jean glanced at Michaela again, seeking confirmation that she was doing the right thing. Michaela had winced when Sadie Jean mentioned her and the money. But she realized that the young woman didn't know she didn't want an account of her financial arrangement with Hagan circulating. She knew, too, that Sadie Jean had to tell all of the facts if she wanted her name cleared. Michaela nodded at the young woman, an indication that Sadie Jean should continue.

"George said Hank tried to keep him from the bounty, too, that Hank almost cost him a lot of money. So he figured he was gonna cost Hank a lot of money. He started beatin' me. Then he pulled out the knife and cut me and. . . ." Sadie Jean drew a deep, shuddering breath. "He said he was gonna cut me up a whole lot more. I was Hank's best girl, George knew that, and he was gonna cut me up just enough that I would live but that nobody would want me."

Matthew passed a hand over his face, rubbing his eyes, then his jaw. He'd had very little sleep, Michaela could tell.

"I got hold of his rifle," Sadie Jean said, tears slipping from the outside corners of her eyes. "I've never killed anyone."

"Ever thought about it?" Matthew asked.

Sadie Jean swallowed. "Sometimes, when my father beat me, I'd wish he was dead. I'd think that him bein' dead was the only way I'd ever feel safe. I fought back sometimes.

221

Once I almost grabbed *his* rifle. I think I would've killed him if I had. I finally just ran away. I thought, 'no one's ever gonna beat me again.'" She sobbed a little. "I didn't see George when I shot him. I saw my father. I shot him, but he kept comin' at me. So I shot him more, and then I ran."

Michaela's heart was breaking for Sadie Jean. She couldn't imagine living through such day-to-day horror, never knowing when the next beating might come, having thoughts of killing a parent because you feared that parent might eventually kill you. Sadie Jean had transferred to George her fear of her father and her need to defend herself; in her mind, George had become her father. And she had grabbed George's rifle and finally defended herself.

Michaela didn't condone violence. All the suffering she had witnessed during the Civil War had shown her the consequences of violence. But in defending oneself, violence was sometimes the only way. It certainly had saved Sadie Jean.

"You had money for Hagan?" Matthew asked Michaela.

"Yes."

"Why?"

"I was paying him to leave town."

"Dr. Mike!" Matthew said, clearly shocked. He shook his head.

"I'd react the same in a similar situation. I was worried that Mr. Hagan might kill Sully."

"Or that Sully might kill Hagan?"

"I never believed that about Sully, Matthew. I believed he would defend his family and friends if the need arose."

"He might have killed Hagan trying."

"And would that have been wrong? It's always better to settle things in a nonviolent manner. But when that becomes impossible, what is the best way to settle something?"

Matthew didn't answer that or even respond to it. She made a good point, he knew. But he still didn't like the fact that two men had been killed within his jurisdiction during the last few days.

222

"Don't leave town or disappear, Sadie Jean," Matthew told the young woman. "I ain't got cause to arrest you, but the circuit judge may have more questions when he comes through."

"I won't leave town," Sadie Jean promised.

"Guess I don't need to talk to Sully," Matthew said. "I'll see you, Dr. Mike."

Michaela nodded. He always seemed uncomfortable whenever something happened that he had to question her or Sully about. She hadn't liked the questions he'd asked these last few days. But she understood that he was sheriff and that it was his job to ask questions whenever trouble arose.

Andrew came that afternoon, and he administered chloroform to Sadie Jean while Michaela withdrew the fluid from the ovarian cyst. She palpated the area, found the cyst, cleaned the skin, then inserted a needle through which she aspirated the fluid into a connecting syringe. It was a relatively quick procedure, and the only mark was a small puncture left by the needle.

Shortly afterward, Sadie Jean began to wake. Once she was fully awake, Michaela was pleased to hear that she had no more pain in her abdomen.

George Hagan was buried beside Levi Willard in the town cemetery that afternoon, and no citizens appeared to protest. Well, no wonder—Loren had made yesterday's protesters feel small, Grace told Michaela when Michaela went to pick up food from the café for Sadie Jean, Katie, and herself.

Michaela knew Matthew must be pleased that this burial was uneventful. She watched him lead the wagon carrying Mr. Hagan's body to the cemetery. The men he'd deputized were with him.

Reverend Johnson saw fit to meet Matthew and the deputies at the gravesite, but not to object to the burial. He had his Bible in hand, and Michaela wondered if the

Scripture he read over the grave after the body was lowered into the ground was a neutral, nonjudgmental one. Most likely it was, especially considering Loren's harsh words last evening. Shortly afterward, Reverend Johnson shut his Bible, said a short prayer, then went toward the church.

17

During the next week, the townspeople went about their business as usual. Loren went back to the relatively quiet running of his mercantile, and Hank went back to his saloon. There, he took up his familiar position behind the bar, serving customers, occasionally tossing out the rowdier ones. He fired a few girls and hired a few new ones.

While Sadie Jean was recovering in Michaela's clinic, Hank brought her flowers, hiding them inside his coat so no one would see them. Sadie Jean's ribs were healing nicely, and so was the stitched wound on her jaw. Michaela hesitated to release Sadie Jean too early for fear that she would return to the saloon and try to start working right away.

Michaela saw Hank coming, and she met him on the porch, at first thinking he was coming to tell Sadie Jean he wanted her back at work. Michaela wouldn't let him do that, not just yet.

She asked what she could do for him, and he shuffled his boots and said, "I wanna see Sadie Jean."

"She cannot go back to work yet."

"Don't get all prim an' proper, Michaela," he growled. "I just want to see how she is. I ain't here to haul her back to the saloon."

He waited, shuffling more, shifting around the bulge in his coat.

"What are you hiding?" Michaela asked.

"Ain't none of your business."

She fought a smile. That must mean it was something for Sadie Jean. Hank rarely wanted anyone to know that he occasionally did nice things for people.

"I'll take you to her," Michaela said.

He followed her to the room upstairs where Sadie Jean had been moved the day after her surgery.

Hank's attention focused on her from the minute he stepped into the room. Sadie Jean sat up on the bed, looking pleased to see him. Michaela wondered if a romance was blossoming, or if Hank simply wanted his "best girl" back at work as soon as possible.

Michaela left them alone and went back downstairs.

They visited for probably ten minutes before Hank came downstairs. He held a bunch of flowers, and Michaela was certain his face turned a shade darker when he said Sadie Jean had told him to ask her if she had a vase for them. Michaela had never known him to bring anyone flowers.

"Well, do you?" he snapped.

Michaela realized she was staring at him and the flowers. She wondered whose flower beds he'd raided. He had tulips and an assortment of other flowers in an assortment of colors. She wondered how long it had taken him to pick them, or to cut them. The rough, grubby-looking saloon proprietor was such a contrast to the soft, beautiful flowers he held. She smiled, and Hank's colored deepened even more.

"It's. . . . What a stupid thing to do," he grumbled, shifting around again. "Flowers."

"Not at all," Michaela said. "They show Sadie Jean that

you care. And they prove that you're not always the blackguard you want people to believe you are. But don't worry"—she lowered her voice—"I won't tell anyone."

He scowled at her. "Got a vase or not?"

The word *vase* seemed so un-Hank. Vases were used and spoken of by refined people, after all, and Hank was anything but refined.

Michaela had him follow her upstairs, to a room where she took a vase from a cabinet. In Sadie Jean's room, she poured water from a pitcher into the vase, then took the flowers from Hank and arranged them in a pretty fashion.

Sadie Jean smiled, obviously thrilled.

Hank mumbled that he had to get back to the saloon—Michaela barely made out what he said—and then he took long strides toward the door. He hurried away so fast, Michaela and Sadie Jean heard him stumble into a table out in the hall. He muttered a curse, then went on, the sound of his boots fading on the stairs.

Michaela and Sadie Jean looked at each other and laughed.

Matthew caught up on sleep during the week following Hagan's shooting. He and Gwennie managed to spend more time together, too. One afternoon while they sat beside the creek, he had thoughts of stealing a kiss. But as things turned out, he didn't have to. His and Gwennie's eyes met and things got real quiet between them. The air felt warmer suddenly, and everything but Gwen became a blur. Matthew reached up and touched her face, she tipped forward, he lowered his head, and their lips touched.

It was a magic moment, and Matthew and Gwennie knew it. When they pulled back, they smiled at each other. Matthew said, "Wooh," and Gwen said, real softlike, that she hoped she hadn't been too forward. After all, she'd heard girls were supposed to resist kisses.

"I'm glad you didn't," Matthew said. "Resist that kiss, I mean."

"I'm glad I didn't, too."

When they walked back to town, they held hands, a sight not missed by many townspeople.

Matthew walked with Gwennie to the café, where she had to resume her work, and when he turned to leave, he caught sight of Brian near the livery stable, talking to Robert E.

Brian didn't see Matthew, so he couldn't run off like he'd been doing for the last week every time he saw his brother. Matthew was determined to talk to Brian about the dress and face paint he'd been wearing that afternoon, and now seemed as good a time as any. Fact was, now seemed a real good time.

Matthew beat a quick path to the livery stable, taking care to stay out of Brian's line of vision.

"Howdy, little brother," he boomed right behind Brian.

Brian jumped nearly out of his britches, at least six inches into the air and clear around to get a wide-eyed look at his brother. "M—Matthew!"

"Yeah, that's right—Matthew. Finally." Matthew laughed. "You've avoided me."

"Have not," Brian said, reddening. Robert E., holding an iron over a fire, looked at them curiously.

"Have, too."

"You've just been stuck on Gwennie. You wouldn't have seen me if I'da been right in front of you."

"Guess what, Brian? You're in front of me right now, an' I see you just fine. I was just thinkin' I need to talk to you. Now ain't that a coincidence?"

He watched Brian swallow.

"W—what do you need to talk to me about?" Brian stammered.

"Maybe you'd rather nobody else hear this. So how about"—Matthew lifted Brian by the front of his shirt and started toward the back of the stable—"if we go off by ourselves an' have ourselves a discussion."

Brian squirmed. "Put me down!"

"Not 'til we do some talkin'."

Robert E. chuckled. "Whatever ya did, Brian, time's up. Ya gotta start talkin', boy, else big brother's gonna put ya on a hook somewheres."

"That's a good idea," Matthew said. He went into the stable instead of around to the back of it, and he hung Brian up by the back of his shirt on one of the hooks over which Robert E. usually hung harnesses.

"Get me down from here!" Brian shouted, kicking and flailing his arms.

"Tell me what you were doin' in that dress an' with your face all painted. No brother of mine's gonna run around town like that."

"Get me down!"

"Brian. . . ."

Brian tried to reach over his shoulders and unhook his shirt. But the back of the shirt was bunched up over the hook and he *couldn't* unhook it.

"I ain't busy right now," Matthew said. "Fact is, I was thinkin' about takin' myself a nap. This looks like a pretty good spot." He plopped down on a nearby pile of clean hay, clasped his hands behind his head, and crossed his legs at the ankles. "Yep, I could get real comfortable here real quick. Might fall into such a deep sleep, nothin' much'll wake me 'til I'm ready to wake. That means you stay there 'til I wake."

"Matthew, get me down," Brian pleaded. "C'mon!"

"Talk, little brother."

"All right, all right! Miss Dorothy couldn't write 'cause of her hands. She needed notes for the story about Mr. Hagan an' Sully. I went to the saloon an' tried to interview Mr. Hagan for Dorothy. Only Hank's girls got me."

That information made Matthew sit up on the pile of hay. "*Hank's* girls got you?"

"Yeah."

"What'd they do to you?"

"What you saw. They put all those clothes on me an' they painted me."

229

That baffled Matthew. "Why'd they do that?"

"So I wouldn't go back in another saloon."

Matthew lifted his brows. Then he laughed. "That's good . . . that's real good."

"I ain't goin' to, neither!" Brian said. "I ain't goin' near another saloon."

"We'll see about that. Boys turn into men an' the saloons get temptin'."

"Not to me they won't! There was a big woman in there with big. . . ." Brian clamped his mouth shut, and his ears turned about as red as Matthew had ever seen them turn. "She was as big as a mountain with big red lips, too!"

Matthew doubled over laughing. "Big ones, huh?"

Brian frowned at him. "It wasn't funny!"

"Maybe not to you. It's funny to me."

"Wouldn't be so funny if she got hold of *you*."

"I wouldn't let her. I run faster than you do."

"Get me down, Matthew." Brian started to kick again. "I'm gonna tell Ma."

Matthew got up and brushed hay off his trousers. In the nearby stalls, horses stirred and poked their heads over the railings. "Does Ma know about you goin' in the saloon?"

Brian glared.

Matthew grinned. "I didn't think so. You don't wanna tell her about this, Brian, 'cause then I'd have to tell her about you goin' in the saloon."

Matthew lifted Brian off the hook and set him down on his feet. Brian looked like he might cry.

Matthew swiped Brian across the top of his head, just enough of a graze to mess his hair more. Brian ducked, but too late. A yell of frustration poured from his mouth, and then he tore into Matthew, lowering his head and butting him in the stomach.

Matthew didn't fight him much. He figured Brian needed to win this one for the sake of his pride. He even let Brian get a few punches in, and then shuffle off.

· · ·

The burn on Sully's back healed, and his gunshot wound was healing nicely. Michaela continued to dress it daily.

Sully put the money back in the bank—and cut off the question that started out of Preston's mouth when Sully told the banker he wanted to redeposit the money. His and Michaela's differences and private business were none of Preston's business. Wisely, Preston quieted and simply took the money.

Sully and Michaela finally discussed her decision to go behind his back and offer George Hagan the money. The discussion didn't go far and it didn't last long. Sully felt she shouldn't have made a deal with George Hagan, certainly not one involving their money. Michaela felt that she hadn't had a good choice at the time. Thinking of Sully's personal safety and health, she did not regret her actions. She told him that she wouldn't normally consider spending such an amount of money unless they agreed on how it should be spent. But he wouldn't have agreed to the deal she'd decided to make with Mr. Hagan, and if George Hagan was still alive and staying away from Colorado Springs the way he had promised he would, she would consider the money well spent.

Dorothy maintained daily appointments at Preston's Turkish steam bath and got more sodium salicylate from Michaela. The two treatments together certainly lessened the pain and swelling in her fingers. She hoped the treatments would one day resolve the rheumatism.

She never said anything to Michaela about her visits to Preston's steam bath, and Andrew didn't say anything either. Dorothy still thought that if Michaela found out she was going to the resort to use the steam bath, Michaela might think she was getting medical treatment there, too. And if Michaela thought that, her feelings might be hurt.

Mouse began to calm down somewhat. He learned Dorothy's tones of voice, when she was happy with him and when she was angry. When she used a stern tone, he hung his head, stuck his tail between his legs, and crawled off. Dorothy managed to train him to lie down, if she told him to, on the pillows she'd piled in one corner of the *Gazette* office. She resigned herself to the fact that she probably had a dog for life, since Hank didn't want the puppy in his saloon and Dorothy didn't have the heart to give Mouse to yet another person. Animals needed stability the same as children, after all.

Piecing together the facts for a *Gazette* article about the George Hagan business was not easy for Dorothy. Sully didn't want to talk about what had happened. He didn't want to talk about his past association with George Hagan; he didn't want to talk about how he'd captured Levi Willard; he didn't want to talk about what had happened the evening Mr. Hagan had been killed and Sadie Jean had been beaten. Michaela wouldn't say how she'd ended up riding in with Hank and Sully, the beaten Sadie Jean, and Mr. Hagan's body. Hank told Dorothy that Dr. Mike had met up with them on their way back into town—and that was all he knew. Although Dorothy didn't quite believe that—mostly because of Michaela's nervousness when Dorothy had asked her why she had ridden in with them—that's what she was forced to include in the article she finally prepared about the bizarre business.

In the end she just put together the facts: A bounty hunter named George Hagan, along with his associates, Curly Bodine and Kenny Standly, showed up in Colorado Springs, claiming to be hunting for Levi Willard, a dangerous robber and murderer. Byron Sully brought the outlaw in days later, and Mr. Willard was shot dead by an unknown person in front of the sheriff's office. Mr. Hagan demanded that the body be turned over to him, but apparently Mr. Sully and Mr. Hagan had a past association and had had differences, and Mr. Sully refused to hand over the body to Mr. Hagan. Sheriff Cooper was told by the marshal in Denver to bury the body, but a number of citizens objected to an outlaw being buried in the Colorado Springs cemetery, where many upstanding former citizens were buried.

Dorothy quoted much of what Loren had said, depicting him as the hero of the day. Then she wrote that at the conclusion of the burial, Byron Sully and Dr. Michaela Quinn rode into town escorting Mr. Hagan's body and Sadie Jean Owens, who had been beaten by George Hagan. Sheriff Cooper investigated Mr. Hagan's death and concluded that Miss Owens had shot Mr. Hagan in self-defense. Mr. Hagan was buried in the town cemetery also, and his fellow bounty hunters, Curly Bodine and Kenny Standly, had disappeared.

Even with just the facts, the article was long. But Dorothy was satisfied with it, considering the trouble she'd had gathering information.

However, the article struck certain people wrong. Loren didn't like being depicted as a hero, and he grumbled to Dorothy about that. But his grumbling wasn't unpleasant at all compared with what followed.

As a reporter and as editor of the *Gazette,* Dorothy felt her job was to document anything newsworthy. But no one in town had liked George Hagan, Curly Bodine, and Kenny Standly, and certain townspeople—Sully included—felt Dorothy made Sully sound almost as bad as George Hagan. They said Sully had brought Levi Willard in to try and make Mr. Hagan and the other two bounty hunters go away—and that Dorothy hadn't included that. Also, the statement about Sully and Mr. Hagan having a "past association" implied that the trouble between the two men was because of that association. The townspeople said the article implied that Sully had withheld Mr. Willard's body from Mr. Hagan because he didn't like Mr. Hagan and because he harbored a grudge against the man.

At least ten people approached Dorothy on Main Street the day the paper came out, and said they felt she should have left that "past association" business out of the article. They said Sully had been worried about his friends and

233

family, and had just wanted Mr. Hagan and those other two men to leave town as soon as possible. Dorothy didn't quite know what to say, except "I just reported what I discovered . . . the facts."

"He could've just handed over the body," she finally snapped at at least the twentieth person—Mrs. Ogleby—who approached her waving the *Gazette* and looking riled. Dorothy knew what was coming, and she was tired of being criticized. She walked off, refusing to listen to another complaint.

Mrs. Ogleby started after her, saying, "And what would that have accomplished? It would have put the bounty money in that man's hands. It would have encouraged him and other bounty hunters to come to Colorado Springs the next time an outlaw decided to hide around here!"

Dorothy spun on the woman. "Why are you—why is *ever'one* so sure Sully didn't want Mr. Hagan to have that money *because* of his 'past association' with Mr. Hagan?" He *does* have a 'past association' with the man. Sully won't hardly talk to me about it, but I get the feelin' he an' Mr. Hagan had diff'rences in the past."

She started to walk off again, and Mrs. Ogleby rushed around and planted herself squarely in front of Dorothy. "You're not supposed to assume things. Maybe the *Gazette* needs a new editor," the woman said with a sniff.

Dorothy and Mrs. Ogleby were in front of the mercantile. People paused from looking through the goods Loren had placed in baskets on the porch, and they stared at the bickering women. During her last remark, Mrs. Ogleby had gotten right up in Dorothy's face.

Dorothy stepped back, putting space between them. "I *own* the *Gazette*," she informed Mrs. Ogleby, who doubtless knew that—everyone in town knew that.

Mrs. Ogleby closed in again. "Maybe we need a new paper, then!"

Dorothy didn't like having to breathe Mrs. Ogleby's

leftover air. She gave the woman a little shove, pushing her backward. Ordinarily, Dorothy wouldn't do such a thing. But how dare the woman bully her!

"We need a new paper, and we need a new reporter," Mrs. Ogleby snapped.

"Ladies," Jake scolded from nearby, "break this up. The damage has been done. There ain't nothin' you can do about it now."

"*Damage?*" Dorothy said.

Mrs. Ogleby sniffed. "There! See?"

Dorothy planned to walk right past the awful woman and Jake, and go into the mercantile. She needed a few things, and that's why she'd come over here in the first place. She'd get what she needed, then she'd go home—and stay home until the unpleasantness about her *Gazette* article ran its course.

She started off, and Mouse decided to tangle himself in her skirt. She tripped, the puppy yelped, and Dorothy lost her footing.

Later, in retrospect, Dorothy was certain Jake was right— it looked like she attacked Mrs. Ogleby. Dorothy felt herself falling, and her hands went up instinctively to try and grab something. She was too far away from the mercantile to grab the porch railing. The only thing handy was Mrs. Ogleby. Dorothy's right index finger hooked between two bodice buttons on the woman's dress. The buttons popped off and went flying. Dorothy, still moving forward, crashed into Mrs. Ogleby.

"Oh! Ooh! Stop that!" Mrs. Ogleby said.

Dorothy knocked the woman clean over. She lay sprawled atop Mrs. Ogleby on the dirt street.

"She's attacking me!" the woman screeched. "Help! Help! Get her off—she's attacking me!"

Certainly, when Mrs. Ogleby had stood in her way in front of the mercantile, Dorothy had given brief thought to shoving the woman clean out of the way. But she wouldn't have done that. That little shove was about as much contact as she wanted with Mrs. Ogleby, and she hadn't really wanted that.

"Dorothy, come on," Jake said, reaching down and taking her by the arm. "This ain't like you."

"She's attacking me!" Mrs. Ogleby screeched again, shielding her face with her forearms.

Shocked by what had happened, Dorothy stared down at the woman, ignoring Jake's tugs on her arm.

"Dorothy, get off," he said.

Dorothy had every intention of doing that. In fact, she started to push herself up, only her hand was planted on Mrs. Ogleby's arm when she pushed, and the woman screamed like she was being murdered. Then she fought. Her other arm flew up and caught Dorothy on the side of her head.

Dorothy saw stars. She was so stunned, she blinked several times and stared down at Mrs. Ogleby, whose face had turned bright red.

"You hit me," Dorothy said. *"You hit me."*

"Dorothy, get off her," Jake said again.

But Dorothy wasn't listening. She saw Mrs. Ogleby's arm start up again, and she grabbed it. Mrs. Ogleby covered her face with the arm, and Dorothy's fingernails scratched the side of the woman's face.

In the end Jake and someone else pulled Dorothy off Mrs. Ogleby. When Dorothy saw that the other person was Matthew, she cringed with embarrassment.

Loren had emerged from the mercantile, and he stood shaking his head at her. "Dorothy, what are you *doin'?*" Other people had gathered, too, probably ten to twenty.

"We'll see if she gives a fair account of *this* in her *Gazette,*" someone said, and a rumble of speculation went up from the gathering.

"She attacked me!" Mrs. Ogleby screeched yet again.

"Would you shut up?" Dorothy snapped. "I tripped!"

"Ladies, I ain't gonna tolerate any more," Matthew said sternly. "I put up with somethin' like this at the cemetery the day I buried Levi Willard, an' that's enough. Mrs. Ogleby, you were in the middle of that scrape, too."

Mrs. Ogleby was sitting up now. She sniffed at Matthew.

"If the two of you can't apologize to each other an' leave each other alone, I'll lock you up."

Stunned by the announcement, Dorothy whipped her head around and stared at Matthew. Lock them up? She didn't want to go to jail. And all because she'd tripped into the woman.

Mrs. Ogleby stared at Matthew, too.

"Guess I got to lock you up," he said.

"That ain't necessary," Loren objected.

"They're disturbin' the peace."

"I'm truly sorry I tripped into you, Mrs. Ogleby," Dorothy said, standing and dusting herself off. She really *was* sorry. She hadn't meant to do that.

"Dorothy?" Michaela said, breaking through the gathering of people.

"Mrs. Ogleby?" Matthew said expectantly.

"Oh, this is absurd," the woman blurted, obviously frustrated. She struggled to get to her feet. "She didn't trip into me."

Matthew tipped his head. "All the same, she apologized. Now you apologize, too, or I'm takin' you to jail."

"I apologize," she huffed at Dorothy, but she didn't look her in the eye. She stalked off, and the spectators mumbled among themselves.

"Are you all right?" Michaela asked, taking Dorothy by the back of an elbow. "Let's go to the clinic. I want to examine you."

Dorothy didn't argue. "That woman has a pretty good punch," she commented, feeling dazed. She shook her head to try and clear it; the shaking gave her a slight headache.

Jake chuckled at the comment.

237

Matthew wanted to, laugh, too, but his position as sheriff dictated that he shouldn't. He turned away and walked to his office to keep anyone from noticing the twitch of his lips as he fought laughter. Mrs. Ogleby was a troublemaker. Still, if he had thrown her in jail, in all fairness, he would have had to put Dorothy in jail, too.

18

Michaela examined Dorothy in the clinic and concluded that she was fine other than the lump Mrs. Ogleby had given her on the head. Michaela applied an ice pack to the lump, and Dorothy scowled as she held it against her head.

"I ought to press charges against her," Dorothy said suddenly. Then she scowled again. "But I reckon that wouldn't be too Christian of me."

"She might do the same against you," Michaela remarked. "Then the two of you would have another fight, this one before the circuit judge."

"I tripped over Mouse! I *fell* into her. Oh dear," Dorothy said, as if something had just occurred to her. "Mouse. Where's Mouse? I've gotta find him." She slid off of the examination table and started for the door.

Michaela stopped her. "I'll find him. You stay here. Your headache will worsen if you wander the streets looking for Mouse. I'll get Matthew if I need help."

Dorothy agreed to let Michaela go look for the puppy. But she still looked worried. No matter how much she and

Mouse had disagreed since she had taken the puppy in, Michaela suspected that Dorothy had become attached to the dog. Of late, everywhere Dorothy went, the puppy went. Her tussle with Mrs. Ogleby probably had frightened Mouse and he was hiding somewhere. He surely hadn't run away. Michaela couldn't imagine that he would go far from Dorothy. He liked her, or at least respected her, otherwise he wouldn't tag along behind her.

Dorothy lifted herself back onto the examination table, and Michaela went to look for Mouse.

She found him hiding behind wooden crates on the mercantile porch. She held her hand out, trying to coax him to her, but he whined and backed up, looking frightened. She might have to move the crates to get him out, then grab him before he raced off.

"Dorothy loves that dog," Loren remarked behind Michaela.

"And how do you know that?" Michaela asked. She wouldn't go that far. She didn't know if Dorothy *loved* Mouse.

Loren handed Michaela a piece of jerky. "I can tell. She'd miss him if he went back to Hank's."

Michaela thanked him for the jerky, then held it out to Mouse.

The meat was a temptation he couldn't resist. He scooted forward slowly but surely, and finally he came close enough to take the jerky from Michaela. As he chewed it, she reached out and picked him up. She felt him stiffen, and she said, "Sssh," and petted his head and back. "I'll take you to Dorothy," she told him, not knowing whether he understood her. He didn't wriggle or struggle.

"Is Dorothy all right?" Loren asked.

Michaela stood with Mouse in her arms. "Well, she has a lump on her head and the beginnings of what might turn into a full-blown headache. Other than that, she's fine."

"Can you give her anything? Y'know . . . to make her head feel better. I feel just awful about tellin' her I didn't

240

like her callin' me a hero. Ever'body's been criticizin' her about that article, an' . . . well, I shouldn't have said anything. I know she meant well. She always means well."

Michaela smiled. Loren's feelings for Dorothy were sweet. Michaela sometimes wished Dorothy felt the same about him. Loren was a lonely man. "I can give her something for her headache."

Loren nodded, still not looking very happy, then went back into the mercantile. Michaela headed toward the clinic with Mouse.

"I heard Dorothy and Mrs. Ogleby were fighting in the street," Preston said, stepping up beside Michaela.

"A misunderstanding," she responded. She regarded Preston as a busybody. He always wanted to know everyone's business, and he was persistent in his attempts to do that.

"You have Dorothy in the clinic," he said.

"Yes." Michaela wouldn't tell him what was wrong with Dorothy. She'd told Loren only because she knew Loren cared about Dorothy. Preston . . . Michaela hated the thought every time she had it, but this was not the first time she had concluded that Preston cared about no one but himself. She wasn't certain why he was interested in what had happened between Dorothy and Mrs. Ogleby, other than the incident being something to gossip about.

"Well, thank God," he said. "I thought she might rush to the resort again. Andrew's busy up to his eyeballs today. So is the Turkish bath. It's better if you see Dorothy today. She's been coming to my medical clinic, you know."

No, Michaela hadn't known.

Why had Dorothy been going to Preston's clinic? For her rheumatism? Dorothy hadn't mentioned that she'd been going to Preston's clinic. Neither had Andrew.

Michaela had been giving Dorothy sodium salicylate. Had it not been helping? Had Andrew been using a different treatment? If the sodium salicylate hadn't worked, Dorothy should have told her. They could have tried a different treatment.

"Excuse me, Preston," Michaela said. She turned away from him and quickened her steps toward the front of her clinic.

Once inside the clinic, she approached the examination table where Dorothy was lying. Dorothy sat up carefully and took Mouse, thanking Michaela.

"He was hiding behind several crates on the mercantile porch," Michaela said. She walked toward her desk, thinking about Preston gloating over the fact that Dorothy had been seeing Andrew at his clinic. She didn't know why Dorothy hadn't told her.

"Dorothy . . ." Michaela turned back.

"He was scared, wasn't he?" Dorothy said, scratching the area between Mouse's ears. The dog nuzzled against her waist. He obviously had missed her as much as she'd worried about him. "Hidin' behind crates? Can you believe what happened with that awful woman?" Dorothy asked Mouse. "She scared you an' me both." Dorothy glanced at Michaela. "I think I'll take him home. Why, he's still shakin'! His pillows an' toys'll calm him."

Michaela thought she ought to let Dorothy know what Preston had just told her. She was due an explanation for why Dorothy had been coming to her for medication, yet seeing Andrew at Preston's medical clinic. But Dorothy was so involved in calming Mouse right now, Michaela wondered if she would hear her if she tried to tell Dorothy what Preston had told her.

"I still have some of those scraps," Dorothy said, sliding off the table, cradling Mouse and talking to him. She seemed to have forgotten about the lump on her head and her slight headache. If she even had it anymore. As large as that lump was, Michaela couldn't imagine that Dorothy didn't still have the headache.

"Grace has been givin' me scraps for him," Dorothy told Michaela as she strode toward the door. "Thanks for lookin' at my head, an' thanks for the ice pack."

Michaela wondered if the headache was really gone, or if

Dorothy planned to go to the resort and see Andrew. Why had she gone to see him in the first place? Why did she continue to see him?

She was jumping to conclusions. Dorothy might be planning to go home from here, exactly as she said.

It's none of my business, really, Michaela thought. If Dorothy wanted to seek the advice of another physician, that was her choice, just as it was the choice of any patient.

But this patient happened to be a good friend.

Michaela let Dorothy go without trying to tell her that she had run into Preston and that he had told her Dorothy was a frequent visitor to his clinic. Dorothy thanked her again, said good-bye, and left, pulling the door shut behind her.

Michaela stood beside the clinic window. She pulled the curtain back slightly and watched Dorothy, just to be sure she turned toward the *Gazette* office and her home. She did.

The sight was a relief.

Michaela began cleaning the clinic, and while she worked, she wavered between thinking Dorothy should have told her she was seeing Andrew and thinking the matter was none of her business. She again concluded that Dorothy should have come to her. Dorothy hadn't exactly changed doctors, after all. She was still seeing her—yet seeing Andrew, too, which was odd. And it wasn't fair to her or Andrew to have a patient bounce back and forth between them.

"Dorothy has been seeing Andrew at Preston's medical clinic," Michaela told Sully that night as they were getting ready for bed. Katie had fussed all evening—teething again—and Michaela felt exhausted. But she had to talk to someone about Dorothy seeing her *and* Andrew. "She's also still seeing me for a certain medication she needs right now."

"Maybe Andrew doesn't have the medication."

That could be.

"Why wouldn't she have told me that? Sully, she's said nothing about seeing Andrew. Why wouldn't she have told me? I saw Preston this afternoon, and he informed me that

Dorothy has been seeing Andrew at the resort's medical clinic. Why didn't *Andrew* tell me?"

"Maybe he felt he shouldn't. You don't normally discuss your patients with people. Maybe Andrew thinks he shouldn't either."

Michaela sighed. "Perhaps."

"Tell Dorothy you ran into Preston an' he told you she's been seein' Andrew," Sully suggested. "Tell her you're wonderin' why, since she's been gettin' her medicine from you."

Straight honesty. That was probably the best way to deal with the problem. But Michaela didn't want to put Dorothy on the defensive. On the other hand, she had to talk to Dorothy about this. Something so troublesome shouldn't be left hanging between friends.

"Dorothy had trouble in town today over her *Gazette* article," Michaela remarked as she settled into bed beside Sully.

"The one about George Hagan an' the bounty business?" Sully asked. He had been strangely quiet regarding the article. He'd read it, then put the paper aside without commenting. George Hagan and the "bounty business" was a touchy subject between them right now, so Michaela hadn't asked what Sully thought about the article. She thought he felt the same way she did about the trouble involving them and George Hagan—that it was over and that she wanted to go on from here and not dwell on what had happened.

"People have been defending you to Dorothy. They don't like the way she portrayed you in the article."

He was quiet.

"They feel she shouldn't have mentioned your past association with George Hagan."

"What happened in town?"

Michaela told him, relating the events as she had pieced them together from Dorothy: that Mrs. Ogleby had approached Dorothy and refused to leave her alone about the matter, even when Dorothy tried to walk away, and that Dorothy had then tripped into Mrs. Ogleby.

"How do you feel about the article?" Michaela hesitantly asked.

Sully was just as hesitant in replying. He rolled onto his back and gazed up at the ceiling. "Michaela, I know she's your friend. But some things're better left alone. Dorothy bothered me an' bothered me for interviews. She got wind that I knew Hagan in the past, an' she wanted to hear about that. I wouldn't tell her about it. I think the article does imply that my past with Hagan was what drove me to keep the bounty away from him."

"But Sully, we discussed that . . . you and I. We discussed it in the clinic after you were shot, remember? You admitted that revenge was part of the reason you—"

"Did you tell Dorothy that?" Sully's eyes flashed, and Michaela knew he was irritated.

"No, of course not."

"Then where'd she get that idea?"

Michaela tried quickly to remember what she had said when Dorothy interviewed her. "I think I told her you didn't like him. But Sully—"

"You shouldn't have said that."

"I can't imagine that Dorothy would turn a statement like that into something more. That—that she would assume from that—"

"I had a 'past association' with him?"

"Yes. Perhaps Mr. Hagan said something to someone about what happened between the two of you in the mining camp. Dorothy interviewed a lot of people for that article. A lot of men who frequent Hank's saloon. Mr. Hagan might have told some of them about your trouble in the mining camp."

Sully shook his head. "She shouldn't have included anythin' from the past in the article, Michaela. If she found out somethin' about the minin' camp trouble, all she had was one side of the story. I didn't talk to her about the minin' camp trouble."

"She didn't write an entire article about what happened between you and Mr. Hagan in the mining camp," Michaela said in Dorothy's defense.

"No, she didn't. She put just enough in there to make people wonder an' ask questions—when I didn't want them wonderin'."

"Sully, Dorothy is our friend. But that doesn't mean she should slant her articles to suit us or to favor us. That's asking too much of her."

"It'll die out, Michaela," Sully said stubbornly. "We need to let it. I haven't said anythin' to Dorothy, an' I'm the one she made the statement about. People need to leave it alone an' let it die."

Which meant her, too. *She* needed to leave it alone and let it die.

Michaela blew out the lamp, then lay back down.

Sully turned onto his side and reached for her, and she went into his arms, pressing her body against his. He made a low sound in the back of his throat, almost a growl. His lips found hers in the darkness, and his hands wandered.

She and Sully. . . . They never allowed a night to settle over their differences.

Sully went hunting and trapping with Cloud Dancing for the next several days.

They rode through the forests, looking for deer and other animals, and they walked through streams, spearing fish. They listened to the trees as the branches whispered and brushed, and they listened to the water as it rushed and gurgled.

Sully thought it was good to see Cloud Dancing roam freely. But he wasn't really free, and both men knew it. If he wandered too far, or if he didn't return to the village when he had said he would, the captain would send soldiers to search for him and bring him back.

The evening of the first day, Sully and Cloud Dancing built a fire and roasted the fish they'd speared. While they ate, Sully told Cloud Dancing what had happened with Hagan, Bodine, and Standly in town: he and Hank had found Hagan's body, and Sadie Jean had admitted to killing Hagan because he had been beating her. He also told Cloud Dancing about the financial deal Michaela had made with Hagan.

"We talk about things," Sully said, shaking his head. "Big things, little things . . . it doesn't matter, we talk about them. After I got to town with the body, she was scared because Hagan was angry that I wouldn't give him the body. She thought she might have to take Brian an' Katie an' hide them out somewhere. I guess she was thinkin' he might take them an' use them to try an' make me give him the body so he could collect the bounty money. I told Michaela I'd promised Willard that I wouldn't let Hagan kill him. I hadn't kept my promise, so there was no way I was gonna give the body to Hagan an' let him collect the bounty. Michaela knew all that—we talked about it. Even knowin', she made a deal with Hagan. He would've come out better than if he'd collected the bounty."

Sully shook his head. More than a week later, he was still stunned that Michaela had made a deal with Hagan behind his back.

"You were wounded, and George Hagan was a threat to your family and friends," Cloud Dancing said. "Michaela thought you should give him the body?"

Sully nodded.

"And you refused?"

Another nod.

"We are friends—we talk freely," Cloud Dancing said.

Sully nodded again.

"Michaela must have felt she could not talk to you about the matter anymore. When people feel so strongly about something, when they have opposing feelings, talk does not help. We know this." Cloud Dancing looked Sully in the eye when he spoke the last sentence. The two men had had enough dealings with the United States government regarding Indian affairs to *know* that talk was sometimes a waste of time.

Sully picked up a stick and scribbled in the dirt, not really drawing anything, not really trying to. He was thinking.

"She couldn't have talked to me about it," he finally admitted. The days that had passed since all the trouble had given him distance. Now, the distance helped give him perspective. "I knew she was scared, but I was angry at Hagan. I let my anger block everything. I couldn't see past it. I dug in, an' I wasn't willin' to compromise, not even for Michaela."

"You have told her this?"

Sully shook his head. "We haven't talked much about it."

Cloud Dancing ate more fish as the fire popped and crackled. "Then you must, so no hard feelings are kept inside. Michaela did not talk to you about the money because your mind was not open. You heard her fear, but you did not respect her fear. She made the deal with George Hagan because she knew your mind was closed. She knew more talk would not help. You wanted Hagan gone because you feared for your family and friends. Yet pride and anger stood in your way. Michaela did not like Hagan either. I saw her reaction the day he came to the village. She wanted Hagan gone for the same reasons you did, but she set aside her pride and approached him. Pride is often an enemy."

Sully hadn't considered that—that Michaela had set aside her pride long enough to approach George Hagan and propose a deal to him. Surely, she hadn't *wanted* to approach him. But, considering that his—Sully's—mind was closed, she'd felt that she had to solve the problem of his standoff with Hagan. She'd set aside her pride and her fear of the man, and approached Hagan with a deal.

"I've been judgin' her," Sully said quietly.

"In your mind, walk in her moccasins," Cloud Dancing advised.

Sully lay back on the blanket he had spread on the ground, propping his hands beneath his head. Stars glittered against a bed of rich blue velvet. Clouds moved in front of the moon, blocking its silver glow, then exposing it again.

Loving him as much as she did and fearing for Brian and Katie, Michaela had felt she had no option but to approach Hagan and offer him money to leave town. Sully *had* been judging her—and that was wrong of him.

19

Dorothy stood staring at Preston, unable to believe her ears.

She'd emerged from the steam bath and walked outside the resort. There she'd run into Preston, who'd asked why in the world a newspaper editor such as herself would involve herself in a tussle; newspaper editors were supposed to be respectable people. Dorothy had snapped at Preston, telling him that she hadn't meant to "tussle" with Mrs. Ogleby, that Mouse had tangled himself between her feet and tripped her into the woman.

She shouldn't have bothered to explain anything to Preston. She might have known he'd turn his nose up at her, no matter what she said, no matter that she had a perfectly logical explanation.

Preston confronting her about the trouble with Mrs. Ogleby wasn't the worst thing, by far. The worst thing was hearing him say that he'd encountered Michaela shortly after the tussle and that she had looked stunned when he'd informed her that Dorothy had been frequenting the medical clinic.

What must Michaela think? Apparently, if Preston had mentioned that to Michaela shortly after the trouble with Mrs. Ogleby, Michaela had known for days but hadn't mentioned it to her. Dorothy wondered why.

Surely Michaela must be wondering why she was going to Preston's medical clinic. After all, Dorothy had been obtaining medicine for her rheumatism from Michaela. Dorothy getting medicine from Michaela, yet Preston insinuating to Michaela that Dorothy was getting medical advice at the resort must have Michaela spinning with confusion.

How horrible!

"If you were gonna take it upon yourself to tell Michaela I've been frequentin' the medical clinic, you should've taken it upon yourself to tell her I've only been usin' the steam bath," Dorothy scolded Preston.

He didn't look the least bit ashamed of himself. Dorothy suddenly realized that he *wanted* Michaela to think she was coming to the clinic here for treatment. Well, she was, but she hadn't sought medical advice here; she'd been treating herself.

Dorothy turned away in a huff, trying to not give Preston a chance to respond.

He responded anyway, once again taking advantage of the fact that she and Michaela were friends: "Maybe you should have told her yourself."

He might also be trying to drive her away, prevent her from returning to the resort to use his fancy Turkish steam bath. Well, she wouldn't be driven away from anywhere, not by Preston Lodge, not by anyone.

She *should* have talked to Michaela and told her that she was using Preston's Turkish steam bath for the sake of her rheumatism. She should have told Michaela to prevent someone else from spilling the beans, especially from spilling them in the way Preston had—making it seem like she was being treated by the doctor at the resort.

As Dorothy walked through town, she took note of the

way people avoided her. At least they weren't flying up to her anymore and demanding to know what she meant by "past association." At least they weren't saying "How dare you insinuate that Mr. Sully brought that outlaw in and refused to hand over his body just to keep Mr. Hagan from collecting that bounty?"

People wanted to believe Sully had brought Levi Willard in only because he'd wanted to protect the citizens of Colorado Springs. The truth was, Sully *had* had other motives. If Mr. Willard had been hiding out on federal land, knowing Sully as well as she did, Dorothy suspected that something about protecting the Indians must have been involved in his bringing the outlaw in to Matthew. Dorothy had learned from Jake that Sully and Mr. Hagan had known each other years before in a mining camp and that the association hadn't been pleasant. And from what she'd squeezed out of Loren, Dorothy had gathered that Sully had been on George Hagan almost from the minute he spotted him in the mercantile. Which made Dorothy believe even more that something bad had happened between Sully and Mr. Hagan long before George Hagan rode into Colorado Springs looking to collect the bounty on Levi Willard.

Dorothy held her head high. She was a journalist, and she had an obligation to collect and report the news even if that news was something a little unpleasant about a friend. She shouldn't discriminate. She wouldn't.

If all the ruckus about her article wasn't enough, now here was this business about Preston blabbing something about her to Michaela, and distorting it, too. How ridiculous!

Well, she'd go to the clinic straightaway and see if Michaela was there. If she was, Dorothy would talk to her and make sure Michaela realized that the only reason she'd been "frequenting" Preston's resort was to use his fancy steam bath.

Michaela and Gwennie Hall came out of the clinic just as Dorothy stepped onto the walkway. Michaela wondered if

Dorothy needed more sodium salicylate. Surely not; she had given Dorothy some only a few days ago.

Gwennie nodded a pleasant greeting to Dorothy. Not everyone in town had been snobbish and judgmental these past days. Grace and Loren hadn't been, and there were other people, too, who were still pleasant and friendly. Dorothy could rarely tell about Jake and Hank. Those two went with the direction of the wind.

Gwennie went on her way, and Michaela invited Dorothy to come into the clinic.

"Is everything alright?" Michaela asked after she shut the door.

Dorothy opened her mouth to say yes, not being one to lay the burden of her troubles, usually not even the heavier ones, on such a close friend as Michaela. What came out of her mouth, however, was not an assurance that everything was all right.

"People're still avoidin' me on the streets, an' this week's sales of the *Gazette* are down. Honestly, if I'd known people would be so fired up by one statement, I never woulda put it in that article! I was just tryin' to be an honest journalist." Dorothy threw up her hands and released a big sigh. She was afraid she might be about to cry. "Now, on top of that, Preston informed me that he told you somethin' about me that's completely untrue."

She *was* crying. She had a sensitive side, but usually she didn't start crying over someone telling a story about her. She brushed at the tears that dripped onto her cheeks, and plopped herself down in a nearby chair.

Michaela went to her desk and returned with a handkerchief.

Dorothy took the handkerchief, blubbered "Thank you," and then blew her nose so hard her ears popped. "Ouch," she said as Michaela sat in the chair beside her.

"Is this about Andrew and the resort clinic?" Michaela asked gently.

Dorothy nodded.

"Dorothy, if you chose to seek Andrew's advice, that's your prerogative," Michaela said, placing her hand on Dorothy's. "I felt baffled when Preston told me, because you've been coming to me for medication. I've wondered if perhaps Andrew doesn't have the medication and—"

"But I didn't seek Andrew's advice! Preston told you that, or maybe he insinuated it, I don't know. But it ain't true, Michaela! He's got a fancy steam bath at the resort, an' I got to feelin' sorry for that Chinese girl who was haulin' all that water for me. Lord knows, I couldn't haul it myself. So I started goin' to Preston's Turkish bath, an' he didn't like it. He thinks it oughtta be for the fancy folk who've come to town since that resort went in. He's just bein' spiteful."

Michaela looked surprised; her brow had lifted. *"That's* why you've been going to the resort? To use the steam bath?"

Dorothy nodded. "Ask Andrew. He'll tell you the truth. He ain't been treatin' me."

Michaela clicked her tongue and shook her head. "I don't need to ask Andrew, Dorothy, you've never lied to me. I have no reason to believe you're lying to me now. Besides, even if you were seeing Andrew for medical advice, it's not unheard-of for a patient to seek a second opinion."

Michaela glanced down at her hands, now folded primly in her lap. "I must tell you that I overreacted when Preston told me you were going to the resort clinic. I—I reacted inappropriately, too," she said, glancing at Dorothy. "I had the terrible thought that because you were my friend, you should have told me. But that wasn't right. Where you seek your medical treatment, and with whom, is your private business. I have a right to know only if you decide to confide in me."

"But Michaela, I wasn't going to the resort for medical treatment," Dorothy objected.

"I know. But if you *had* been, it wouldn't have been my business unless you chose to tell me about it. That's why I haven't mentioned to you what Preston told me. I was upset for a few days, wondering why. Then I became ashamed of myself because I realized I didn't have a right to know why."

Dorothy wiped her eyes with a corner of the handkerchief. Michaela could be so understanding.

"Where is Mouse today?" Michaela asked.

"I'm teachin' him to stay at home sometimes," Dorothy said. "I can't have the silly dog tailin' along behind me to church an' to certain other places. We have dances sometimes, an' I worry that he might trip me up again like he did the other day. That was horrible, just horrible. He has to stay home sometimes."

"I think you have a friend for life."

"I *hope* I have two friends for life—you an' Sully." Dorothy watched Michaela, measuring her reaction.

"Of course you do!" Michaela said, smiling. "But I believe that makes a grand total of three. I think Mouse is permanantly attached to you."

"I never thought I'd have a *dog,*" Dorothy said. "I thought maybe I'd have a cat, maybe even more than one someday. I never figured on a dog."

"Grace had Gwen bring tea over. Would you like some?"

That made Dorothy smile. "You're always so mannered. I'd love some tea."

"Wonderful," Michaela said, standing. She strode across the room to a far cabinet, and Dorothy followed her.

Dorothy watched the delicate way Michaela lifted Grace's tin pitcher and poured the tea into pewter cups. She marveled, as she didn't do quite so often anymore, that a woman who'd grown up surrounded by fancy things didn't mind settling for less. That was just one more thing that made Michaela special in Dorothy's eyes.

When Michaela handed Dorothy one of the pewter cups, Dorothy decided they needed to talk about the other matter that was troubling her. She had to take the subject by the horns right off; otherwise, she was ashamed to admit, she might turn tail and run like a scared chicken.

"Sully . . . Michaela, how does Sully feel about the article?"

Michaela had turned away and lifted her cup, then turned back, obviously meaning to take a drink of tea. When Dorothy asked the question, Michaela paused with the cup halfway to her mouth.

Before Michaela said anything, Dorothy knew the answer to her question: Sully didn't care for the article. She hadn't talked to him since the paper had come out. In fact, several times when she'd seen him in town, she'd gotten the distinct impression that he, too, was avoiding her.

"He . . . he wishes you wouldn't have mentioned—"

"The 'past association,'" Dorothy finished for Michaela.

"Dorothy, people will read the *Gazette* for as long as you publish it, and they might not always like or agree with what they read. It doesn't matter. If you report the news, you've done your job."

"It does matter, Michaela." Dorothy sighed. "I've done some thinkin' these past few days. How unbiased was it of me to mention Sully and Mr. Hagan's past association? When I really thought about it, I started thinkin' that was just slipped in there for the sake of gossip. Whether or not I intended it to be gossip, that's what it was. I put a piece of personal information in the article that didn't need to be there."

"If you had left it out, people who knew that Sully and Mr. Hagan knew each other from the past . . . those people might have been offended if you had left the information out. Don't you see, Dorothy? You can't please everyone. If you try, you'll go mad.

"Drink your tea," Michaela advised. "The hard feelings will ease with time. Hard feelings usually do."

"You're the best friend I've ever had," Dorothy said. "Or ever will have."

Behind her cup, Michaela smiled. "Drink up. Grace will send Gwennie back soon for the pitcher, and she'll expect it to be empty. I can't drink it all by myself. I'm glad you came along!"

Dorothy had the distinct impression that Michaela was talking about much more than just coming along in time for tea.

A few mornings later, Sully rode into town with Michaela to get supplies at Bray's Mercantile. They left Brian at the school, then went on from there. In front of Loren's store, Sully got down from the wagon seat first. He took Katie from Michaela, then handed Michaela down.

Matthew approached them at a pretty good clip. At first Sully thought something was wrong. Matthew had a serious look on his face, and he leaned close to Sully as he said, "I've got bounty money for you."

Sully's reaction was immediate: "Send it back, I don't want it."

Matthew shook his head. "Send it back?"

"That's what I said. I don't want it. I don't want anything to do with it."

Michaela and Matthew exchanged glances.

"It's a lot of money, Sully," Matthew said. "If you don't take it, it'll just go back into the fund for bounties. It'll eventually go to someone, probably to some bounty hunter who makes his livin' collectin' bounties."

"I don't care."

Sully turned away to walk up onto the mercantile porch.

Michaela stopped him with a gentle hand on the inside of his elbow. "Sully, let's talk about this. I know you don't like the idea of taking that money. But we could donate it to a charity in Denver . . . perhaps to a place like that art school Hank's son is attending. And there are orphanages and hospitals."

"You could use it for the clinic, Dr. Mike," Matthew said.

Sully shook his head. He couldn't believe they were trying to talk him into taking the money.

"Sully . . . you heard Matthew. If we don't take it and

do something good and worthwhile with it, another bounty hunter will collect it eventually."

Michaela had a good heart. But Sully wished she'd let this subject go.

"There's a hospital for the indigent in Boston," Michaela said. "There's also one in Philadelphia, where I studied with Elizabeth Blackwell—the first degreed and licensed female medical doctor. And I know of plans for another hospital for the poor in Denver. A committee has already formed, but it needs funds, much more than it has."

Michaela wasn't going to leave the matter alone, Sully could see that. And if he let her go on, she'd come up with about a hundred other causes that might benefit from the money.

"I'll think about it," Sully said finally. Katie squirmed against him, wanting to get down. She'd learned to take two and three steps at a time, and she was ready to exercise the new discovery that she could do something with her feet besides play with her toes. She wasn't quite as headstrong as Sully had heard Michaela had been as a baby. But he imagined Katie would grow up into the same kind of stubborn, independent woman.

"I'll hold the money," Matthew said, looking less tense now. A faint smile crossed his face. "Come an' see me when you decide what you wanna do."

Sully nodded. Michaela smiled at him, melting him, and he lowered his head and kissed her.

"Something . . . something I should warn you two about," Matthew said, looking uncomfortable. "Sadie Jean an' Hank, too."

Sully and Michaela stared at him. Matthew glanced down at his boots, shuffling them in the dirt.

"What?" Sully asked.

Matthew looked up at him. "Circuit Judge James Morgan's comin' through next week. I'm bettin' he'll wanna talk to ever'one involved about Hagan's shootin'."

Sully had thought the troublesome business was behind

259

them for good. But it made sense that the judge might want to ask questions and then make an official statement or report about Hagan's death. A death was a death, after all.

Sully nodded. "You know we'll be around town."

Matthew headed toward the saloon, and Sully and Michaela went into the mercantile to collect their supplies from Loren. Sully would take them home while Michaela went to the clinic for the day. Sully had hides to tan and meat to salt and hang in the smokeshed. Later in the day he'd return with the wagon.

After picking up the supplies and after leaving Michaela at the clinic, Sully started out of town. Up ahead, he saw Dorothy in front of the *Gazette* office.

She was feeding her puppy, and while the dog wolfed down the food she'd put in a metal bowl for him, Dorothy took up a broom and began sweeping her walkway. She glanced up, spotted Sully, and waved him down. Not to try and get another interview, he hoped.

"Fine day, ain't it?"

"Sure is," he responded. The sun was shining. Up ahead, just beyond town, trees were dressed in new leaves. The grass was thick and green again, and household gardens were starting to come up. Out at the homestead, Michaela's was.

Dorothy rubbed her hands against her skirt. "I was thinkin' I owe you an apology. Y'know, for puttin' that statement in the *Gazette* article about you an' Mr. Hagan. I had no business doin' that. I shoulda concentrated on reportin' the facts of what happened durin' the time he was here."

This was a surprise. "Apology accepted," Sully said.

"I have a tendency to gossip, an' maybe that's what that was—me tryin' to get in a little gossip. I sure didn't mean to start more trouble around town."

"We'll forget about it," he said.

"Really?" She looked hopeful. He'd heard from Michaela about her skirmish with Mrs. Ogleby. He'd also heard from

Michaela that some people were snubbing Dorothy, avoiding her on the streets and refusing to talk to her in places like the bookstore and the mercantile.

"I talked to Cloud Dancing the other day about somethin' me an' Michaela weren't seein' eye to eye on. I didn't understand somethin' she almost did," Sully told Dorothy, wanting to help somehow. "Cloud Dancing told me to walk in Michaela's moccasins."

Dorothy had tipped her head, and her eyes had gotten wider, like she was real interested in what he was saying.

"Your job ain't always easy," he continued. "I understand that. When you first started the *Gazette,* an' when you got your book published, too, you had a hard time makin' ever'one happy. Now there's even more people, an' there's no way to keep ever'one happy. You do your reportin' an' hope for the best. Those people who are sayin' bad things an' ignorin' you . . . they haven't walked in your moccasins."

"Oh," Dorothy said, and the sound was more like a squeak than the actual word. A smile broke out across her face, and her eyes turned glassy, like she might cry.

Sully shifted on the wagon seat, always uncomfortable when women cried.

"That's the wisest thing I've ever heard," Dorothy said. "Thank you."

Sully nodded. A second later, he shook the reins he held and clicked his tongue at the horses so they'd move. If Dorothy started crying, he'd be tempted to get down and do something about it — maybe mop up her tears or something.

That evening, Sully told Michaela about his encounter with Dorothy, how she'd apologized. He said nothing about telling Dorothy what Cloud Dancing had told him — that before judging someone, he should walk in that person's moccasins.

Michaela planned to stay home tomorrow because she wanted to spend the day with Sully. He suggested that they go off where no one would bother them, where they absolutely would be left alone. Michaela agreed, giving him a bright smile that lit her eyes. She looked like a thrilled girl, and Sully laughed at her excitement.

The next morning, they left Katie with Grace and Gwennie, and they went up into the low mountains, foothills compared with the snow-topped peaks in the distance. They alternately rode and walked alongside their horses through the lush forest. They splashed in an icy stream, then built a fire to warm themselves. It was summertime, but the higher into the hills and mountains they went, the cooler the air became. Sully and Michaela giggled and laughed as they romped in the stream.

Afterward, they rubbed each other's hands and faces to warm them. Then they kissed long and numerous times to warm each other's lips.

They spread blankets on the ground beside the stream, and they made love out in the open, which was something Michaela would never have considered doing in the early months of their marriage. Now she was more confident of their marriage, and of herself as a woman. One intense look from Sully always told her that he found her beautiful and desirable, and she found their openness thrilling and delicious.

"I should have walked in your moccasins," he said after their lovemaking. They lay staring up at the sky, so rich and baby blue, so clear.

"What?" Michaela truly didn't understand what he was talking about.

"I should have walked in your moccasins," he said again. This time he rolled onto his side and pushed her hair back from her face. "I didn't try to understand your fear an' desperation when Hagan was in town. When I found the money you meant for him, I judged you without tryin' to understand why you'd arranged to pay him. I was wrong. I didn't put myself in your moccasins."

He was sweet and endearing, and Michaela loved him

more than ever during those moments, more than life. Without him, life would not be as rich and fulfilling.

She snuggled against him, and he brought a second blanket up over them, covering her shoulders as she laid her head on his chest. Nearby, the fire popped and glowed, the stream trickled and lapped, and the horses grazed beneath the trees where they were tied. Overhead, a few puffy clouds drifted by. Michaela closed her eyes, feeling content and secure.

She and Sully slept. After a time, they rose, helped each other dress, mounted their horses, and headed in the direction of Colorado Springs.

So Sully put aside his pride and stubbornness and agreed to the interview and the article. Dorothy sat down with her pen and paper beside Michaela, across from Sully.

Sully told Dorothy how Matthew had told him and Michaela that the bounty money had arrived, and how Sully had at first told Matthew he didn't want the money. Then Michaela had suggested several charities, and the idea had taken root from there. Sully didn't like the way he'd come by the money. But donating it to the medical committee in Denver was a way to put it to good use.

After the article came out in the next issue of the *Gazette*, the shock and speculation died down about Sully's accepting the bounty money. Mrs. Ogleby became quiet—probably only until the next time something happened for her to gossip about, Dorothy figured.

Just as Dorothy, Michaela, Sully, Loren, Hank, Jake, Grace, Robert E., Reverend Johnson—who had kept to himself pretty much since the burial of Mr. Willard's body—and others began discussing plans for the upcoming Independence Day celebration, the circuit judge arrived in Colorado Springs.

He listened first to Matthew's testimony against the two rustlers he had been holding in the jail. Matthew hadn't actually caught the two men stealing, although several times he'd followed their trails away from the ranch where the cattle had been stolen.

Judge Morgan didn't like the fact that Matthew had no evidence—no stolen cattle to show for the arrest—and Matthew was irritated when the judge announced that he'd have to let the two men go.

The men whooped and hollered all the way outside, where they waited for Matthew to finish with the judge so they could collect their personal belongings from him. When Matthew handed them what little cash he'd found on them, he figured they'd probably go straight to the saloon and raise the roof so much Hank would end up booting them out before midnight.

Judge Morgan scanned Matthew's report about Levi Willard's death. Willard had been a wanted outlaw, and as Matthew had anticipated, the judge didn't give the report of his death much notice.

He gave the report about Hagan's death quite a bit of attention, however, maybe because it was the only halfway interesting case in Colorado Springs that afternoon.

Judge Morgan questioned Sadie Jean, who was nervous and skittish and even tearful when she talked about how Hagan had told her he was gonna cut her up so Hank's customers wouldn't want her anymore. Sully and Hank testified about how they'd found Hagan's body and how Hank had found Sadie Jean. Michaela testified about Sadie Jean's medical condition, saying nothing about what Sadie Jean had revealed to her and Matthew about her childhood and the beatings she had endured from her father. Matthew and other townspeople testified that Sully, Hank, Sadie Jean, and Michaela had arrived in town with Hagan's body shortly after sundown the day of the shooting.

As Matthew had hoped wouldn't happen, the judge's ears perked at mention of Michaela arriving in town with Sully, Hank, Sadie Jean, and Hagan's body. The judge wanted to know how Michaela had come to be with the party that had brought Mr. Hagan's body into town.

Before Michaela could say a word, Hank stood up and said, "Your Honor, she was out callin' on—"

"No!" Michaela objected, stopping Hank. She shook her head at him. "Don't," she said, and Matthew, Sully, Hank, Loren, Dorothy . . . everyone who knew anything about what really had happened that day knew Michaela was telling Hank not to lie for her. She told the roomful of people, "I was there that day, in the forest, because I was supposed to meet Mr. Hagan."

Hank made a sound like a disgusted snort. He took his seat, shaking his head at Michaela.

"Mr. Hagan wanted the bounty money that had been offered for Levi Willard," Michaela said, clasping her hands

268

in front of her. "He had threatened my husband, and he had threatened one of our closest friends. I—I offered Mr. Hagan money if he would leave town, and I was there, in the forest, to meet him and give him the money. I was at the old miner's shack a mile east of town, where I was supposed to meet him. He didn't arrive, and then I heard shots, and I found Mr. Hagan's body. He was already dead. My husband and Mr. Claggerty arrived within minutes of that, and Mr. Claggerty went off to look for Miss Owens."

People who had come to witness the proceedings whispered among themselves. Mrs. Ogleby was there, and doubtless she would be running around town again, asking what people thought of Dr. Michaela Quinn *now*.

What people thought of Dr. Michaela Quinn now soon became evident.

Judge Morgan pounded his gavel on the desk behind which he sat. When the crowd quieted, the judge cleared his throat and shifted his position on his seat. "Dr. Quinn, every man should have such a devoted wife," he commented.

More whispers rose among the spectators, this time whispers of agreement.

"While I don't condone your withholding your entire part in what happened that evening," the judge continued, "I can appreciate your not wanting to air something so personal."

Sully squeezed Michaela's hand. She squeezed his back. She was a bundle of nerves. Her palms were damp, and she was trembling inside.

"Let's see . . . I have a confession from someone who says she did the killing in self-defense," Judge Morgan said, looking down at his notes and at Matthew's report. "I have testimony from Mr. Claggerty, who claims that almost as soon as he found Miss Owens she confessed to killing Mr. Hagan in self-defense. I have testimony from Dr. Quinn about the girl's medical condition and hysteria—that Miss Owens feared Mr. Hagan might kill her if she didn't defend herself. . . ."

Judge Morgan read for another minute, then he glanced

up and looked out over the crowd. "I would say there's nothing more to do here. Miss Owens clearly killed Mr. Hagan in self-defense. This case is closed."

With that, the judge banged his gavel on the desk and shut the folder that held the reports and his notes.

During the ensuing days, the only gossip that went around town involving Michaela's confession in the courtroom was about how marvelous her love for Sully was. People talked about her devotion, about her unwavering commitment to her family, about her contribution to Colorado Springs in helping plan the upcoming Independence Day festivities.

Michaela humbly went about the her medical practice and planning activities for the celebration, humorously watching Sully whenever he stopped to talk to people about her. He wasn't a social individual, and she felt proud when she heard him talk about her devotion to their friends and family, and to the community. Several times she shook her head and told him he was embarrassing her with all the talk.

Mrs. Ogleby went off to her husband and house on the outskirts of town, where she remained unseen for the rest of the week. Hank remarked that it was a good thing the woman's husband was deaf, and Michaela commented that she hadn't known Mr. Ogleby was deaf.

After learning more about Mrs. Ogleby, Michaela felt sorry for the woman. Gossip often hurt people, but Mrs. Ogleby seemed to have little to do for entertainment other than gossip. Her children were grown and gone. Several had died. As far as Michaela knew, the woman had no grand-children and no other relatives. So what was she to do with herself?

Well, Mrs. Ogleby was a good cook, Michaela had heard. So she talked to Grace about asking Mrs. Ogleby to help with food preparations for the picnic and barbecue that would be part of the Independence Day celebration.

"Ain't she fortunate you're such a forgivin' person," Grace remarked.

Dorothy was seated nearby during the conversation—she and Michaela were having dinner—and she agreed with Grace. But then she cleared her throat and said she'd be willing to go with Michaela to ask Mrs. Ogleby if she'd like to help with the food. "That would be wonderful." Michaela said lifting her brows in surprise.

Dorothy flushed and said, "One shouldn't hold grudges, after all." Certainly all of Colorado Springs had known about Dorothy's tussle with Mrs. Ogleby in front of the mercantile, especially since Mrs. Ogleby claimed that Dorothy had attacked her when actually Dorothy had tripped into her.

Michaela and Dorothy went straight to the Ogleby home. They knocked on the door of the tiny white house, and when Mrs. Ogleby answered the door, she almost reeled with shock at seeing them on her porch. She looked alarmed, her eyes flaring and her hand going to her throat, until Michaela informed her that they had heard she was a wonderful cook and had come to enlist her aid in food preparations for the upcoming festivities.

Mrs. Ogleby said, "Oh!" then "My!" and finally, "I never expected this!" She fluttered around some more, patting her hair, then her skirt, then her cheeks. Finally she opened the door wide and invited Michaela and Dorothy to come inside the house.

The three woman shared tea, and they talked about the food Michaela and Grace had in mind—ribs and potatoes and several vegetable dishes and desserts.

"It might be better if you and Grace put your heads together," Michaela told Mrs. Ogleby, who agreed that would probably simplify things, since Grace was in charge of food for the celebration.

That night, when Michaela told Sully what she and Dorothy had done, Sully shook his head at her in wonderment. Then he pulled her into his arms and told her she had the biggest heart of anyone he knew, the biggest and the kindest.

Plans for the festivities grew, as plans are inclined to do. Michaela hired several townsmen as musicians, one of them being Mr. Britton, the pianist from Hank's saloon, who agreed to entertain the Independence Day gathering with his harmonica and his accordion. Sadie Jean agreed to sing several songs, and Robert E. constructed a small platform on which the musicians could sit as they played. Loren provided the red, white, and blue banners that would decorate the tables and the platform. Hank had a friend in Denver from whom he arranged to purchase fireworks, and Michaela put Hank and Loren in charge of setting off the fireworks after sundown. Brian and Gwennie would serve lemonade, and Grace, Dorothy, and Mrs. Ogleby would serve food.

Preston was so busy at his resort while the plans were being made, and Michaela was so caught up in making the plans, she totally forgot to delegate a task to him. He felt insulted, but rather than say anything to Michaela about the fact that she'd left him out, he went back to his resort, where he pouted for several days. After that he busied himself with his own plans for a celebration at his resort, plans he had begun months ago and hadn't thought to mention to the citizens he felt were beneath him and the resort.

He had huge banners hung, and he paid handsomely—in advance—for musicians and cooks to come from Denver on Independence Day. He advertised resort specials in the Denver newspapers, as he had already done in newspapers in St. Louis, Chicago, and Philadelphia, in which he described the resort as being set among "majestic peaks, healing springs, and mountain air." He ordered champagne and hired additional servants. Since Dr. Quinn and the other council members had decided to snub him in planning the town celebration, he would simply outdo them. No plans were too small for Preston.

No one had known for certain whether Colleen would be home from medical college for the holiday, and her family was beginning to worry that she might not be. But Michaela and Sully received a telegram from her just days before the celebration, in which she gave the time of the train on which she would arrive the day before Independence Day.

After reading the message, Michaela jumped up and down several times with joy, and Katie giggled, bouncing up and down on her mother's hip. Brian said he sure had missed Colleen—they hadn't seen her in a good two months now because she'd been so caught up in school and in her studies. He rushed from the clinic over to Matthew's office, to tell his brother the news.

Matthew grazed a hand over the top of Brian's head and told him that was great, that was real great. He was thinking he'd introduce Colleen to Gwennie and see what his sister thought of his sweet new interest.

Colleen arrived, exactly as planned, and Michaela shook her head at the sight of her. With each passing month, Colleen grew prettier and became a more poised young lady. Michaela wished Charlotte, Colleen's birth mother, were alive to see her daughter. Charlotte would be incredibly proud. Michaela told Colleen that as she greeted her on the train platform and kissed her cheek.

Michaela and Colleen sat up talking late that night, later than Michaela knew either of them should stay awake, considering the celebration planned for the following day. But Michaela wanted to hear Colleen's news about medical school. She wanted to hear about Colleen's instructors and her classes, and she wanted to hear about any new friends Colleen had made and the physician with whom she was beginning a preceptorship. It felt so good to have Colleen in the house again, warming her feet before the low fire burning on the grate, sipping tea from the china cups Michaela's mother had sent from Boston last year. Both Michaela and Colleen were nodding off by the time they finally made their way to bed.

They woke the following morning to bright sunshine beaming into the house through the curtains Sully had tied

273

back on the windows. Michaela hid her head under the pillow, not ready to wake yet; Sully laughed and snatched the pillow away from her. He plopped Katie down on the tick beside Michaela, and Katie squealed and climbed onto Michaela's stomach, sat there, and clapped her hands as if she had done a great thing.

"She's adorable," Colleen said, smiling at Katie over breakfast.

"She's gettin' into everythin'," Sully said, offering Katie a spoonful of scrambled eggs. Instead of opening her mouth and letting her father feed her, she took the eggs off the spoon and fed herself. "She's independent, too, just like her mother."

Colleen laughed. "I see that."

The family finished breakfast and dressed for the celebration. They rode into town in the wagon, which they left at the livery stable, and then busied themselves with putting everything in place for the afternoon and evening events. Sully and Brian helped set up tables, while Colleen and Michaela helped Grace and Mrs. Ogleby with the food.

By noon, the serving tables were lined with food, and Robert E. turned ribs over the huge grill he'd made especially for today's celebration. On the platform, Mr. Britton played a lively tune on his accordion.

"No, no, you've gotta stagger them," Loren told Hank as the two men walked toward Michaela and her family. Michaela presumed they were discussing the arrangement of the fireworks and how they would set them off.

"Reckon I'd better get to the lemonade booth before too long," Brian said. "There's already a lot of people out."

There were. They milled here and there, on the church grounds, on the school grounds, on the bridge leading to the cemetery. They wore colorful clothing, and some women carried parasols decorated with ribbons and lace to ward off the bright sunshine.

Brian started off, and Loren called to him, saying, "Hold on, Brian. Wait just a minute. Can't walk as quick as I used to. Got a hitch in my step today." He held his back as he hurried toward Brian.

"Is something wrong with your back, Loren?" Michaela asked.

"No, no. Don't be fussin' over me."

"Nothin' he can't work out with a little dancin' or a little hanky-panky. Eh, Loren?" Hank teased.

Color brightened Loren's face suddenly. "Don't be talkin' like that," he grumbled. "There's decent folk here."

Hank pulled a sour face. "Preston wouldn't think so. He's angry 'cause no one included him."

"This isn't a by-invitation-only event," Michaela said. She immediately realized how harsh that sounded, and she set about remedying that. "I simply forgot. He's been busy at the resort, and I've been busy at the clinic and with making plans for today. I would have been glad to have him to help."

"Brian, your printin' press is in," Loren announced. "I've got it sittin' pretty as a peach on a counter in the mercantile. It's just a little thing, though—thought I oughtta warn you about that."

Brian was already in a festive mood, his eyes aglow and his face flushed with excitement. But Loren's news made his face brighten even more. "Can we go see it?"

"You mean right now?" Loren asked.

Brian's head bobbed up and down.

"I s'pose. If your ma don't mind."

"I don't mind," Michaela said. "But Brian, when you return, you must tell us all about it."

Brian and Loren started off together, and as they walked away, Michaela heard Loren telling Brian he'd sold several of those music boxes that Brian and Katie liked so much to a tourist lady from Baltimore.

"Hank, I haven't had the opportunity to thank you for trying to protect me when Judge Morgan questioned me about Mr. Hagan's death," Michaela said.

Hank scowled. "I had a real good lie goin', an' you messed it up."

Colleen laughed in astonishment. Michaela didn't. She had known Hank long enough that nothing he did or said astonished her. She smiled at Hank. "I don't advocate lying, but you were trying to do a noble thing."

He snorted. "Noble, huh? I ain't never done nothin' noble in my life. An' I ain't gonna start now, either."

"You were trying to protect my reputation."

"I'd sure never do that—protect a woman's reputation," he said, walking away.

"I think he doesn't like you complimenting him," Colleen told Michaela in a low voice.

"He doesn't know how to take a compliment," Sully remarked. Katie squirmed in his arms, pulling at her bonnet strings. She'd get irritated in a minute. Michaela had tied the double strings to keep the bonnet on Katie so she wouldn't get burned by the sun.

"Let me take her," Colleen offered, and she held out her arms, beckoning Katie to come to her. Katie lost interest in the bonnet strings and went to her sister.

"Good," Sully said, tugging on Michaela's hand. "That means we can start the dancin'."

She laughed and let him gently pull her toward the open area in front of the platform.

Mr. Britton saw them coming, and he began a waltz.

Michaela and Sully danced, smiling at each other, glowing in the warmth of their love and the festive atmosphere.

Matthew and Gwennie began dancing, too. Then Robert E. pulled Grace out from behind the food tables and waltzed her around near the platform. Jake and Dorothy appeared, and other couples joined the dancing, one by one.

That evening, Michaela watched the fireworks as she sat on a quilt surrounded by Matthew, Colleen, Brian, Katie, and Sully.

When the first fireworks exploded, glittering in the sky and lighting the mountains in the background, the sleeping

Katie stirred a little, then settled. Brian said, "Ooh!" and Colleen said, "Oh, it's so pretty!" With the third burst, Matthew laughed and remarked that he was sure Hank was having fun lighting the fireworks and watching them explode, and Michaela wondered if Matthew was envious of Hank.

Katie was lying on her stomach, and Michaela rubbed the baby's back, unconsciously soothing her with a mother's touch. Sully tugged Michaela toward him. She settled against him, and a moment later, she felt his warm breath on her ear.

"I love you," he whispered as the sky lit again.

She smiled and whispered that she loved him, too.

Moments later, as she glanced around at the bright faces of her family and friends, she marveled that she had so much to be thankful for—and so much to celebrate.